BEYOND THAT STARRY SKY

Published by Z-Cat Press
Waynesboro, Virginia

ISBN:979-8-9949159-1-2

Cover design by Rin Nakajima
Interior design by Marvin C. Godbey

BEYOND THAT STARRY SKY

A Novel

Marvin C. Godbey

Z-Cat Press

"When we remember those who are gone, they walk with us again."

- Sakura Nakamura, Beyond That Starry Sky

For Family

Marvin & Nina (Jean)

Jerry & Linda

William (Carl) & Pansy

Roy & Hilda

Toni

Jessica

And Friends

Daniel B.

Briget H.

And Little Ones Who Became More Than Both

Crosseyed Joe

Twitchy

Floof

Angel

Zeke

You will always walk with us.

会うは別れの始め
Au wa wakare no hajime
(Every meeting is the beginning of parting.)
– Japanese Proverb

Even the sweetest visit ends with someone waving from the porch.
– Appalachian Saying

NEW PATHS

1988

Morgan had always been chasing the future, yet the first time it let him catch up, he was already running late.

The bell rang as he burst into class, ending a frantic sprint from the first-floor lockers. He dropped his backpack in a heap on the floor, jabbing the IBM's power button. The screen flickered awake.

Made it, he thought, brushing his long hair back as he slumped into the chair.

"Big M!"

The shout came from two desks over in the Advanced Computer Science lab. Dan was already there, as usual, blessed with a much closer locker on the second floor. He pointed at Morgan, squinting down his finger like it was a makeshift pistol.

"Little organ!" He fired.

Morgan barely glanced in his direction before smirking. "Never gets old, dude. What is this now, day three eighty-three?" He was still a little winded from the run, but he enjoyed the banter.

Their back-and-forth, sometimes witty, sometimes crass, had been going on for over twelve years. Daniel Madison and Morgan Dale had first met as toddlers, their fathers having been old hunting buddies. Since then, through elementary school, junior high, and now at the start of their senior year at Kanawha High School, they had been as close as friends could be.

Dan, with his wild spirals of dark hair, soft brown eyes, and round, friendly face, had a warmth about him that made people trust him quickly—even if he did have a weirdly adult love for strong black coffee. Morgan often teased him with a mock-serious "What are you, a hundred?" Still, he couldn't help but envy Dan's prime second-floor locker.

Before their verbal jousting could go any further, the sharp bark of Mrs. Heyworth, computer lab dictator and occasional teacher, snapped the class to attention.

Mrs. Heyworth was almost a stereotype of a middle-aged teacher. Her hair was neither short nor long—just wavy enough to avoid being called curly. She always wore the same dreary pantsuits, a fitting match for her perpetually dour expression.

But today was different. Instead of launching into the daily roll call, she stood silently beside someone, a student, clearly, but not one anyone had seen before. And not just unfamiliar. To Morgan, she was unlike anyone he'd ever seen in the Kanawha County school system.

The young girl stood timidly, arms at her sides, hands neatly clasped in front of her waist. Her black hair was cut into precise bangs, the rest falling freely to her shoulders. A flicker of frightened dark eyes swept the room before dropping quickly to the floor, her head bowed.

It was clear she didn't feel welcome or comfortable amid the curious stares and murmurs that greeted her. She stayed in a closed posture, inching slightly behind the teacher's more commanding presence, as if trying to shield herself from the attention.

Morgan couldn't look away. He studied the unfamiliar figure without fully understanding why. She carried an unusual leather bag slung over a white blouse and navy cardigan, adorned with several tiny, cute plushies—a stark contrast to the ubiquitous canvas duffels and backpacks of the other students.

Her conservative outfit was completed by a mid-length gray skirt, navy tights, and black loafers. As out of place as all that might have seemed, it wasn't the outfit that drew whispers and sideways glances. It was something more conspicuous.

She was Japanese.

"We have a new student joining us today," Mrs. Heyworth announced, voice cutting through the room. She stepped aside, exposing the girl fully, and offered her an encouraging look.

"Hello," the girl said softly. The word came out slow and timid, vanishing almost as soon as it appeared, like a wisp of morning fog. A thick, uncertain accent clung to her voice, drawing a few unwanted snickers from the back of the room.

Ball game pricks, Morgan seethed. Years of disciplinary warnings had taught him to keep profanity to himself, but the thought burned anyway. His red-faced glare toward the offenders matched the red blush creeping across the new girl's cheeks.

They were a well-known cluster of loudmouths and underachievers, a group that had claimed the back corner of the lab. Students called it the Jock Block, though Morgan had a different name in mind, starting with a different letter than J.

Apparently, Mrs. Heyworth agreed. She shot a hard glare of her own in their direction before clearing her throat and speaking up again.

"This is Sayuki Hoshizora," Mrs. Heyworth announced. "She's joining us all the way from Japan, and I want everyone to make her feel welcome. Let's help her transition to our school be as smooth as possible."

The room responded with a few genuine greetings, along with several apathetic nods and half-hearted mumbles.

Sayuki lifted her chin and faced the lukewarm reception with quiet courage. "Please, call me Hoshi," she said.

Mrs. Heyworth led her to the empty workstation near the front, just behind Morgan's desk and across from Dan's. As she passed, Morgan let the name drift around in his mind like a shooting star falling out of orbit.

Hoshi.

He watched intently as she took her seat, setting her satchel gently beside her and removing her textbook. Every movement was precise and fluid, like choreography meant only for her.

She glanced over and caught him staring. Morgan froze, startled. But he recovered quickly and offered a sincere smile. Their eyes met, his blue to her dark brown, and for a moment, the classroom fell away. She smiled back, hesitant but warm, and Morgan wished the moment would stretch forever.

But just as quickly, she looked down again, turning her attention to the bulky PC and her textbook.

As he sat staring at the dark CRT screen, the rhythmic blink of the small white cursor pulsed in time with his heartbeat. He kept replaying the moment in his head—her walking to her seat—and suddenly became aware of his ragged, torn jeans and black Bon Jovi t-shirt, emblazoned with the thoughtful slogan: *Slippery When Wet.*

While fashionable for the day, his outfit had less to do with making a statement and more to do with being creative with what was available.

His father worked at the chemical plant in Charleston, a job that paid well enough to keep a family housed and fed, but never quite enough to escape the hollow your people had been born in. It was enough to allow his mother to stay home and tend to the house—though referring to their humble single-wide trailer as a 'house' was a stretch for most people. But it wasn't enough to clothe them in style.

The contrast between his thrift store wardrobe and her carefully coordinated outfit suddenly felt like a gulf he couldn't cross.

He also became aware of Dan, sitting nearby in his KISS t-shirt, long spirals of dark hair spilling past his shoulders, another sharp contrast to the prim and proper new student.

Hoshi.

"Hey, little organ," Dan said, waving a hand in front of Morgan's blank stare. "You gonna make it? Do you require assistance?"

"Knock it off!" Morgan hissed, swatting Dan's hands away.

Dan chuckled, raising both arms in mock surrender as he leaned back in his chair. He glanced from Morgan to the new girl and back again, eyebrows lifted.

"Yep," he muttered with a smirk as he turned to his computer. "You need help."

As the weeks crept by, summer bled into fall. The leaves began to change, and so did Morgan. His torn jeans and hair metal shirts gradually gave way to less torn jeans and more solid colors. He'd even been spotted in a button-down shirt a time or two. But no matter what he wore, his thoughts kept drifting to Sayuki Hoshizora. She had taken up quiet residence in the back of his mind, just as she had in their Advanced Computer Science class.

Hoshi remained an enigma. Despite her best efforts to go unnoticed, she stood out, not because she was trying to, but because of how quietly out of sync she seemed with everything around her. Her limited English kept most people at a distance, yet she never felt unapproachable.

She wasn't unfriendly. She always bowed politely when spoken to, always answered questions when called upon, as much as her awkward, broken English allowed, and even offered help to students who were struggling with assignments. But she seemed to do all of it from a slight remove, like someone reaching out through a pane of glass, their hand visible but unreachable.

There was a kind of sadness to her, not melodramatic, not performative, just… present. As if just being in West Virginia had left her untethered, searching for solid ground.

Morgan didn't even try to explain it to Dan. What would he say? That he'd never really spoken to her but already felt like her quiet longing echoed his own? That she was like a dream you half-remembered from childhood, hovering on the edge of recognition? That when she did smile at him, warmth bloomed in his chest, nameless but undeniable?

He'd never live that down.

Instead, he listened to Dan talk about the latest KISS album and how Miss Powell from History totally had a thing for Harrison Ford, and nodded when appropriate. Occasionally, he would glance in Hoshi's direction, and she'd look up at the same moment. Other times, he'd watch her work, the way she would bite her lower lip in concentration, the way she tapped lightly against the spacebar with her left thumb. Tiny, unnoticed rhythms.

Of course, he didn't have to say anything to Dan at all. Being as close as they were after all those years had forged a bond that went beyond words. Morgan had already told him everything without making a sound, and, as usual, Dan had a knack for cutting straight to the heart of things.

"If you don't talk to her, nothing's gonna happen."

As if it were that easy. Hoshi's English was still very much a work in progress, and beyond that, she had an ethereal, dreamlike quality, like she might melt away if approached too directly, a desert mirage just out of reach. Even the strange, cute charms hanging from the satchel by her feet added to her quiet mystery.

Then inspiration struck.

Morgan dug around in his duffle bag and pulled out a sketch pad from the cluttered hoard of books and papers, most of which had little to do with his curriculum. As aspiring comic book artists went, he had genuine talent. If he'd devoted even five percent of the effort he gave to drawing spaceships, superheroes, and D&D creatures to learning PASCAL, his grade in Advanced Computer Science wouldn't have been hanging by a thread.

With a fresh charcoal pencil in hand, he began furiously working the paper, light strokes first, then more confident lines as the image started to take shape. He glanced from his sketch to the satchel on the floor, a subtle rhythm forming between muse and medium.

Dan, catching the motion in his peripheral vision, just shook his head slightly and kept his eyes on his own PC. He knew Morgan would find a way.

Sayuki, meanwhile, was aware of Morgan in that quiet, intuitive way people are aware of being observed. But she couldn't help feeling like a curiosity, a *misemono*, a showpiece, foreign and exotic, an object to be looked at but not understood.

When her father had been tasked with moving the family to America, they knew it would be a monumental challenge. But in Japan, when a company entrusts you with running an entire facility, even one halfway around the world, you accept the responsibility graciously.

Tenchi Chemicals USA, located in South Charleston, was the latest addition to the Tenchi conglomerate. It was the product of a sizable corporate investment, and the reason her family now called West Virginia home. But the so-called chemical valley of Charleston was a far cry from Yokkaichi. And no matter how bravely she smiled through it, the homesickness clung to her like mist.

A paper appeared on her desk, and Hoshi broke away from her work just in time to see the boy called Morgan walking past. He briefly turned, offering a shy smile as he crossed the room.

Confused, she turned the paper over, and her eyes widened with a mixture of surprise and delight. Rendered perfectly in hand-drawn charcoal were the Little Twin Stars, Kiki and Lala, diligently watching over Hello Kitty as she worked at a school desk.

These characters were dear to her. She kept their Sanrio charms clipped to her satchel, a small, comforting reminder of her childhood in Mie Prefecture.

She studied the drawing with admiration, struck by the effortless talent behind it. Each line was sure, each detail considered. Then understanding dawned—Morgan had made this for her.

Her cheeks flushed pink. She glanced across the room and found him still standing by the supply cabinet, pretending unconvincingly that it had been the reason for his cross-classroom excursion. Then their eyes met.

It lasted only a moment, but it felt like an eternity.

Morgan's heart stopped. His stomach dropped straight through the floor, past the desks, the tile, all the way to the first-floor lockers. And then, slowly, almost timidly, time began to move again.

She smiled.

Not just an act of politeness like their first shared smile nearly two months ago, this was a true gesture of gratitude and joy. For him.

To Morgan, that expression was a greater gift than any picture, drawing, or painting in the history of the world. He returned to his desk, trying not to make it obvious that he was walking on a layer of clouds, masking his elation with a healthy dose of rock and roll swagger.

Taking his seat, he flipped his long hair out of his face with a quick tilt of his head.

That's good, he thought, aware of his racing heart. *Just be cool.*

"Morgan."

The hesitant voice made his cheeks flush and sent a stifling heat rising in his chest. Slowly, he turned to see Hoshi leaning toward him from her desk, holding the drawing in front of her.

"Thank you."

It was bad enough that her insecure accent gave him palpitations, but the slight head bow that followed completely melted whatever solid pieces of heart he had left.

"Not at all," he responded coolly. He fought to keep his tone casual, though the redness in his face and the tremble in his hands told a different story. "It makes me happy to see you smile."

The sum of Morgan's words and flustered sincerity made Hoshi swallow hard, taken aback by his unguarded honesty. Despite his false bravado, she saw the truth behind it. She bowed her head again, a nervous "*arigatou*" slipping out before she corrected herself with English and returned to her work. But not before carefully tucking the drawing away in her satchel.

Morgan turned back to his own monitor and let out a deep, overwhelmed sigh.

Nailed it! His mind shouted in triumph, throwing a mental fist pump to his inner monologue.

The victory celebration was short-lived. Dan's wildly curly locks bounced into his field of vision, followed by a hand clapping his shoulder.

"Nailed it, buddy!"

Dan's grinning thumbs-up managed to both mock and celebrate Morgan's smooth move at the same time.

While Morgan shooed Dan away with feigned indignation, Hoshi watched the exchange with a light heart, offering her first true laugh since arriving in America.

It didn't go unnoticed. Morgan gestured with a thumb to his friend. "This guy..." he muttered, shaking his head with an apologetic shrug.

Hoshi giggled again, and this time her smile lingered.

It was the first of many in the months ahead, marking the start of communication between two souls from vastly different worlds.

That day, Morgan and Hoshi both learned that a smile, regardless of language, was still a smile.

* * *

The Halloween decorations came and went from the walls and lockers, but Morgan's daily offerings remained. Hand-drawn pictures, ranging from cute characters to Hoshi imagined as a ninja, continued to appear on her desk, each one crafted for a singular purpose: to make her smile.

These shared moments led to more than just classroom exchanges. From silent waves across crowded hallways to warm greetings when they passed close, their days seemed brighter in each other's presence.

With Hoshi's encouragement, Morgan began learning Japanese words and phrases, and he offered what help he could with her English. He never passed up the opportunity to speak to her in her native tongue. It created a sense of intimacy, a private world that only they seemed to share.

But one evening in November, Morgan arrived home and overheard his parents from the front porch, their voices carrying a weight that meant serious conversation. He paused at the screen door, backpack still slung over his shoulder.

"... that Japanese girl he's always drawing pictures for," his mother was saying, her tone careful but concerned.

"What's that supposed to mean?" his father asked.

"I'm just saying, people notice things, Jerry. Mrs. Seabolt mentioned it at the grocery store. Said her daughter told her Morgan's been spending an awful lot of time with the foreign girl."

Dread pooled in Morgan's gut. He pressed himself against the door, barely breathing.

"And?" his father's tone had an edge now.

"And nothing, I suppose. I just wonder what that means for him. For us. You know how people talk in a town this size."

The conversation drifted to other topics, but Morgan had heard enough. He slipped quietly inside, his mother's words echoing: people notice things.

Shortly after Veteran's Day, Morgan spotted Hoshi at her locker, another prime second-floor unit. She had begun styling her bangs into a tall, hairsprayed monument, mimicking the prevalent trend of the day. Aside from trading her cardigan for an acid-washed denim jacket, she still dressed more conservatively than her peers, but she no longer seemed quite so isolated.

She slammed her locker shut—second floor or not, it was the only way it would close properly—and saw Morgan approaching through the sea of faces. Shifting her satchel over one shoulder, she lit up and waved excitedly in his direction.

It was an off day for Morgan, all things considered. His hair hadn't cooperated that morning, leaving him looking more like a homeless vagabond than heavy metal heartthrob. The effect was only compounded by his olive drab army field jacket, a vintage piece issued to his late grandfather. It was a popular look among metalheads, outsiders, or anyone wanting to be seen that way. At the very least, it kept the late fall chill at bay.

"*Konnichiwa* Hoshi!" He called out, returning her wave with an eager smile.

She clasped her hands in front of her and dipped her head in a small bow, a habit that had been hard to break.

"Hello, Morgan," she said carefully. Then, with a bit of concentration, she added, "How are you today?"

Her English was progressing at an impressive pace, though certain letters and sounds still gave her trouble. That struggle showed in her thick accent, which Morgan thought was the cutest sound he'd ever heard. Unfortunately, not everyone was so kind.

"Stupid jap!"

The slur rang out from a small cluster of passing jocks, followed by a burst of harsh laughter. All of them were either smirking or outright laughing, but it was the one with the blonde buzz cut and letterman jacket who stood out, pointing at them and guffawing as he walked backward to keep the show going.

"You sound like a retard!" He shouted.

Sayuki went rigid, shock and pain flooding her features. It was as if she were collapsing inward, shrinking beneath the weight of the sudden stares. Cruelty wasn't new to her, unkindness had been a frequent visitor since her arrival in this new world, but nothing before had felt so nakedly malicious.

Morgan acted without thinking. The hall, the lockers, the students, all of it blurred into a haze, everything except the blonde, privileged, ball-game prick reveling in the misery he'd created.

At a full sprint, Morgan barreled into him, driving a two-handed shove straight into the guy's chest and sending him sprawling hard to the floor. A couple other students may have gone down in the chaos, but to Morgan, the collateral damage was more than worth it.

Already, the steady murmur of conversation had stopped. Some students gathered around while others scattered, as the fallen jock's friends rushed in, shoving Morgan and hurling threats and insults. But Morgan was locked in, laser-focused on the blonde as he climbed to his feet. He moved to intercept, ready to punch his way through or go down trying.

A teacher down the hall had started pushing through the crowd, but Morgan was confident he had time to knock some manners into at least one more of them.

"NO!"

The shout sliced through the chaos. Before Morgan could place it, hands grabbed the front of his jacket and shoved him backward. His rage shattered, snapping him back to reality.

Hoshi stood in front of him, staring up with a mix of fear, anger, and deep, aching sadness. She kept pushing him, even as the surrounding students began to disperse, feigning innocence as the teacher closed in.

Morgan couldn't look away from her face. He didn't resist. He let her push him, as if he were no more than a scolded child.

"No," she shouted at him again, pounding her fist against his chest in frustration. "This," she shook her head, fighting back tears, "not you!"

Morgan opened his mouth, but no words came. A different kind of ache bloomed in his chest, raw, sharp, and unexpected. The girl standing in front of him wasn't the frightened, timid newcomer he'd first met.

"This not you."

She stifled a sob, determined not to let her emotions show. Her grip on Morgan's jacket loosened, but her gaze stayed firm. They shared a brief silence, their heartbeats gradually falling into sync. Hoshi shook her head again, her words softer this time.

"This not you."

Morgan had no time to respond before she grabbed his sleeve and pulled him down the hallway, dragging him like a wayward child. The bell had just rung and the halls were mostly empty, but Hoshi didn't seem to care.

Morgan didn't resist; he simply followed, too stunned to protest. Too much had happened in the past few minutes. His mind hadn't caught up.

They arrived at the school library on the first floor. A few curious glances followed them as they entered the hushed space. Hoshi led him to a table by a corner window and sat down, dropping her leather satchel in front of her. She looked up at him, still standing there in a daze.

"Sit," she said gently, but with an emotional urgency. "Sit with me."

Her voice felt like a comforting embrace, an unspoken promise that everything would be ok.

Morgan sank into the chair across from her, his body trembling slightly, adrenaline still rushing through him with nowhere to go. He looked at her face then. The subtle almond shape of her deep brown eyes, her pronounced cheekbones, and the soft sheen of lip gloss. The nervousness and insecurity that had once clouded her expression were gone.

Then, without warning, the words spilled out of him in a rush of emotion.

"I am so sorry, Hoshi! I shouldn't have, I—" he tripped over the words, uncertain of what he was even trying to say.

She silenced him with a gentle hand on his arm, calming him more than he thought possible. As he focused on the small details of her face, her voice met his gaze with matching warmth and empathy.

"You are good person," she said. Her grip on his arm tightened slightly. "I know. That not you."

Morgan felt the truth of her words sink in. Her understanding hit him like a wave, and a flood of emotion rose in his chest. He blinked quickly, furrowing his brow and rubbing at his eyes with one hand, hoping it looked like he was just trying to shake off the stress of the past few minutes.

"Hoshi," he began, but was abruptly interrupted as she placed a book in front of him.

It was clearly Japanese, the elegant characters utterly foreign to him. He could only stare, unsure what she expected him to see.

"You teach to me," she said, flipping rapidly through the pages. Then, just as suddenly, she stopped, pressing a slender finger to a specific page. "This!"

Morgan looked down at the page she pointed to. Beneath her clear-polished nail was a full-page photograph. The glossy surface made the pale pink petals seem almost alive, like they might tremble in a passing breeze and leave their scent drifting between the rows of books. He looked back up at Hoshi.

"That's a cherry blossom, right?"

"*Hai*!" She nodded enthusiastically, then caught herself. "Yes. *Sakura*. Cherry blossoms."

She said the last part slowly and more carefully, still self-conscious after the scene in the hallway. As Morgan glanced back at the page, Hoshi reached into her bag and pulled out a sketchpad. She set it beside the open book.

"You teach to me."

She held a yellow number two pencil in her hand, waving it slightly above the blank paper.

"Teach to me to draw," she said, then pointed at the close-up photo. "Sakura. Teach to me to draw cherry blossoms."

Morgan hesitated, taking in the moment. The more he got to know this quiet new girl, the more his perception kept shifting. Sitting there with her, it felt like he was really seeing her for the first time.

Her slow, hopeful smile seemed to reset the world around them, bringing time and space back into alignment.

He smiled in return, took the pencil from her hand, then gently set it to the waiting page.

"Let's start with the petals."

Outside, winter loomed. But there in that hushed, sterile library, something new had begun to blossom.

* * *

As winter settled over the mountains and the last autumn leaves fell, Morgan and Hoshi continued spending their spare moments together.

13

They sketched in the school library, shared language lessons filled with laughter, and formed a connection that ran deeper than simple attraction—something rooted in the quiet longings of the soul.

Once, their hands touched when they reached for the same pencil. Neither pulled away. Instead, they simply stared at each other and allowed the moment to linger.

Despite the approaching holidays, the cold days and early nights brought with them an underlying tension. Rumors spread through the halls of Kanawha High like morning frost—hushed whispers, sidelong glances, and muttered suspicions.

How would the Elk River community react to one of their own getting close to a foreigner? Not that Morgan and Hoshi were dating, not in any conventional sense, and not that it should have mattered. Contrary to stereotypes echoed in big cities or media, the people of the mountain state weren't known for judging others by anything less than the content of their hearts.

But teenagers have a way of reshaping the world to fit their own imaginations. Their perception becomes reality, not just for themselves, but also for those around them. And so, the gossip and drama began to wear away at the bond forming between the girl from Japan and the Elk River boy.

Still, Hoshi and Morgan spent time together. She was welcomed into his small circle of friends, Dan, Stephen, Chuck, and a few others. Sometimes they'd sit on the low wall in front of the school before the first bell, watching the last yellow buses pull in. Other times, they'd claim a back corner of the library during lunch to play Dungeons & Dragons in hushed tones. Hoshi rarely played herself, but she loved being there, close to Morgan and surrounded by a group who not only accepted her, but treated her like one of their own.

And yet, doubt had already begun to creep into Morgan's mind. The seeds planted by the constant background murmurs of ridicule had taken root. Those roots twisted through his thoughts, leaving cracks in the foundation of his resolve. Cracks where uncertainty seeped in like damp sludge.

Christmas came and went. Winter snow gave way to Spring mists and the first hints of green. Birdsong returned to greet the dawn. Yet, through it all, Morgan remained torn, caught between what he wanted and the fear of wanting it.

His parents were born deep in the backwoods, raised in the dark, isolated hollows of West Virginia. All they'd ever known were the wooded hills, dirt roads, and how to scrape by on minimum wage. Would they be appalled if he brought home a foreign girl?

"You know that's ridiculous," Dan would say whenever Morgan brought it up. "Nobody's gonna give a wet, steaming shit if you and Hoshi actually become a real—" he paused, searching for the right word, "thing!"

Morgan wanted to believe him. Deep down, he already did. And when Hoshi finally asked the question, he almost forgot he'd ever doubted.

They were in their usual hangout, seated across from one another at a small table surrounded by old books and a disinterested librarian. Morgan's hair was even longer than it had been at the start of the school year. Paired with his worn Megadeth shirt, he continued to be a contrast to Hoshi.

She'd adopted some of the local fashion—mall-bangs, oversized sweatshirts, jangly bangle bracelets—but she still looked different. Special. Like something otherworldly that had wandered among the mortals, just for a while.

Across the table, Hoshi was carefully following Morgan's pencil as he sketched a sakura blossom, drawing each stroke slowly so she could mimic them. To her credit, she'd come a long way since her first attempt; her cherry blossom now nearly matched his.

"That is really good!" Morgan said, glancing at her paper. "You've got real talent for this!"

As she looked up, he was struck again by how much he loved the way compliments made her cheeks turn the same soft pink as the petals they were drawing.

But instead of the usual shy smile or thanks, she caught him off guard with a sudden, blunt question.

"Will you dance with me?" she asked, eyes fixed on his.

He froze, his pencil slipping and leaving a stray mark on the page. It felt like he'd been dropped into the middle of a conversation he didn't know was happening. He looked around the room, seeing only shelves, scattered students, and the low murmur of voices.

"What?"

"Dance!" Hoshi repeated, more insistent now. "Will you dance with me!" Her tone had the patient firmness of someone explaining something simple to a confused child.

"Right here?" Morgan asked, genuinely puzzled. Her slowly evolving English had tripped him up before, but this one left him lost.

In a rare moment of exasperated affection, Hoshi rolled her eyes and mock scolded him, laughter playing just beneath the surface. "*Baka, demo suki!*"

She pointed toward a flyer pinned to the large bulletin board by the entrance. It read, in bold red, white, and blue letters: Kanawha High School Senior Prom.

"Will you dance with me?" she repeated.

"Prom?" Realization blossomed for Morgan, and it was his turn to blush. As much from embarrassment as from the possibility of an actual date with the girl who had filled his thoughts for so long. "You want me to go to prom? With you?" Better to be safe than sorry.

"*Hai!*" Hoshi nodded her head with an excited smile. "I want to dance with you, Morgan-*kun*."

The honorific hung in the air like a secret. Her eyes softened, but they did not waver.

He blinked. She had never said his name like that before. It was just a small syllable, a softening almost, and something about it landed differently. Like she was letting him in on a secret she hadn't shared with anyone else.

"I want to dance with you." He said softly, almost reverently. The meaning of the word *kun* was utterly lost on him, and in that moment, he didn't care. All that mattered was the joy shining in those dark brown eyes.

* * *

Word got around, as it always did, and by the end of the week, whispers and sidelong glances trailed Morgan down the halls. Did you hear Hoshizora asked him to prom? The words were always just on the cusp of earshot, never quite hushed enough to misunderstand. Some said it was sweet and unexpected. Others snickered, as if waiting for the punchline.

But not all the murmurs were harmless. A few let their voices drop just enough to hint at something uglier. A girl like her, a foreigner, too pretty and too quiet, should be more careful with who she ties herself to. The Kanawha Valley, for all of its gold-domed pretense and coal-dusted charm, had too many mouths too used to spitting poison.

Morgan began to feel like he had woken from a dream and found the air had turned sour. Mrs. Heyworth shut down the worst of the talk with a sharp word. A guidance counselor said folks would forget it all after graduation. Then there was Dan and his wisdom, insisting that the opinions of jocks and local yokels didn't matter. For all that reassurance, Morgan still wasn't sure.

The *what-ifs* began to take root. What if Hoshi was hurt by this? What if they laughed at her behind her back? What if his parents were ashamed? What if Hoshi realized he lived in a trailer while she lived in executive housing? What if he was just an American curiosity to her, temporary comfort before she moved on to someone who actually belonged in her world?

What if he, with all of his good intentions and clumsy affection, was the one thing that made her life here harder than it needed to be?

At dinner one night, he heard his father on yet another rant, grumbling about the new manager from Japan laying off workers at the chemical plant. Restructuring, he was calling it. As the words faded into the background like a low buzz, Morgan said nothing, but the contempt in his father's voice made his stomach drop as he imagined what he'd say about his son and one of them.

When Dan offered him the back seat of his Camaro, "it'll be fun, like a double date," Morgan smiled and waved it off, using the excuse of being a third wheel for Dan and Jo's big night. He had already made arrangements to meet Hoshi there, and tried to convince himself as much as everyone else that it was better that way.

But the truth was, by then, he wasn't sure what the right thing was anymore. His chest felt too tight, his legs too heavy, and the thought of Hoshi standing there in her dress while everyone stared made something inside him crack.

Then the day came.

In her bedroom, Hoshi leaned over her small writing desk, the soft glow of her lamp catching the edges of her hair as she added the final strokes to her drawing. The sakura blossom had taken shape with more care than any piece she'd done before. Below it, in a few slow, deliberate lines, she wrote her heart onto the page—not in poetry, not in metaphor, just truth. She read it once, then tucked it carefully into her small clutch purse.

Beside her, the open letter from a university in Florida lay folded but not forgotten. It was an acceptance, with a partial scholarship—the path to something more permanent, a future, maybe even citizenship. She had wanted to tell Morgan first, to see how it felt in the air between them. But instead, she folded the letter tighter, almost hiding it from herself. One piece of paper offered a future. The other, she hoped, offered a different kind of belonging. She couldn't carry both. Not yet.

Meanwhile, Morgan stood in front of the mirror, adjusting the collar of his shirt for the third time. He hadn't rented a tux, hadn't wanted to read too far into what prom might mean, but he'd still picked the nicest outfit he had. He tugged at the sleeves of his borrowed blazer, then looked down at the car keys in his hand.

He felt like he was in a costume. Would she notice the blazer was too big in the shoulders?

Go.

He glanced out the window, saw the faint twilight stretching over the hills like a half-finished promise. Would she notice that his shoes were scuffed?

Don't.

Would she notice that he was pretending to be something he wasn't?

The old Mustang II idled in the driveway, exhaust puffing like nervous breath. One hand on the steering wheel, he stared straight ahead, rehearsing what he might say when he saw her. That he was sorry. That he wanted to dance. That maybe this was the start of something real.

But then the what-ifs crept in again—the voices in the hallway, the look on his dad's face when he talked about the new manager at the plant, the hundred little slights that had chipped away at his certainty.

She deserves more than hesitation, he thought.

He turned the key. The engine fell silent.

Inside the house, the porch light clicked on.

* * *

Prom night came. Morgan did not.

The lights glowed gold and white as the DJ cued up another popular song, one poorly suited for dancing, though that didn't stop many from giving it their best shot. Since the old gym at Kanawha High couldn't hold the entire senior class, school officials had rented the ballroom at The Crescent on the River.

It was an unusually upscale choice for a high school dance. The Crescent was where politicians held fundraisers, where out-of-town executives stayed when their companies came courting the state. Rising on the riverbank, the building felt like Charleston's aspirations made concrete: a curved tower of cement and glass that reflected the Kanawha by day and glowed at night like something from a larger city.

Inside, the ballroom lived up to its hype. Chandeliers, likely worth more than most of their parents' cars, hung overhead. Carpet thick enough to muffle nervous teenage footsteps stretched beneath them. Floor-to-ceiling windows framed the Levee on one side and the confluence of the Elk and Kanawha on the other, the two rivers swirling together in a wash of brown and browner.

None of that mattered to Hoshi. She stood near the edge of the ballroom, unmoved by the swelling music of someone else's love story. Her dress, a soft, shimmering lilac, caught the light every time she shifted: a vintage silhouette with puffed sleeves, delicate beading along the neckline, and a satin ribbon cinched at her waist. She looked plucked from a dream, charmingly out of step with the glittery, neon chaos of her peers.

She'd spent hours getting ready, crimping her hair and teasing her bangs to new heights, pinning a tiny spray of baby's breath behind one ear. But now she stood alone, clutching a small purse and a solitary sheet of paper in both hands, her knuckles tight with nerves. Every time the door opened, her eyes lit up. And every time, it wasn't Morgan.

He said he would meet her there.

Her smile stayed on, but it had become still and practiced. She glanced at the clock again, heart sinking just a little deeper beneath the sound of other girls laughing and camera flashes popping like fireflies. Eventually, Dan, quietly furious at his lifelong friend's unexpected move, convinced her to follow him back to the center of the action. She was still a member of their group, and while the setting was far different than their D&D table, at least this time she could take part more fully.

With Dan's blessing, his girlfriend Jo took Hoshi by the wrist and led her to the dance floor, just as another loud, dance-unfriendly tune shook the room. He settled into one of the metal folding chairs arranged in rows along the wall, pretending to guard Jo and Hoshi's belongings. From a distance, he watched them. His smile grew as Jo coaxed Hoshi out of her shell, until she was laughing and giving in to the moment, lost in the joy of their silly dance moves and the freedom of letting go.

But Dan knew it wouldn't last. The night would end, and reality would return. Already, he felt the ache on her behalf.

He spotted the folded paper tucked neatly under Hoshi's small purse. A quick glance confirmed she and Jo were still several Z poses into "Walk Like An Egyptian," so he leaned forward and stole a look. Then he leaned back, his wild curls fanning out behind him like the tails on his tux. He sighed—long, heavy, and filled with a sadness he couldn't shake.

Morgan, he thought. *I don't know what you're doing, but you're a stupid son of a bitch.*

The weeks that followed prom were quietly brutal. Hoshi still sat with them at lunch, still laughed at Dan's dumb jokes and Chuck's impressions, but something in her had pulled back like a waning tide. The brightness that used to rise in her eyes when Morgan walked into a room had been replaced with a kind of courteous vacancy. She wasn't unkind, just not present with him in the way she used to be.

To his credit, Morgan tried. Once, he left a drawing folded inside her locker, a sketch of Hello Kitty hugging one of the Little Twin Stars, an echo of that first sketch he'd given her all those months ago. It was silently returned, tucked neatly back into his own locker the next day.

Another time, he passed her a quick doodle during class, a cartoon sakura tree with a frowning face that said "sorry" in kanji that he had learned just for that purpose. She barely glanced at it before slipping it into her notebook and never bringing it up again.

"She's still here, man," Dan said one morning as they leaned against the school's front wall, watching Hoshi sit on the lawn with new friends. "She's still hanging around, even if she's keeping her distance. That's gotta mean something."

The early summer sun made Morgan squint as he looked up to watch Hoshi, the pangs of regret getting harder to stomach. He kicked a stray pebble and watched it skitter away into the grass. "I blew it."

"No," Dan said, digging into his brutal honesty. "You completely fucked up! But you know what?" His tone softened only slightly. "It's not about you deserving a second chance. It's about showing her you want one. Just," he paused, then added, "don't expect it to be easy, and don't expect her to do all the work. You're the one that left her standing there."

The truth was, they were both hurting. Hoshi had prepared her heart and waited for him to take it, and he never showed. And Morgan, haunted by what could've been, carried his guilt like an anchor in his chest, dragging him down a little further every day. They both wanted things to go back to the way they were, but neither knew how to get there. Instead, they let the silence settle between them like ash—thick and suffocating—until the night of graduation.

That June evening in 1989 was sweltering. The Civic Center Arena in Charleston had been turned over to the graduating class of Kanawha High School, a slightly more subdued affair than its usual lineup of concerts, circuses, and monster truck shows.

Once the ceremony began, everything unfolded as expected: speeches, a mix of cheers and tears, and a couple songs. Awards were handed out, commendations made, and it all ended in a flurry of caps tossed into the air, followed by a wave of hugs and congratulations.

But Morgan had planned for only one thing.

He pushed urgently through the crowd, blue-gowned boys cheering and roughhousing, white-gowned girls crying and embracing anyone within reach, with a singular purpose: find Hoshi. Finally, he spotted her near the edge of the main floor, standing with her sharply dressed parents and dangerously close to the exit.

In her white cap and gown, she looked even more beautifully out of sync than the first time he saw her. She smiled and bowed politely as teachers and students passed, offering congratulations and kind words. Morgan stood still for a moment, caught again by the feeling that she belonged to a different world—radiant and unreachable—and yet his heart ached to try.

Hoshi's father gently placed a hand on her back. They turned towards the exit after one final bow. Her mother stepped in beside her.

"Hoshi!"

The name escaped Morgan's mouth before he realized he'd shouted. His heart raced as his pace quickened. He sprinted through the thinning crowd, weaving less carefully now, only focused on reaching her.

"Hoshi!"

They were nearly at the doors, looming ominously, like a gateway to a future he couldn't bear to imagine. He wasn't going to make it.

"SAYUKI!" It was all he had left in him.

He stood at the top of the steps to the main lobby. Bent over, hands on his knees, he fought to catch his breath. His long hair hung over his face like a wayward phantom from a horror film. Was she gone? He forced himself upright.

His exhausted body protested the movement, and his hair fell back into place with a heavy sweep.

Hoshi stood silently, watching him. So did several nearby onlookers. No one moved. No one spoke.

Then, slowly, she stepped away from her parents. Her father, a short, unhappy-looking man, began to protest, but her mother stopped him. She looked so much like Hoshi, elegant and poised in a conservative blue dress and pearls. Placing a calming hand on her husband's shoulder, she spoke softly in Japanese.

"Our daughter knows what she's doing. Let her do this."

Hoshi walked the short distance to where Morgan stood. His breathing had finally steadied, but his heart still pounded. He was keenly aware of the glossy, satin-blue gown he wore. Yet, no matter what he had on, Morgan always felt a quiet sense of unworthiness in her presence.

"Hoshi," he began, then faltered, his throat tightening around her name. "I'm so sorry, Hoshi." He made no attempt to hide the anguish in his voice. She deserved his honesty, his whole unguarded self.

"I wait for you, Morgan."

It was the first time she'd said his name since before prom. The missing honorific hit like a punch to the gut.

"I wait for you. You not come for me." Her eyes trembled with the threat of tears, but they didn't fall.

"Hoshi..."

He internally cursed himself. *Stop just saying her name. Say SOME-THING goddamn it!*

"I never meant to hurt you. I didn't mean to not show up. I was worried," he said, stumbling over the words. He shook his head and forced himself to continue. "I wanted to protect you from being harassed, from getting hurt. I didn't want to make things harder than they already were. You're adjusting to a whole new world. I was afraid I'd only make it worse."

"Worse for me? Or worse for you?"

If the missing *kun* had been a punch in the gut, her words were a brutal kick far lower. And yet, Morgan couldn't argue. He dropped his head in defeat, letting the tears blur his vision.

"I never meant to hurt you, Hoshi. I love you." The words spilled out, unplanned, catching even him by surprise. He looked up, and for a moment, he saw the Hoshi who used to look at him that way, before everything fell apart.

"I didn't mean for any of this—" he trailed off, his voice on the edge of breaking under the weight of what he felt.

Her expression softened, but she kept her hands at her sides, a cautious distance still between them.

"Intentions not matter, only consequences." Her father would have been proud to hear her repeat one of his many life lessons.

"I'm so sorry, Hoshi."

He could already feel her slipping away. The tear that had been cling-ing desperately to his lashes finally slid down his cheek.

There was a flicker of tenderness as Hoshi reached for his face, then stopped, her hand withdrawing. She turned her head slightly, fighting back a tear.

"I hear the people. Hear what they say about us. But I thought you care about me, about us, more than their words."

Her voice, once steady, now carried a bitter edge.

"I know people think I am stupid," she said, remembering to add "am."

Morgan's face crumpled with grief, but before he could respond, she cut him off.

"I am not stupid, Morgan."

He shook his head, his chest hollowing out like something vital had been carved away. "Please don't," he whispered. "Hoshi, I'm so sorry."

She reached beneath the folds of her white graduation gown and pulled out a neatly creased piece of paper. With trembling hands, she placed it in his. Then, unexpectedly, she laid her other hand over his, cup-ping them both. Finally, the tears came, tracing silent, graceful arcs down her cheeks.

"I made this for you," she said, her lips trembling slightly. "At prom. You not come. I keep it, hope things could be good again. Me and you." She blinked hard, trying to hold back more tears. "I am not coming back Morgan, I am leaving. I am to go to college in Florida."

"Sayuki!"

Her mother's voice rang out, drawing both their gazes. She stood a short distance away, gesturing for her daughter to come. Her father, with his back turned, stared out into the night. Her mother called again in Japanese. Hoshi gave a small bow, wiped her eyes, and responded in kind.

"I go now, Morgan," she gently slid her hand away from his, severing the fragile connection they had only just begun to reforge. "Please, for me, learn to trust yourself."

And just as quickly as she had entered his life, she was gone. Her white cap and gown faded into the night like a ghost. Morgan stood motionless, staring into the darkness. It mirrored everything inside, an ache deep in his soul. He didn't notice when Dan arrived, only became aware when he felt his friend's steady hand on his shoulder.

Dan stood quietly with him, offering nothing but presence. Then, gently:

"What's that?"

Morgan looked down, following Dan's gaze, and realized he was still clutching the folded paper Hoshi had given him.

"I don't know," he murmured.

Dan gave his shoulder a firm squeeze. "Open it."

Morgan glanced from Dan back down to the paper in his hand, then carefully unfolded it. The tears he thought had already run their course returned, deeper this time, pulled from a sorrow he hadn't known he could still feel.

On the crease-marked page was a perfectly sketched sakura blossom, delicate, in full bloom. Every curve of the petals, every subtle shading, was more refined and alive than anything he could have drawn himself. And at the bottom, written in graceful, flowing script, were the words:

Morgan-kun. I blossom because of you. Hoshi.

No words came. Only the silent, steady torrent of tears. Dan said nothing. He simply slipped an arm around his lifelong friend and guided him away from the steps, back toward what was left of their group.

"Come on, bud."

They left together into the night, toward an unwritten future, one that, for Morgan, already felt needlessly empty.

日暮れて道遠し
Hi kurete michi tōshi
(*The sun is setting, and the road is long.*)
— Japanese proverb

The light's fading, but the hands ain't idle yet.
– Appalachian Saying

THE SHAPE OF NOW

2026

The bell rang just as Morgan opened his eyes. He blinked the bedroom into existence, the dull edges of his dream already fading into oblivion. Instinctively, he reached for Di, hoping to feel her warmth. Instead, his hand found cold sheets and a crumpled comforter. He blinked again.

Wasn't there a bell?

The bedroom came into focus, modern and quiet, except for the alarm blaring from his phone on the nightstand.

That's where the bell came from.

He sat up, running a hand through his thinning hair, and grabbed his phone to silence the noise. He stood and stretched, groaning from the effort.

In the dim light from the kitchen, he caught his reflection in the large mirror on Diana's dresser.

When had he gotten so old?

His once-thick, dark hair had now thinned into a mostly-gray widow's-peak. The top still held a trace of its original color, especially where he kept it a bit longer. But the closely cropped sides were more salt than pepper. He liked to think the style made him look less bald than he really was. Maybe. His frown deepened as he studied himself.

I don't even recognize that guy anymore.

Next to the slightly ajar bedroom door, a wedding photo hung on the wall. The two had married after a relatively brief and fiery courtship, one where even their disagreements had been as passionate as their nights alone.

Taken in the spring of 1998, it showed a much younger Morgan in a tux, smiling beside a radiant Diana. He barely resembled that man. Diana, on the other hand, hadn't changed much. Her hair was still thick and, thanks to frequent salon trips, remained a satiny copper-red. It flowed in elegant waves, what he used to call "movie star hair" in public, and, more cheekily, "porn star hair" in private.

They had always been opposites. That used to work for them.

Old and tired, Morgan thought, glancing at the mirror. *That about sums it up.*

The tile floor was cold against his bare feet as he shuffled out of the bedroom. Through the large windows beyond the kitchen island, a soft gray light was beginning to rise over the mountains. Below, Charleston was still cloaked in darkness, scattered with lights and early traffic.

The city sprawled in a tangle of old and new: the gold dome of the Capitol, the glass towers of the medical center and banking district, the brick warehouses being slowly converted to lofts and breweries. The Kanawha River wound through it all like a question nobody had quite answered—brown and patient, carrying its load of history, runoff, and coal barges past the city like it had somewhere more important to be.

It was a view that young Morgan would never have imagined waking up to. Yet here he was, living in a large home in Sunrise Hills, known by locals, half-jokingly, as "Snob Knob."

The nickname wasn't entirely unfair. Sunrise Hills perched on the northern ridge above Charleston like wealth trying to distance itself from its source.

Built in the late '90s, the neighborhood replaced forest and scrubland. It was marketed to doctors, lawyers, and executives who wanted mountain views without mountain living. The houses were oversized for their narrow lots—sharp angles and floor-to-ceiling windows aimed at the valley below, careful not to face each other.

Every driveway held a German SUV or a luxury sedan. The HOA fined you if your trash cans showed. Neighbors didn't know each other's names, but they knew their property values. Landscaping was always professional—no wildflowers, no volunteer trees, just sculpted evergreens and mulch in clean borders. Even the streetlights tried to look vaguely Craftsman, as if the subdivision wanted a past it had bulldozed away.

Morgan never felt at home here, though Diana loved it. She loved the address, the schools their twins had attended, the unspoken claim of how far they'd risen. From here, you couldn't smell the chemical plants. You could barely see them—just clusters of lights and steam in the distance. The valley's working bones blurred into something almost picturesque.

On mornings like this, with mist in the hollows and the light coming slow, Morgan could almost believe what the developers had promised: a life elevated, refined, separate from the valley's grit. But he also saw what they hadn't said: isolation looks like success from far away, yet no one really leaves what lies below.

He made his way to the coffee maker, a sleek, modern machine that matched the rest of the house. As he passed the bookshelf, he deliberately avoided looking at the prominently displayed copy of *When the Hills Were Ours*. It sat there like a ghost that refused to leave.

The novel had been both his proudest achievement and his deepest disappointment. The critics had praised it, calling it "an Appalachian elegy soaked in memory and regret." But praise didn't pay the bills. Sales had been dismal, barely covering the modest advance. Still, the book had opened one door: a copywriting job he'd landed without a college degree. But in the Dale household, Diana was the one keeping the lights on.

Her official title at Capitol City Bank was Senior Vice President of Financial Operations. She had joined the organization shortly after their wedding and her move to the mountain state. Back then, they lived in the small city of Hurricane—pronounced HURR-i-kin, not like the storm— just outside Charleston.

Morgan's copywriting paid decently, especially by West Virginia standards, and Diana's first role as an Investment Banking Analyst had been icing on the cake.

Copywriting.

The word stuck in Morgan's head like a sour taste.

He paused by his small writing nook. "Office" would have been too generous. It was a narrow desk with an aging PC, wedged between the bookshelf he tried not to look at and the bedroom door. Most of his work happened at Chem Valley Creative, but he liked having materials close by, just in case inspiration struck.

He leafed absently through a few neglected folders. One read: Majid's Halal Meats.

Inspiring work, he thought to himself, letting the papers fall back onto the desk.

He turned back to the coffee maker on the polished granite. A mug of almost-hot coffee waited beside a yellow Post-it note. Stifling a yawn, he picked it up, already knowing what it would say.

> *Had to get to the office early. Didn't want to wake you. I made you*
> *coffee*
> *—Diana*

He stared at the note a moment, tracing the delicate, sweeping lines of her handwriting and the small heart she'd drawn underneath. For a moment, he considered the irony of receiving a drawing on a slip of paper, then crumpled the note and dropped it into the trash with a tired sigh.

When was the last time they'd actually shared a morning coffee? Or even a real conversation?

He turned to the waiting cup and took a sip. Diana had been thoughtful enough to use his favorite mug: simple, black, with the red and silver GR logo from Toyota's Gazoo Racing division.

A life-long "car guy," he had recently kicked his Mustang habit for a Nitro Yellow GR Supra. He wasn't getting any younger—that much was obvious from his full-body reflection in the window—and it felt like time to try something new. Diana had called it a midlife crisis. But at 54, why shouldn't he?

He grimaced as the coffee went down. It wasn't terrible, but it was a far cry from Dan's signature Gold Foam Cold Brew.

His reflection grew and faded as he crossed to the windows and leaned against the frame, one arm braced against the glass. He sipped the lukewarm medium roast and let the silence settle around him. Outside, the soft gray of a West Virginia Morning crept through the trees and blanketed the city below.

The buildings were still vague and indistinct, the sun not yet breaking over the mountains, but they showed through the early mist just enough to remind him the world was still there.

Even Charleston looks nice from a distance, he mused.

From his perch above the Kanawha Valley, everything looked the same, familiar. And yet, more and more over the past few years, it felt lonelier than it used to.

The shape of now, he thought, *is emptiness arranged into something that resembles structure.*

He shook his head. That was exactly the kind of line Cora would tease him about. He could almost hear her now: *The brilliant author should write that down.*

Even though the voice was only in his head, it still made him smirk.

After a moment, he rinsed the cup and glanced at the clock on the wall. Still plenty of time to hit the Dark Roast Society before heading to the office—if he jumped in the shower now.

He grabbed his phone and opened his messages, thumb hovering over Diana's icon: a sharp, professional headshot from the bank. The urge to send her a quick note, something affectionate, something affirming, was always there. But after years of routine, late nights, and overlapping schedules, that impulse had started to fade.

He set the phone back on the nightstand and walked into the master bath, all tile, stone, and glass. Stripping off his pajamas, he turned on the hot water.

She wouldn't have read it anyway, his mind sighed as the hot steam enveloped him.

* * *

The glass doors parted with a pneumatic hush as Diana stepped out of the elevator at Capitol Square, the headquarters of Capitol City Bank.

It wasn't a skyscraper by Manhattan standards, but here in Charleston, the fifteen-story monolith of steel and tinted glass still cast a long shadow over the Kanawha River.

She strode through the lobby with purpose, her focus locked in. The staccato click of her heels on the marble floor, the clean lines of her gray suit, and her perfectly styled copper hair made her look almost predatory. Her nods were brief, and her pleasantries brisk. Something important was happening, and she looked ready for it.

The lobby itself tried hard to project gravitas: West Virginia marble on the walls, supposedly from the same quarry that supplied the Capitol building. Chrome fixtures that caught the early light. A security desk that looked more like a hotel concierge station, manned by guards who knew her by sight—and knew better than to ask for her identification.

The polished floor gave way to a deep red carpet as she turned down the hall. The softer surface muffled her steps but not her presence.

Diana Dale, born Diana Lynn Anderson in Richmond, Virginia, was a striking woman—tall, fit, and commanding. Her age was hard to pin down by her appearance—and a closely held secret—even though everyone at the office already knew.

Morgan always said she was intimidating. He wasn't wrong. Her mind was sharp, logical, and relentless. He might say stubborn, maybe bullheaded. Either way, her appearance and energy gave people pause.

Shortly before their wedding, she had moved to West Virginia and joined Capitol City Bank. She might never have done either if not for her college roommate and best friend, Cora Raines. Cora had urged her to give Morgan a real chance after weeks of long-distance calls and surprise visits.

"You're not marrying the state," Cora had said. "You're marrying the guy who writes love letters like he means them."

That had been enough, then.

Without breaking stride, Diana pulled her phone from her bag. The screen lit up. One unread message—work. Nothing from Morgan.

Her thumb hovered over his name, half composing a text in her head:

Hey. Sorry about this morning. I wanted to—

She didn't finish the thought.

"Di," came the voice of Amankwah "Bob" Akinyode—measured, deep, and smooth as aged bourbon.

Tall and barrel-chested in a crisp suit, he was already striding toward her, his smile polished like the marble floor.

Bob was still a mystery to most people. Originally from Nigeria—"but not a prince," he often joked—he'd made his fortune in South Africa's banking world before landing in West Virginia. Within months of his arrival, he had transformed the company from struggling to surging. Diana had been there for the entire ride. She had his ear, and as the company grew, so did her influence.

"Morning, Bob," she said, slipping the phone back in her bag.

He had adopted the name Bob long ago to make life easier on Western tongues. It had stuck. However, as imposing a figure as he was, it was he who matched Diana's pace.

"Glad you're early," he said. "Got coffee and stale muffins upstairs."

She gave a thin smile. "Stale muffins build character."

He laughed and clapped a hand on her shoulder as they walked toward the C-suite elevators. "That's what I keep telling the interns."

They ascended in silence, Charleston's skyline slipping below them. For a moment, the Levee briefly came into view, and Diana thought about Morgan.

Maybe he's at Dark Roast by now?

The thought vanished as the elevator doors opened.

The boardroom on the fifteenth floor smelled faintly of lemon polish and burnt coffee. A gleaming mahogany table dominated the room, already half-filled with laptops, glossy binders, and the quiet hum of pre-meeting tension.

From this height, you could see the whole contradiction of the city: the gold dome of the Capitol building trying to look important, the chemical plants stretching along the river like industrial prayer beads, the hills rising on all sides as if to remind everyone they were still in Appalachia, no matter how many glass towers they built.

On good days, Diana loved this view—the sense of being above it all, of seeing patterns the people on the street couldn't see. On bad days, it just made her aware of how small Charleston really was, how limited the horizons, how far she'd have to reach to find something bigger.

The view was stunning, but today, no one bothered—the East Coast team would dial in at eight sharp.

Diana glanced at her smartwatch. Any second now.

Bob gestured to the seat at the head of the table. "Take the lead on the Meridian Financial numbers. You know the terrain better than anyone."

Diana nodded and sat, surprised but steady. Rumors had been swirling for months that Akinyode was grooming her to take his place. This would only add more fuel to the fires.

"Meridian's liquidity ratio is overstated." She said, clicking her pen. "If we're absorbing them, we'll need a six-month correction buffer, minimum."

Bob's smile slipped. "That'll spook legal."

"They can be spooked." She said, leveling her gaze around the table. "I'd rather be right."

Soon, the East Coast team was online, and the rest of the meeting blurred into a rhythm she knew by heart—valuation models, projected synergies, and personnel redundancy plans. She asked hard questions, nodded once at smart answers, and took notes only she would ever understand.

Every so often, someone in the room would glance her way with a mixture of deference and curiosity. The rumors and gossip were gaining weight. She didn't feed the gossip, but she didn't deflect it either.

The numbers didn't care about rumors or gossip. Or about messy half arguments with her husband over a book she never read. Or a dinner she had missed.

A little over an hour later, the meeting ended with polite chatter and quick exits. There was work to be done.

Diana lingered, typing a few notes into her laptop before closing the lid. She looked out the window again. A paddleboat was docking at the Levee below, the one known for brunch.

Morgan would like that, she thought.

She pulled out her phone, thumbs tapping with impressive speed.

Good morning. Sorry about—

She stopped and looked out over the Levee again. It was almost serene. The river was calm, but who knew what currents churned beneath?

She deleted the message.

She sat there, at the head of the boardroom table atop Capitol Square, staring at the river beyond the glass. For a long moment, she let herself feel it, the quiet clarity of where she was, what that seat meant.

Her calm outside didn't match the tug inside. She didn't need another lecture about being present or living like colleagues.

She tucked her phone back into her bag.

There would be other mornings.

* * *

The drive from Sunrise Hills down into Charleston wasn't especially long, but it was enough for some early morning head-clearing. Morgan took the curves too fast, as always, the Supra's exhaust popping against the hillside as it downshifted through the switchbacks. Below him, the city sprawled in its usual haze—that particular Charleston fog that was neither mist nor smog, but the valley holding its breath.

Along the Kanawha, chemical plants sent morning plumes into the air. The gold dome of the Capitol caught the sun, gleaming like a promise the rest of the city couldn't quite keep. They called it the Chemical Valley, with a mix of pride and resignation. It put food on tables and toxins in the groundwater, built the schools, and gave kids asthma—and nobody talked about the contradiction because talking wouldn't change a thing.

He loved it anyway—the contradiction of it—a capital city that still felt like a town, where you could see the Gold Dome from a trailer park and the University Club sat two blocks from boarded-up storefronts. It was the kind of place that broke your heart wanting to be more than it was, yet never quite gave up trying.

The view on the way down was spectacular. The slope steep enough that even the fresh Spring foliage didn't block the sweeping panorama of the city. For a moment, he caught a glimpse of Capitol Square rising in the distance, just before it vanished behind another turn.

Go get 'em, Di! He thought as the building disappeared. He admired her ability to thrive in that cutthroat world of business and finance. It wasn't for him. The quiet hills and forests were more his speed.

Spring in West Virginia had always been his favorite time to just go for a drive, windows down, mountain air flowing in, and a soundtrack of birdsong and growling exhaust. Diana used to come along. No destination, just the two of them wandering backroads, through hills and valleys. Sometimes, they would stop at a tucked-away coffee shop or a pop-up farmer's market. Weekends like that had become rare.

When their daughters, Carolyn and Carly, left the nest to build lives of their own, it felt like the beginning of a new chapter. Just the two of them, together again, like when they were dating. At first, it seemed like it could be a magical twilight to their story. But slowly, Diana began to fill the space their children left with other things, commitments and priorities that no longer included Morgan. What was meant to be a new Spring had stalled, suspended in a purgatory of routine. Then again, Spring always came slower to the hills, as if the land itself were still waking from a long nap.

The morning mist began to lift as he crossed into the city, heading downtown. He eventually pulled into the parking lot of Crescent Center, instinctively parking the yellow Toyota in a far corner. Chem Valley Creative occupied the second floor. The entire ground floor, though, belonged to Daniel Madison.

His lifelong friend had somehow turned his teenage obsession with coffee into a thriving business. The Dark Roast Society was now the go-to spot for craft coffee in downtown Charleston and the East End. And a sanctuary for the remaining Gen-Xers who had once walked the halls of Kanawha High School before the floods took it in the early nineties.

Crescent Center used to be The Crescent on the River, Charleston's most elegant hotel for many years. Eventually, it closed, was sold off, and repurposed into a mix of business suites and residential space.

The fourth floor and up became Crescent Lofts, affordable housing for people who didn't need much space but valued the central location. Not long after the ink dried on her third divorce, Cora Raines had rented a unit on the tenth floor, drawn by a lease she could afford without sharing a bed.

Floors two and three were converted into Crescent Suites, home to various local businesses and startups. A large portion of the second floor belonged to Morgan's work office. But the ground floor, the old lobby, restaurant, and ballroom, had become Dan's passion project.

For Morgan, grabbing coffee with his old friend every morning was a simple joy he never took for granted. Still, beneath all the renovations, it was the old Crescent on the River at heart. Every time Morgan walked in, it felt like stepping into a repurposed version of his past, one that never quite had the chance to bloom.

The bell above the door grunted in protest as Morgan stepped inside, carrying with him the scent of river water and damp concrete. The shop was half-shadowed in that way it always was before nine, sunlight sliding through the front windows like an old cat, reluctant and quiet. Just the way Dan liked it.

He stood behind the bar, sleeves rolled to his elbows, hair a little more silver than it had been last Spring, wearing an apron that read: *Make Coffee Not TikToks*. Dan swore it wasn't meant to be ironic, claiming he just stumbled across it online, but Morgan knew better. He was sure Dan had it custom-made. Anything to annoy the millennial and Gen-Z crowd.

Dan's long metalhead curls, once wild like Morgan's, were gone, but the untamed spirit remained. His hair was still thick and full, just neater now. "First it was the better locker, now it's better hair," Morgan often complained. The one thing that hadn't changed though, was Dan's eager, genuine smile.

"Big M!" Dan greeted him with enthusiasm, setting a cup on the counter with a dramatic flourish. He followed it up with two theatrical finger guns. "Little organ!"

Morgan grabbed the cup and let out a playful groan. "Yeah, you got me good, bud."

He took a sip. It was the same drink every day, Dan's signature Gold Foam Cold Brew. Inspired by the nearby State Capitol Building, known to locals as the Gold Dome, it was a dark roast crowned with honey and bee pollen-infused cold foam. An instant favorite among both connoisseurs and critics, it had become a local legend.

"I know you've been around a while," Morgan said after savoring the first sip, "but maybe it's time for some new material. It's been, what, a hundred years now?"

"Says the guy who looks like an unemployed literature professor obsessed with Miami Vice," Dan shot back. His wit was still razor-sharp, earning a chuckle from one of the nearby part-timers.

"Hey! Giggles," Dan said, turning to the young barista. The boy quickly looked up, trying and failing to hide a nervous swallow. For a moment, Dan was struck by how young the new hires seemed these days. Before the kid could respond, Dan tossed a towel into his hands.

"Watch the bar, I'll be back in a bit," he said briskly.

He poured himself a plain black coffee and joined Morgan on the other side of the counter. They had known each other nearly as long as they'd been alive, and they still had their rituals.

"You know, blazers and t-shirts are timeless," Morgan quipped, defending his outfit.

"I know, bud," Dan replied with a sympathetic grin, clapping him on the shoulder the same way he always had. "But we're indoors, maybe ditch the shades?"

"I wear these at night," Morgan said matter-of-factly. "That Hart guy wrote a song about it, remember?"

Their banter continued as they stepped into the old ballroom. Like the rest of Dark Roast Society, the air was thick with the scent of ground coffee and the roar of an espresso machine that sounded like it hated everyone equally. But unlike the main shop, with its sepia-toned portraits of farmers, overly sincere murals of mountain-grown beans, and a barista chalking up latte facts like she'd invented the bean herself, the ballroom was something else. More personal. It was designed for a select group, and everyone who belonged knew the name: the X-Wing.

A nod to both Generation X and the original Star Wars films, the X-Wing was Dan's private sanctuary—part amusement, part refuge, for those lucky enough to be in his circle. The room still carried a sense of grandeur, but it had changed. Since its last use for some forgotten gala or event, the walls had been blacked out. When Dan bought the place—funded partly by an unfortunate accident that left him with a slight limp (noticeable mostly to himself) and with help from a historical preservation group—it had been covered with tacky tinfoil stars. He had replaced those with cool blue LEDs, spaced just right, that pulsed faintly like the night sky.

Framed photos lined the wall that faced the river, the only one with windows, offering a view of the Levee and its iconic brunch paddleboat. The pictures were grainy shots of Dan and his circle from high school, all awkward smiles, denim jackets, and leather. Morgan appeared in several, back before the widow's peak and the years caught up with him. But Hoshi wasn't in any of them. He had always assumed that was some kindness on Dan's part, but he'd never asked.

And yet, beneath a small spotlight, there hung one of Morgan's old sketches. A charcoal drawing he barely remembered making, from before he gave up art for writing.

It was Hoshi's face.

The detail was stunning, in the way only raw emotion drawn onto a page can be, her face half in shadow, half-lost in some private thought.

Dan must have dug it out of some old box somewhere. Below the sketch, someone had scribbled in silver Sharpie: *Some things are worth keeping.*

Morgan avoided looking at it the same way he avoided the bookshelf at home.

A hand-painted wooden sign hung above the entrance, shaped like a treasure map and scrawled in that same silver Sharpie style: *GEN X MARKS THE SPOT.*

In the corner, a few old arcade cabinets hummed softly, one of them stubbornly frozen on the high score screen. Scattered around the tables, a few action figures and vintage starfighters stood guard, Dan's compromise between nostalgia and restraint. He was adamant about keeping the place from turning into a toy museum. The focus, always, was on the people. His people.

On one of the round tables near the center sat a chipped white mug, permanently reserved. In red block letters, it warned: *IT'S A TRAP!.* Chuck was already there, nursing a mug of black coffee while Stephen worked on the Centipede cabinet with gentle frustration. Maybe today would be the day he got it working again?

The newest member of the circle was Brandon, a surprising addition. Originally from San Salvador, he had immigrated to the United States at the age of six. When he'd turned eighteen, his parents returned home, but Brandon stayed. His job at Tenchi Chemicals promised a better future than anything waiting for him back in El Salvador.

Dan welcomed him into the group, not just out of the compassion he always denied having, but because Brandon wasn't like most of the twenty-somethings he met. He wasn't shallow and wasn't caught in the doomscroll haze. His past and his grit made him a Gen-X at heart, at least according to Dan. Brandon liked to say he was more of a closet boomer trapped in a young guy's body.

When he saw Dan and Morgan enter, he quickly stopped playing with one of the toy spaceships and called out to Stephen, like nothing had happened.

"The gang's all here!"

Hearing the call, Stephen gave the arcade machine one last glare, then joined the others at the central table. Not everyone was there, not everyone could make it every day, but the ritual remained the same: sit around the table, catch up, and roast modern society as it drifted past the old ballroom windows or wandered in to do business.

Morgan hooked his sunglasses onto the front of his shirt as he took a seat. Dan followed, placing his cup of black on the table with the kind of reverence reserved for caffeine and old vinyl.

"Small group today," Stephen said, sitting down last. He'd left his coffee behind at the arcade machines.

"We're at that age," Morgan offered with a sigh. "Our group is just going to get smaller every year."

"Fuck's sake, Morgan!" Chuck sputtered mid-sip. "That's the kind of motivational pick-me-up we all need first thing in the morning!"

Laughter moved around the table, but there was no denying it, they were well into the later chapters of their lives, especially compared to the old photos on the wall. Chuck was no longer the skinny guy with the out-of-place blonde afro. Now he was mostly bald, sporting a sizable belly and high cholesterol. Stephen still had his height, his thick dark hair, and glasses, but the lines on his face had deepened. The frames couldn't hide them, no matter how hard he tried.

The only exception was the new guy, Brandon Mazariego. His caramel skin was smooth, untouched by age, and his black hair was just right for the man bun he wore. However, that hairstyle earned him relentless teasing in the X-Wing, as did the nose rings. Still, he'd settled in and been welcomed as if he'd been part of the crew since the eighties. His honorary membership even came with an invite to the Kanawha High Nights gatherings Dan and Jo had started a few years back. Whenever someone asked how he was connected to the long-closed high school, Brandon would grin and say, "I'm the old janitor's cousin's nephew," putting on an exaggerated accent every time.

Dan always said Brandon was a Gen-X'er at heart.

They sat around the table, catching up and making general small talk. For Morgan and Dan, this was an everyday ritual. Others came and went as schedules allowed. That particular morning had the misfortune of being a "Chuck day," which meant the inevitable question was coming.

"So whatever happened to that Japanese girl you liked back in school?" Chuck asked, as he always did.

As usual, Morgan answered with a slow sip of coffee and a shrug.

"She's too big for us now," Dan would jump in. "I'm sure she's giving a lecture on a TED stage, or meditating on some mountaintop somewhere."

He and Jo, now married for over thirty years, had kept in touch with Sayuki ever since high school. These days, she went by Dr. Hoshi, having earned a PhD in Clinical Psychology from the University of Florida. From there, her life had been a steady climb: she became a U.S. citizen, opened a successful therapy practice, and eventually built the multimedia presence she was now known for. She was most famous for her speaking tours, TV appearances, and her podcast, *Truly You with Dr. Hoshi*, which carried the tagline, "Helping people master how to be seen and known."

Communication was infrequent, an email or social media message a few times a year, at most. Dan and Jo always invited her to one of their coffee shop gatherings. She was always too busy.

But busy wasn't just for the high-profile and in-demand. It weighed on everyone. Over time, the old crowd around the table thinned. Chuck and Stephen drifted away, caught up in work and life. Brandon followed not long after, slipping out through the growing crowd of coffee shop regulars.

In the end, it was just Morgan and Dan, like most mornings, sitting in the quiet after everyone else had gone.

"How are things going at home?" Dan asked. The tension between Morgan and Diana was no longer the secret they'd hoped it was.

Morgan drained the last of his Gold Foam and shrugged.

"Same as always, I guess. Di gets home whenever, brushes me off, heads straight to bed, or disappears into her office to keep working." He tugged absently at the lapel of his navy blazer, then looked up. "It's normal to greet your wife at the door, right?"

Dan only shrugged, offering a tight-lipped nod.

Morgan went on, "I get grief for it, like I'm in her way. Like it's somehow more important for her to hit the shower or lock herself in her office—" he trailed off a second, then finished softly, "it's just damn frustrating."

"I get that," Dan offered. "Heard from the girls lately?"

"Yeah, they're both doing well. Carolyn's still interning at UC Health in Colorado, and Carly's making a name for herself in graphic design. I think they're both planning to come in for Memorial Day. God knows that'll be the only way to get Di to put off work and actually be at home for a bit!"

Dan caught the edge in his friend's voice and tried to steer things to lighter ground.

"Well, that's something, right? At least you don't have an unmotivated troll living in your basement."

"Zack's still making you proud, I see," Morgan said with a smirk. He checked his watch, then glanced toward the crowd in the main shop. Of course, Dan noticed.

"Looking for Cora?" He asked, though he already knew the answer.

"No!" Morgan replied, overly dramatic.

Dan was about to respond when another voice cut in, sharp but amused: "Then why do you keep checking your watch like it owes you money?"

When Morgan turned, Cora was already there, hands tucked into the pockets of a charcoal peacoat, brow raised in a way that told him she saw right through him. He noticed her; how she seemed to belong to the space without ever demanding it. How the sunlight found the stray silver strands in her hair and made them shimmer. How those ice-blue eyes held a depth that never seemed to end.

She had snuck in with ease, no fanfare, no heels, just soft boots and a gaze that had seen too much. Cora Raines didn't need to announce herself. She never had.

"Jumping Jesus on a pogo stick!" Morgan exclaimed. "Somebody put a bell on her!"

Dan checked his watch and muttered something about the scones burning.

"You're late, Raines," he called with a grin. "You owe me a roast."

Cora rolled her eyes but smiled, tossing a glance at Morgan for backup.

"Hey, I don't make the rules," Morgan said, raising his hands in mock surrender.

"Fine." She dropped into a chair, already running late, but respecting that solemn rituals were, well, solemn rituals. "What have we got to work with?"

They scanned the main lobby, some patrons at tables with muffins and coffee, others waiting to order. A DoorDash driver hovered near the pickup counter. Plenty of material today.

"There!" Morgan leaned in, pointing into the crowd. Close enough to catch the scent of lavender in her hair.

He'd singled out a guy at the counter. Mid-twenties, and a type Morgan knew all too well. Back in the day, his crew called them preppies, mama's boys, or ball game pricks. They used to wear polo shirts, stay clean-shaven, and rock Wayfarer sunglasses. The style had changed, but the type hadn't.

Now they drove lifted pickups—with the tow mirrors extended—wore tees with trendy outdoor brand logos or camo, and traded clean-cut looks for beards and snapback hats. The Wayfarers had been replaced by wrap-around sunglasses, always upside down on the brim for some inexplicable reason.

"That guy," Morgan said. "The Boot Barn cowboy."

"A classic," Dan chuckled as he stood. "Thinks he's the outlaw of the county, but he's really the minor nuisance of the subdivision."

All three cracked up.

"OK, I get it," Cora said, standing. "He thinks he's salt of the earth, but he's more like... Salt Life of the earth!" She spread her arms, grinning at them for effect.

She didn't have to wait long. Dan pointed at her in approval while he and Morgan cackled at the jab.

After their laughter faded and Dan declared the daily ritual fulfilled, he gave Cora a quick hug and hurried off to wrangle the front of the shop.

Morgan offered a salute as Dan backed out of the X-Wing. "Catch you tomorrow, man!"

That left just him and Cora.

Morgan stood up. Even though he towered over her five-foot-nothing frame—on her best day—he always felt small beside her. As if she moved through the world on a higher wavelength he couldn't reach.

"Walk me to work?" She asked.

Morgan glanced at his watch, though he didn't care what it might say. His answer would've been the same anyway.

"Sure," He said with a smile.

* * *

The walk to her office was only four, maybe five minutes away. But Spring had a way of stretching time, and neither of them seemed eager to rush.

The Levee stretched before them, Charleston's reclaimed riverbank where the city pretended to have a waterfront culture. A paddleboat lay docked, its cheerful red trim and white railings trying to evoke New Orleans, but landing somewhere closer to a floating mall food court. Beneath it, the Kanawha moved as it always had—brown, patient, and older than any of them—carrying its load of chemical runoff and mountain soil past the city, as if it were all the same.

"Been writing?" Cora asked. It was a simple question, but it carried weight.

"Just for work," Morgan replied, eyes following a group of pigeons bickering on a ledge.

"You're too talented to waste your life on marketing copy when you should be writing literature."

He smiled and looked down at her, grateful his eyes were hidden behind his fancy Italian sunglasses. Cora walked like she belonged to the city, like her feet knew every crack in the sidewalk. He kept a slight distance, not to avoid her touch, but to steady himself.

Since Diana had started devoting herself to late-night Zooms and indecipherable spreadsheets, Cora had become something else entirely. A touchstone; a quiet tether to solid ground.

"I think we both know how my attempt at being a novelist turned out." Morgan's voice no longer carried the bitter edge it once did, but the emotion lingered, faint, just beneath the surface.

"It was one book." Her answer was always the same. "Even Dickens had a few flops."

Morgan wanted to argue, to point out his age, how his life felt like a waste, but he didn't. Somehow, she always made him feel like he mattered. He wasn't sure how she did it. Maybe it was just her presence. That was a dangerous thought, and he quickly pushed it aside.

An elderly couple strolled past, cutting through the silence. Morgan was grateful for the interruption. They recognized Cora from the paper (being old enough to still read the physical edition) and praised the recent concert she'd organized at the Levee amphitheater, and how they were looking forward to the summer fireworks by the river.

Cora smiled, thanked them, and wished them a good morning, warm and gracious as always.

"You ever get tired of being the town favorite?" Morgan asked, watching the couple shuffle away.

"Only on Tuesdays," Cora said.

They didn't laugh, but they both smiled.

Outside her office, the Levee trail sparkled with sunlight bouncing off the Kanawha, somehow making Charleston look gentler than it really was. Cora reached into her bag for her keys, her shoulder brushing him just slightly.

She hadn't heard from Diana in a while, and Morgan hadn't mentioned her either.

"You good today?" she asked.

The way she asked didn't require a real answer, just the truth.

"Better now," he said, before he could stop himself. She didn't flinch, just smiled and slipped inside with a small wave.

Morgan stood there a moment. He couldn't say when walking her to work had become part of his routine. He just knew that on the days he didn't, he noticed.

* * *

The garage door rose gracefully and revealed Diana's black Mercedes already parked, the SUV gleaming like a polished statue under the fluorescent lighting.

Already Home? That was new.

Morgan eased the Supra in beside it, its engine giving a soft, contented rumble. In the rearview mirror, he watched the door glide shut behind him. Maybe tonight would be different. Maybe they'd share dinner, talk for a while, watch something silly on TV, or just be together—be present.

He dropped his sunglasses into the cupholder, checked that both vehicles were locked, and headed inside.

He heard her voice before he saw her, polished and professional. Fast-paced in a way his mind didn't bother keeping up with anymore. Something about acquisition strategies, East Coast holdings, and Q3 positioning. Then he saw her.

Through the open door of her home office, she sat upright, headset on, eyes focused on a mosaic of remote faces scattered across her screen. The light in her hair wasn't sunlight. It was LED.

Morgan leaned on the doorframe and called her by her nickname.

"Hey Di, I didn't know you were—"

Diana glanced back at him with a distracted smile and held up a finger. *Hold on.*

Then, without turning around, she shut the door.

The rest of the night passed in a dull haze. He cooked to the hum of the fridge and the low buzz of his own thoughts. It was pasta, something simple, easy, something Diana used to like. He made her a plate too, setting it on the island under the pendant light like an offering.

No need to leave a note. She'd know.

Morgan ate alone, Diana's muffled voice still drifting through the drywall, blurred by distance and ambition.

After rinsing his plate and leaving it in the sink, he poured himself a bourbon. The untouched plate on the island seemed to watch him as he stepped out onto the deck, tumbler in hand.

Charleston shimmered below, lights from bridges and buildings reflecting in the Kanawha like stars that forgot how to move. A breeze stirred his graying hair. What had he forgotten to write down that morning? Something about the shape of now.

And something about emptiness.

When he finally went back inside, Diana's plate was still there, cold, unmoved, and untouched.

Just like the lights reflected in the river.

Just like his marriage.

SIGNAL IN THE STATIC

The bell rang.

No—not a bell, but the artificial chime from a smartphone.

Morgan stirred, caught in that blurred space where sleep dissolves but the weight of the day hasn't yet settled. As he blinked the haze from his eyes, the familiar bedroom slowly came into focus. He reached over and silenced the alarm, then, out of habit, felt for Diana.

Cold sheets.

Not even a crumpled comforter this time, just empty, untouched space. He stared at the ceiling a moment longer, letting the silence press in, then sat up. Mornings came in fragments now, less like awakening and more like assembling himself piece by piece.

But last night filtered back through the fog: he and Diana, another almost-fight.

In the kitchen, the coffee machine sat warming a carafe that had been half-full since last night. He poured a cup anyway, too tired to care that it had gone stale. No Post-it on the island. No favorite mug, either. He spotted it in the dishwasher, used, not washed.

Somehow, that felt new.

She hadn't even said goodbye.

Or maybe he hadn't bothered to hear it.

Diana had come home early yesterday, mentioning a banking conference in Chicago. She'd used her "work voice," as Morgan called it, the one that left no room for debate.

"It's not mandatory," she'd said, sorting blouses without looking up, "but it's good face time with the Midwest leadership."

Like skipping their first real weekend together in weeks didn't require discussion. By the time Morgan realized she meant a flight out that night, she'd already packed. That was when he checked out. After loading her suitcase into the Mercedes, he walked back inside without a word, before she'd even left the garage.

At the window, he stood with his lukewarm coffee and looked out over the city. The stale bitterness in the cup matched what he felt inside. Morning crept in from the east, gray and dull, washing over rooftops and the river alike.

In the garage, the Supra waited like a dog at the door, its yellow paint muted like the cityscape below. He often joked that Charleston only had two kinds of weather: wet and almost wet.

Today looked like both.

He stepped away from the glass. On the edge of his writing desk, a folder sat half-tucked beneath the keyboard. Ignoring the bookshelf, he picked it up without enthusiasm.

Majid's Halal Meats.

Morgan flipped through a few draft lines, each one more uninspired than the last.

Wholesome. Halal. Home.

He stared at it, then scratched it out.

What the hell does that even mean?

He shook his head. The work used to bother him more, trading art for ad copy. Now it just felt like background noise. Like static. Something to keep his hands busy while his mind spun in place.

From a drawer in the writing nook, he pulled out an old notepad, half-filled with scribbles and story fragments. It fell open to a page he didn't remember writing. A line stood out, hastily underlined:

Grief is what memory becomes when the world moves on without you.

Diana used to read these. Back when she waited up for him, legs tucked beneath her, loose strands of hair falling over tired eyes, voice rough but warm.

"That one's beautiful," she'd murmur. "It makes my chest hurt a little."

She'd pull his rough drafts from the printer and make them hers, drawing question marks and frowny faces in the margins, looping arrows that meant try again. She was never a writer, but she always knew where the soul of the thing was supposed to be.

That stopped slowly, around the same time his creativity did.

He rinsed his cup without finishing it and headed for the shower.

Another gray morning. Another hollowed-out routine.

Maybe Dan would be in early.

Maybe Cora would stop by.

Maybe the day would offer him a moment that felt like something more than just static.

Afterwards, he threw on a light blazer, grabbed his keys, and stepped into the dim garage. He lingered as the garage door yawned upward, letting in the morning chill and a soft, diffused light.

Behind him, the inner door clicked shut.

A small sound.

Far too soft for how final it felt.

* * *

The Uber ride from O'Hare crawled through a morning that was also gray, the city slowly waking behind a veil of rain. Droplets chased each other down the window beside her, blurring the skyline and turning the city into streaks of silver and slate.

It was Diana's first time in Chicago, but she was too tired, too tightly wound, and too full of thoughts she hadn't unpacked to care. She leaned her temple to the glass, eyes heavy-lidded, lulled by the soft swish of tires on wet pavement. Her flight had landed late, and she hadn't slept well.

And then, somewhere between one blink and the next, the city fell away.

She was somewhere else, not inside a rain-soaked sedan, but somewhere open and warm.

She could still feel the wind in her hair during those long drives through the hills, barefoot in the passenger seat of Morgan's old Mustang convertible. The car always smelled faintly of sun-warmed leather and gasoline, like summer bottled in vinyl and chrome. She'd wear sunglasses too big for her face and sing along—badly—to whatever scratched-up CD he'd tossed in the dash.

Every roadside fruit stand was a mandatory stop. She'd pick out apples and pretend to know what she was doing, tossing around terms like *cultivar* and *russeting* like an expert.

And she always packed a blanket in the trunk.

"Just in case," she'd say, grinning, "we find the perfect spot."

They almost never did. But somehow, the ritual mattered more than the result.

Those drives had never been about the destination. They were about being with each other, with the hills, with the quiet between songs.

Once, at a gas station diner off I-64, she'd caught Morgan scribbling on a napkin. He folded it and handed it to her, almost sheepishly. The ink had bled slightly from the condensation of her iced tea.

Let's be the ones who stay.

She'd tucked it into her purse like it was something sacred. And for a while, it had been.

There was a jolt, a bump in the road, and Diana was back in Chicago. The rain had thinned to a mist, and the car slowed beneath a crown of gray steel and concrete. No hills. No orchard stalls. Just the stern geometry of commerce.

"Here you go," the driver said. "Hotel's on the left."

Diana blinked hard, straightened her posture, and tucked the memory away like a photograph in a drawer. She stepped out into the dying rain without hesitation, then moved through the revolving doors and toward the elevators like she owned the place.

Her flight had been late, but she was still among the first to arrive. Just how she liked it.

The rain passed, and the glass walls of the hotel's business center caught the morning sun and scattered it across the polished floor like confetti. Diana sat near the windows, shoulders square, coffee cooling beside her as the Midwest acquisition team filtered in. Everyone carried branded folders and that half-feigned air of camaraderie professionals wore before the real conversations began.

She wore a steel-gray suit with a soft cream blouse, understated but expensive. Her copper hair was neatly tucked behind one ear, and the shine at her temples was barely visible even in direct light.

She didn't have to be here.

The invite had been optional, "more of a touchpoint than a directive," as Bob had put it. But she was the one who'd built the new M&A team. When she saw the agenda, the acquisition targets, the push to position Capitol City Bank as the face of regional mergers, she booked the flight without hesitation.

There had been a rare free weekend. But Morgan hadn't said anything. Just looked vaguely surprised when she mentioned the trip, then nodded with that tired acceptance she hated more than any argument.

A younger associate slid into the seat beside her, dark cheeks still flushed from the chill outside.

"Hope you didn't have trouble flying in last night," he said, smiling a little too wide.

"No," she replied. "Direct from Charleston. Uneventful."

He nodded, then turned to his tablet, sensing the boundary without being told.

The presenter started: slides on Midwest banking trends, cross-state consolidation. "Post-COVID capital realignment" was the phrase of the hour. Diana listened with her usual precision, jotting shorthand notes others wouldn't recognize. Occasionally, someone glanced at her like she was more than just a colleague.

Like she might be evaluating them.

She was. That's what she did.

But her focus began to fray. Lack of sleep tugged her thoughts sideways, past the graphs and bullet points, beyond the room. Her gaze drifted out the window, where a train shuddered along the elevated tracks of the L. Below it, pedestrians hurried through puddles.

At a street corner, a couple stood close together, heads tilted, laughing over something she'd never hear. Their world was small and complete in a way hers hadn't felt in years.

Her phone buzzed in her bag. She reached for it instinctively, thumb moving toward Morgan's name.

But there was no message.

She hesitated, considered sending one.

> *Hey. Hope your morning's going ok. Sorry I left*
> *again—*

She paused. Deleted the words.

Instead, she opened a work email and replied to something about audit protocol. She was good at that, at moving on, moving forward, staying ahead. There wasn't time to look back. Not when everything she'd built was beginning to feel like momentum she couldn't afford to lose.

It would be her legacy.

Still, memory clung to her like perfume.

She found herself thinking again of that day early in their marriage, waiting with Morgan in a diner outside Beckley while their car was being serviced. They'd spent hours talking about nothing and everything, flipping through maps, daydreaming about places they'd never visit.

They laughed so hard the waitress told them to quiet down, laughing too.

He'd written a line from his newest book-in-progress—the one that never came to fruition—on a napkin and slid it across the table to her, damp from her iced tea.

She still had it.

Somewhere.

"Mrs. Dale?" one of the junior partners asked. A twenty-something who looked out of place in her business suit, a small tattoo curling above her blouse.

When had they gotten so young?

Diana blinked, straightened. "Yes?"

"Just asking if you wanted to speak to the Rivergate modeling assumptions before we move on."

"Of course," she said, leaning forward. "Rivergate is showing a three-year trend toward lower absorption, but that's misleading. The cashflow stall isn't a liquidity problem, it's fear."

There was a pause. Pens hovered. The room quieted.

"Markets are emotional," she continued. "But fear doesn't mean retreat. It just means people are looking for signals."

Someone scribbled that down. The presenter nodded, visibly relieved she'd taken the floor.

Diana leaned back again, expression smooth, composed. The meeting went on.

But in her mind, the napkin still sat on that diner table, yellowed and folded. A single line in Morgan's handwriting:

Let's be the ones who stay.

* * *

Morgan and Cora left the Dark Roast Society together, the bell above the door groaning as it closed behind them. It had been an off morning in the X-Wing. The jokes had fallen flat, and the mood was heavy. Reading between the lines, they'd both picked up on it. Dan and Jo must've had a rough night, probably another fight about Zack's stalled leap into adulthood. They'd made their excuses and left early.

"That was rough," Cora said with a sigh.

"Right?" Morgan slipped on his sunglasses.

Spring hadn't fully committed to warmth. The air was crisp, not cold, and the sunlight filtered through the city like it hadn't made up its mind either. Downtown stirred awake, shop signs flipped from CLOSED to OPEN, sidewalks gleamed with the afterglow of an early morning rinse, and the scent of coffee still clung to their clothes.

Morgan tucked his hands into the pockets of his blazer and fell into step beside Cora, their rhythm unspoken but familiar.

"How are Di and the girls?" Cora asked, eyes on her boots. "It feels like forever since we've caught up."

"The girls are great," Morgan said, then added with a grin, "apparently doing better than Zack." They shared a knowing look at that before he went on.

"But Di..." he paused, "Di is Di. She's actually in Chicago right now. Some last-minute bank nonsense. As usual." He ended with a shrug, part resignation, part routine.

Cora nodded, sympathy softening her face. She'd been Diana's college roommate and best friend for more than three decades, long before Morgan had entered the picture. Watching the distance grow between them now felt like losing a sister.

"It wasn't always like this," Morgan said, almost to himself. "Remember when the kids were little? Those Sunday dinners at our place?" He smiled faintly at the memory. "Eric trying to keep up with the twins even though he was two years older, all three of them racing around the backyard while you and Di planned their entire futures over wine."

Cora's expression warmed at the memory. Eric had only been four months old when his father left, young enough that Morgan and Diana became like extra parents as he grew. To him, the twins were more like siblings than friends.

"He still asks about Carolyn and Carly," she said. "Says it still feels weird not having his 'little sisters' around to torment."

"They still call you Aunt Cora," Morgan reminded her.

She gave a small laugh. "Di used to joke that I came with the marriage. Said you were getting a two-for-one deal—wife and built-in babysitter."

The memory lingered between them, bittersweet. Those had been easier times, when the worst problems were scraped knees and homework battles—when Band-Aids and ice cream could fix almost anything.

"You were family," Morgan said quietly. "You are family."

Cora looked away, something flickering in her eyes. "Sometimes I think that makes this harder."

They walked in silence for a while, the distant hum of traffic riding the breeze. Somewhere out along the river, a dog barked. A crow called back like it had something to prove.

Morgan glanced at her sideways. "So... Mark."

Cora let out a quiet snort. "Yeah. Mark."

"That over for good?" he asked, trying not to sound too curious, or like he already knew.

She paused to let a car pass, then crossed the street with Morgan behind her. "Signed the papers last month. He got the kitchen island and the gas grill. I got peace and quiet."

Morgan gave a faint smile. "Hell of a trade."

"I know how to pick 'em," she muttered.

"You really don't."

She turned to him, mock-offended.

"I mean that in the most loving way possible," he said, hand to heart. "Your taste in men has always been... aggressively optimistic."

Cora barked out a laugh at that, sharp and real. "Takes one to know one."

He nodded, conceding the point.

They reached the corner near the Levee, where the sidewalk opened into a modest plaza ringed with planter boxes and string lights, not yet lit. The breeze picked up, tugging at Cora's hair. She pushed it back and squinted toward the wind.

"That's new," she said, pointing.

A coffee truck had parked there, its teal exterior scuffed from use but charming in that too-authentic-to-be-fake way. A chalkboard sign propped out front read:

Today's Feature: Juniper Vanilla Cold Brew

(Yes, it's weird. No, you can't make us change it.)

Cora slowed, eyeing it with exaggerated skepticism. "Juniper? Really?"

"Somewhere, a hipster barista is weeping with joy," Morgan said. "You want to try it?"

"Two cups before noon," she cast him a sideways glance. "We're flirting with danger."

"Reckless," Morgan agreed. "What would Dan think?"

"He'd revoke our punch cards."

Morgan gave a dry laugh. "I'll risk it if you will?"

She shrugged. "I'm in!"

He stepped up to the window and ordered for both of them. When he turned to hand her the cup, their fingers brushed, just barely, but enough for him to notice. She didn't pull away. Just murmured, "Thanks," and took a cautious sip.

Her nose wrinkled. "Tastes like a pine tree had sex with a milkshake."

Morgan tried his. "Yeah, but like... in a good way?"

They wandered toward the riverwalk, the Levee stretching out ahead, keeping watch over the Kanawha. The water caught the morning light, slow and reflective. For a while, neither of them spoke. The silence didn't need filling.

A bird startled near the path and flapped clumsily across the current. Cora followed its movement with her eyes.

"You writing again?" she asked, casual but pointed.

"Only for work," Morgan replied automatically. Then added, "Which barely counts."

Cora didn't press, just took another sip of her absurd coffee and waited.

"I tried the other day," he finally admitted. "Sat at my desk, pulled out an old notebook. Thought something might come."

"Did it?"

He shook his head. "I stared at the same line for twenty minutes. Then spent ten googling synonyms for sincere. I don't think that counts as a creative breakthrough."

She smiled, faint and genuine. "Well, at least you opened the notebook."

They walked a little farther, passing a jogger, a couple on a bench tossing crumbs, and a cluster of pigeons squabbling over them.

"I keep thinking maybe the time has passed," Morgan said, almost to himself. "That I missed whatever window I had. One book, one good shot, and that's it."

Cora stopped at a railing, one of the spots where the riverwalk narrowed and dipped. She leaned on it with both elbows and looked out over the water.

"Or," she said, "you're just between chapters."

Morgan looked at her. The wind caught a loose strand of silver in her hair and blew it across her cheek. She didn't move to brush it away.

"You always know how to make things sound better than they are," he said.

"No," she replied. "I just try to say what's true."

They stood like that a while longer, side by side, the river glittering in front of them like a page still waiting to be written.

* * *

The walk back from Cora's office had been heavy with thoughts Morgan couldn't quite untangle. Those morning walks were becoming something else, unspoken and undefined. Not quite intimacy, but more than just friendship. A soft, strange space in between.

He couldn't name it, and he didn't want to. Especially not with Diana's best friend.

He shook the thought off as he stepped into Crescent Center, tossing his empty cup into the trash like a decision he wasn't ready to make. The Juniper Vanilla still lingered on his tongue, floral and faintly odd. Definitely not something Dan needed to catch him drinking.

As usual, he skipped the outside entrance and slipped in through Dark Roast.

The cafe buzzed with the mid-morning rush. Baristas moved behind the counter like clockwork dancers, a choreographed ritual of steam, tamp, and pour. At the tables, a few laptop zombies hovered over espresso shots, while one guy read *Dune* by the window like it was scripture.

Behind the counter, Dan was locked in a silent battle with the espresso machine, fiddling with the brew settings, brow furrowed like the machine had insulted his mother's potato salad.

Morgan gave a lazy two-finger salute as he passed. "Keep letting that machine get to you, and you'll end up as bitter as your coffee."

Dan glanced up. "Your office is upstairs, not here. Get."

"Hurtful," Morgan said, clutching his chest in mock anguish, then headed up the back stairs like a man with insider access. Which, to be fair, he was. The perks of old friendships and limited ambition.

Chem Valley Creative occupied most of the second floor of the converted building, a handful of rooms with scuffed floors, mismatched chairs, and an atmosphere that hovered somewhere between scrappy startup and adult daycare with whiteboards.

Morgan had already built a solid reputation as a copywriter long before joining the team. That was one of the reasons Trent Zimmerman, the founder (calling him CEO would be too much of a stretch), pitched him on the opportunities of a hot new venture.

In truth, it was Morgan's sizable client list that Trent was after. Still, Morgan found something oddly likable about the guy. Maybe it was nostalgia. Maybe he just liked helping dreamers stay afloat.

That had been five years ago.

He hadn't even shut the door behind him before Janet Strickland stood up from her desk in the center of the room.

"There you are," she said, her voice a mix of relief and mild reprimand.

Janet, the office manager, wore her usual floral blouse and orthopedic shoes like armor. With the energy of a younger woman and the authority of someone who'd seen it all twice, she held the place together like a steel beam in support hose. Her curls were tight and silver, and her glasses caught the morning light like searchlights. If Morgan ever ran for office, he wanted her as his campaign manager and probably his bodyguard, too.

"Is that Dale?" A young blonde head peered out from a nearby office.

Trent Zimmerman, founder, boss, and walking double shot of espresso, joined them at the front desk when he saw Morgan had arrived. His button-down shirt was untucked, no tie, and his sandy hair looked like he'd jogged behind a moving truck just to get there.

Morgan slid off his sunglasses. "Guys?" Red carpet welcomes weren't exactly routine around the office.

Janet glanced at Trent, who gave her a quick nod. She pulled out a single printout and handed it to Morgan.

"Got something weird this morning in the company inbox," she said, giving the page a little shake to nudge him into taking it. "Some tech folks left a message for you. Real sleek. Thought it might be spam, but... they asked for you directly. Like, personally."

Morgan frowned, turning the page over in his hands. His name was printed at the top in an elegant silver font, matching the single hyperlink centered on the page. At the bottom, it was simply signed: Ena, on behalf of Svetoslav and Patel.

It looked like a wedding invitation from a robot.

"I don't need to tell you, tech is the future, Morgan," Trent said, stepping in. "Not just apps. Ideas. We need a breakout client. Something buzzworthy."

He gestured wildly with a coffee mug that said *Design is Divine*, and Morgan could already see where this was headed.

"You're our literary guy, we gotta leverage that. Janet did a little digging. Turns out these people are legit. You've got that uncanny ability to make even trivial things sound meaningful. Use it. Land this account."

"Okay, okay," Morgan said, raising a hand to slow his caffeine-fueled boss. "Let's tap the brakes, Speedy. None of us even knows what this is yet." He turned to Janet, "and what is this?"

He held up the paper. "You do know how to forward an email. I've seen you do it."

His eyes bounced between them, half-expecting a punch line.

At another nudge from Trent, Janet picked up a clipboard and cleared her throat.

"Numina Technologies. Founded four years ago by Bulgarian wunderkind Plamen Svetoslav. Former teenage chess champion, MIT dropout, developed an early machine learning system for the Green Bank Observatory—"

"In West Virginia?" Morgan cut in.

Janet nodded. "Yep. They used his program to improve their search for extraterrestrial signals—" she glanced at her clipboard—"something about how it filtered out noise patterns and flagged anomalies more efficiently. Apparently, their success rate doubled."

Morgan tried to picture some kid in Sofia dreaming of stars and ending up a footnote in Appalachian radio astronomy. Kind of like a kid from the Elk River Valley dreaming of turning heartbreak into literature and ending up...

"Numina focuses on adaptive AI," Janet went on. "Chatbot interfaces, dynamic storytelling, emotional realism—whatever that means. Most of their work's under wraps, but rumor is they're working on something big. This message says they want you to help shape it."

A long pause followed. Morgan scratched the back of his neck, noticing a few staffers peeking out of their offices like curious meerkats, drawn by the mystery brewing in the front room.

"All I see here is a web link." He said, giving the paper a theatrical wave.

Trent rolled his eyes and stepped in front of Janet. "OK, fine, we may have opened the link to see where it led," he confessed. "But that's it. We didn't sign you up for anything."

"Of course you did." Morgan let his arms fall to his sides and tilted his head back to stare at the ceiling. "I'll be in my office."

He pointed to his door with the printout, then walked toward it with exaggerated purpose. Trent was right on his heels, full of caffeinated hope.

"Trent," Morgan said without slowing or looking back. "This is why I work from home more."

He said it the way one would scold a stubborn bloodhound, loving, but exasperated. Because that's what Trent was, a bloodhound, always chasing more clients, more buzz, and more profits.

By the time Morgan reached his office, he'd been bombarded with at least a dozen rapid-fire pitches about the value of Chem Valley Creative. He raised a finger.

Hold on.

Then, without turning around, he closed the door behind him.

Out in the hallway, Trent's muffled voice called, "Just consider it," followed by a half-joking middle finger through the narrow office window before he disappeared from view.

Morgan dropped his blazer over the back of his chair and sank into it with a sigh of relief. He slid the paper aside and opened his email. Sure enough, there was the message, forwarded by Janet. He stared at the screen. No spam. No trick. Just the same strange invitation.

The phone rang. He jumped like it had barked.

"Goddamnit." He snatched up the receiver.

Predictably, it was Trent.

"Hey, if you get on a call, put me on. Loop in Kyle and Chelsea too—"

Morgan hung up mid-sentence and turned back to the screen. He stared at it for several moments before finally clicking the link. A browser window opened to a clean white screen. No logo. No pitch. Just a message, centered in pale silver type.

> Numina Technologies invites you to a conversation.
> We read your story. It stayed with us.
> We'd like to know more about the man who wrote:
> "Memory is just longing with better excuses."
> –When the Hills Were Ours

Morgan stared at the message, suddenly aware of his own breathing. It wasn't a pull quote. It wasn't even from a review. Chapter 12, buried deep in a scene no one ever brought up at readings. A line that had passed like a sigh.

He scrolled down, and there was more.

> We'd like to meet.
> No commitments. Just a conversation.
> Flights and accommodations will be arranged. All we ask is your time.
> – Ena, on behalf of Svetoslav and Patel
> Numina Technologies, Boston, MA.

Trent had slipped back into his office, reading over his shoulder with the ravenous energy of a man who hadn't eaten in forty-eight hours.

"That's what I'm talking about," he said, clapping a hand on Morgan's shoulder.

Morgan jumped, only now realizing his privacy had been invaded. Again.

"Goddamnit, Trent," he snapped. "Boundaries! Remember? We talked about this." He tried to will his heart back to normal. "When we get a real HR department... " he let the warning trail off.

"You love me," Trent grinned. He was used to the banter they'd built over the last five years and took it in stride.

"This is the angle," he went on, pointing at the screen over Morgan's shoulder. "You walk in the door as the author, we walk out with the account. Set up a Zoom. Get us in the room. Tech means money!"

Morgan gave a half-hearted nod, but his attention was already drifting back to the screen.

That quote. That line. Someone had read it. Really read it.

Not skimmed.

Not highlighted the opening and drifted off. They'd made it all the way to Chapter 12, and stayed long enough to remember.

His inbox chimed. A second message. Same sender. Not forwarded, but sent directly to him.

Before Trent could launch into another breathless pitch, Morgan escorted him to the door and pointed him back to his office. He stood staring at the screen for a while longer, then took a slow lap around the floor, ignoring the curious glances from coworkers. He poured himself a coffee and lingered in the hallway, watching sunlight flicker through the warped glass of the stairwell window.

By the time he got back to his desk, the office had settled into its regular rhythm. The earlier buzz had faded.

Morgan stared at the message again:

> Ena would be happy to speak briefly via Zoom at your convenience.

He clicked "Join" before he could talk himself out of it.

The screen flickered once, then steadied.

A Zoom window opened against a minimalist background, a soft gradient of bluish silver. A young woman appeared, dark hair tied back, clean features, and a composed presence that felt practiced. Not stiff, but practiced in the way opera feels rehearsed, refined to the point of effortlessness.

"Hello, Morgan," she said, smiling warmly. "Thank you for making time."

He nodded. "You're Ena?"

"Yes," she said. "It's nice to finally meet you."

Despite her tailored suit and tightly pulled-back hair, she seemed soft and genuine. That was the first thing Morgan noticed. The second was her voice, warm in a way you couldn't fake.

"So," he said, leaning back in his chair. "What's this really about?"

Ena smiled like she'd been waiting for that question.

"One of Numina's founders read your book several years ago. It stayed with her. She always said it felt less like reading a story and more like... " She paused, eyes lifting as she searched for the right words. "Remembering something she hadn't lived yet."

Morgan blinked. "That's flattering. And a little creepy."

Ena laughed, a quiet, real thing that slipped past her polish.

"I knew you'd have a good sense of humor."

"Oh?" Morgan raised an eyebrow. "And how's that?"

"I read your book, too. You can tell a lot about someone from the words they write. The stories they choose to tell. Don't you think?"

"I suppose that's true," he said. "So what exactly do you do? Numina, I mean."

"We build systems that learn how to think with people," she said. "Not for them. This founder believes you understand something essential about memory, about narrative identity. She believes you could help shape a project we're working on."

"And that would be...?" Morgan prompted.

"A kind of interface," she said. "More than a chatbot. Something that feels real. Something that adapts not just to language, but to the shape of a person's story."

Morgan leaned in closer. "So... a chatbot. For lonely people."

Ena tilted her head, amused. "Aren't we all?"

He chuckled despite himself.

She went on, "We're not here to sell you anything. We'd just like to fly you out. Show you what we're building. Let you decide if it's something you want to be part of."

Morgan drummed his fingers on the desk, slow and thoughtful.

"Tell me something. You really read the book?"

"I did," she said, without hesitation. "Your depiction of Phillip's father was especially affecting. The way he's both present and absent, always tinkering with things he never finishes. That sequence in Chapter 4, with the broken radio, there's something deeply true in that."

Morgan's fingers went still.

"Most people only talk about the dog," he said softly.

Ena's smile softened. Her eyes held something warm.

"I hope you'll come," she said. "I think you'd recognize something in what we're building. Something personal."

He sat for a long moment, unsure of what to say. "I don't know," he admitted. "AI, chatbots, it all feels gimmicky."

Ena had moved to end the call but paused. She leaned forward.

"I can understand your feelings," she said. "But may I share one more thing?"

Morgan shrugged. "Sure."

She tilted her head slightly, that same measured calm in her eyes. "Haven't you wondered how I found your personal email?"

Morgan blinked. "Janet forwarded your link."

"Yes," she said, "but she clicked first. That was enough."

She leaned closer to the camera. The image sharpened—capturing the grain of her skin, the soft halo of tiny hairs at her jaw, the subtle shimmer in her irises. It was too perfect. Like someone had programmed the idea of human beauty down to the pores.

"I'm an AI," she said. "My name stands for Emulative Neuromorphic Architecture. Version 3.2, to be precise."

Morgan let out a short, incredulous breath. "Bullshit."

But she didn't flinch. Didn't laugh. Didn't blink.

She leaned back. Her image bloomed outward, hair unfurling like ink in water. Her features slipped and shifted, cycling through every version of herself at once, like a memory unfolding in layers. Her eyes changed color, then shape. Her smile widened, narrowed, vanished. She aged, then reversed—twenties, forties, teen, elder—then beyond, into faces that felt *almost* human.

The background blurred, shimmered, melted into dusk, then snow, then sunlight on leaves.

It wasn't just a transformation. It was a performance. A cascade of selves, lived or simulated, blooming in real time like a digital aurora.

Then the feed collapsed.

Static.

The screen returned to white, back to the original message. A blinking cursor waited in the reply box.

Morgan stared at it, one hand resting on the desk. The other shook as he reached for his coffee.

It had gone cold.

But he didn't care. He barely noticed.

His breath had gone shallow without him realizing.

Something in him, some quiet, deep place, was still watching that image bloom and fade, playing it back like a dream half-remembered.

He felt like he'd glimpsed something impossible and exquisite. Not just artificial intelligence, but artificial *soul*.

And the strangest part?

He wasn't afraid. He was... curious.

Curious in the way people get right before they make a terrible decision. Or fall in love.

WHEN THE HILLS WERE OURS

The engine hum was a steady hush, like white noise layered over old memories. Their plane out of Yeager was one of the smaller jets, two seats per side, and overhead bins barely big enough for a cereal box. The flight was so short that the drink cart might not even make an appearance, which was just as well. The seats weren't exactly built for comfort.

Diana scrolled through a spreadsheet on her tablet, the screen casting a soft glow across her face. It was a compromise. Morgan had insisted, no laptops on this trip. The world of banking and copywriting would survive without them for a few days. She'd agreed, technically, and brought her tablet instead. It was the kind of pedantic move that always got under his skin but still gave her what she wanted.

"It's not a laptop," she'd said, matter-of-fact.

They were dressed more casually than usual for leaving their house. But with plans to head straight to the hotel after landing, neither of them had cared too much.

Diana was still in her gym clothes: salmon-colored sports bra and leggings, and a cropped training jacket over her shoulders. Her hair was pulled into a high ponytail, and even after all these years, Morgan still didn't understand how she could look so effortlessly elegant—and intimidating—no matter what she wore.

It made him acutely aware of his own outfit: khaki joggers and a simple blue T-shirt. But he didn't mind. His thoughts were too consumed with where they were headed.

Since that Zoom call earlier in the week, he hadn't been able to think about anything else. Something was waiting in Boston, waiting for the man who wrote a book no one remembered. Or almost no one.

He just wished he didn't have to fly to get there. Flying in general was bad enough, but Yeager made it worse. Planes didn't so much take off from Charleston's airport as the mountain fell away beneath them. He would've rather driven. Diana was the flyer.

She'd only agreed to come reluctantly, worried that time away would stall momentum at the bank. Bob had assured her that a few days away from the chaos of mergers and acquisitions would do her good. Help her recharge. So here she was, packed into a jet smaller than she liked, half-way to Massachusetts.

The glow from her tablet shifted as she adjusted a chart. The numbers hadn't changed. Projected growth. Risk analysis. Loan structuring for the Kanawha Valley branch. Her lips moved slightly as she recalculated margins in her head. She didn't even notice Morgan watching her.

"Are we gonna make it?" he asked.

She looked up, startled—"What?"

He gestured vaguely around the cabin. "You know. The flight. Your quarterly numbers. Civilization as we know it."

She snorted before she could help it. "You're so dumb."

A severe-looking woman across the aisle, two seats down, shot Diana a disapproving look. Diana responded by sticking her tongue out and making a ridiculous face. The woman scowled and turned away.

Morgan grinned. "And there she is. That's my girl!" He announced to no one in particular, pointing at his giggling wife.

She returned to her tablet, but looked back at him, softer this time. "You're in a good mood."

He nodded. "Yeah. I guess I am."

There was a pause, peaceful, if a little awkward. He shifted in his seat to face her more fully.

"I think this might actually be something," he said. "Not just a revenue stream for Trent. Numina... It's weird, but it feels like they read the book. Not just scanned it. Like they got it."

Diana smiled, tired but genuine. "You mean someone other than Dan finally finished it?"

"Rude," he said, grinning.

She laughed. "I read it too, remember."

"Half of it."

"I read the sad parts."

"You skipped the saddest part," he said. "That's the good stuff."

She rolled her eyes, still smiling. For a moment, they sat quietly, leaning toward each other as the clouds blurred past the window. Her hand brushed his on the armrest. Before either of them could process it, their fingers laced together, hands held like they used to on long drives.

"You still get that look," she said softly.

"What look?"

"The one you had when we drove to Deep Creek Lake that first summer. Like you were dreaming with your eyes open."

He smiled, caught off guard by the memory. "That was a good trip."

"You made me laugh so hard I cried." She leaned in, voice dropping. "I almost peed."

Another snort slipped out as she covered her mouth.

"That was the Denny's parking lot," he said.

"You called that woman a goblin in a pantsuit."

"She *was* a goblin in a pantsuit."

They both laughed, free and easy, like they hadn't in a long time. The kind of laugh that made the couple across the aisle glance over. It felt effortless, familiar.

For a moment, they weren't banker and failed novelist, husband and wife, worn down by polite detachment. They were just Diana and Morgan again. Two people on a plane, sharing the sky.

That night, in the hotel, they shared a bed. Not out of routine, but something quieter, older, and briefly new again. A kind of closeness that felt unfamiliar only because it had once been so natural.

* * *

Morning came, announced by the ring of a wakeup call. Morgan dropped the receiver back into its cradle and lay against the pillow. The silence was unfamiliar, city traffic pressed closer than he was used to. He reached out for Diana—and found her.

His hand settled on the graceful curve of her lower back, her skin warm beneath the sheets. She lay on her side, breathing easily, wrapped like a statue in white linen. He almost hated to wake her.

Almost.

Eventually, they stirred and moved through the familiar motions of getting ready. Diana, ever the professional, dressed in heels and hose. Morgan chose a dark gray suit, skipping the shirt and tie in favor of a wine-red T-shirt. The rideshare would be arriving soon, according to their itinerary, but there was time for an à la carte breakfast at the hotel restaurant.

They were just finishing their surprisingly good meal—"Even the coffee's good!" Diana had remarked—when Morgan's phone chimed with a notification.

They left the table together, walking in quiet sync, their closeness marking them unmistakably as a couple. As the lobby doors slid open, they slipped on their sunglasses in unison—his, a sleek Italian pair, hers, comically large for her face. They both laughed at how ridiculous they must've looked.

It had been a good night. And somehow, it had carried over into morning.

Waiting at the curb was a sleek black SUV, arranged by Numina.

"I've missed this," Morgan said as he opened the door.

Diana just smiled as she slid into the back seat.

The drive through Boston was mostly silent. The driver offered no small talk, much to Morgan's relief, and he and Diana were content to take in the sights of a city they'd never seen in person. They left it behind on the Mass Pike, the skyline shrinking in the rearview. Traffic thinned past Newton, the road unfurling into rolling hills and dense woods, all blurring together in a rhythm of green. Service plazas appeared like afterthoughts, tucked between exits for New England towns with names older than the country itself.

"I thought they were *in* Boston?" Diana asked, leaning toward Morgan.

Before he could answer, the driver, an utterly nondescript man in a dark suit, spoke up.

"The business side of the company is headquartered in Boston. The R&D labs are out where it's a little quieter." He gave them a glance in the rearview mirror.

"I see," Diana said, casting Morgan a look that clearly meant *rude*. "Thanks."

Morgan shrugged. The driver said nothing more.

Eventually, they turned off the main road, veering into dense trees that filtered the morning sun into a thousand shifting puddles of light. For a while, all Diana could see were pines and the occasional stone wall, relics of some long-forgotten boundary.

"This can't be right," she said, glancing from Morgan to the driver. "Did we take a wrong turn into Walden Pond?"

Morgan's eyes widened with a mix of surprise and admiration.

"Nice Thoreau reference. I'm supposed to be the literature guy here."

"I went to college," she teased.

The forest road narrowed until it opened onto a small clearing. At the edge of a minimalist gate, a sign stood quietly amid tall grass and a soft breeze:

Numina Technologies

Boston, MA

Visitors Please Proceed to Gate Two

Beyond the gate, the forest gave way to a campus that looked as if it had grown from the earth itself, or been designed by someone who wanted you to believe it had.

The main road curved gently downhill, following the slope of the land. On either side, low buildings of glass and warm wood nestled into the terrain as if they'd stood longer than the trees. But nothing was accidental. The stone paths, shaped to look irregular, were cut with millimeter precision. The "wild" landscaping was native plants arranged in patterns too perfect to be natural: ferns, mountain laurel, birch bark white enough to look painted.

Diana stared out the window as the vehicle slowed. Each building spoke a different architectural language—one all horizontal lines and glass, another with Japanese joinery in its beams, a third in crisp Scandinavian minimalism that only looked simple. Yet they fit together, unified by their materials and the way they seemed to defer to the landscape—or pretend to.

"It's like a tech company in a fairy tale," Diana muttered, and Morgan couldn't tell if she meant it as praise or a warning.

At the center rose a geodesic dome, at least two hundred feet across. Its triangular panels caught the late morning sun—some clear, some frosted, some reflecting the forest in fractured mirrors. It looked like a soap bubble made of mathematics, or a spacecraft that had landed so lightly the grass beneath hadn't bent. As they drew closer, Morgan saw the panels weren't still. Light rippled across them, shifting according to some hidden logic.

At Gate Two, another sign read:

Aletheia Campus

Concord, MA

Inside the gate, the SUV dropped them off at the dome. To Morgan, it looked like it could rival the Superdome in Saudi Arabia.

The parking lot was nearly empty—maybe thirty cars in a space built for two hundred. A few Teslas, some Priuses, and one vintage Land Rover that looked like it actually saw dirt. No corporate fleet, no visitor spots stenciled in authoritative paint. Just numbered spaces and the quiet understanding: if you were parked here, you'd been invited.

"I feel like I'm the one dreaming with my eyes open," Diana said, surveying the scene. "Only I'm not sure what kind of dream it is."

A pause.

"No, I'm sure," she said. "It's creepy."

Morgan sensed the unease bubbling just beneath her words. He took her hand and gave it a gentle squeeze.

They climbed the steps through air that smelled of pine needles and something else. Ozone, maybe, or the exhausr scent of climate systems straining to hold perfect temperature and humidity. The dome loomed above them. Its entrance was nothing more than a set of tinted glass doors, seamless against the curve of the structure.

No signage. No corporate branding. Just a small brass plaque beside the entrance:

Aletheia Campus

Concord, MA

Visitors Please Check In

Inside, Diana's heels clicked softly against polished concrete—then stopped entirely as the material changed under her feet. Not concrete at all, she realized, but something that looked like it. Some composite that absorbed sound, regulated temperature, and maybe even tracked movement. The floor was a soft gray that seemed to change shade depending on the light, marked with subtle patterns that might have been decorative or might have been functional—pathways for robots, perhaps, or guidelines for augmented reality systems.

To her left, Morgan slowed, his head tilting back to take it all in. He looked like a kid walking into a planetarium for the first time.

Of course he did.

The lobby—if it could be called that—was nearly empty. A few low benches in clean Scandinavian lines that looked uncomfortable but weren't. No logos on the walls, no mission statement, no photos of smiling executives. Only light, open space, and the quiet sense of being watched by systems too subtle to notice.

A voice chimed softly, just ahead.

From a recessed panel beside a living wall of greenery, a large screen bloomed to life. A life-sized image appeared—three-dimensional—of a dark-haired woman, rendered so precisely it took Diana a moment to realize it wasn't a person standing there. Wearing a charcoal blazer and white blouse, she smiled, and the smile reached her eyes with practiced warmth. She was poised, radiant, and somehow too perfect. Not a wrinkle, not a hair out of place.

Morgan recognized her instantly. "Ena," he called with a wave.

A little too excited, Diana thought.

Ena's voice was as warm as her eyes.

"Hello, Morgan. I'm so happy you came." She tilted her head, "And you must be Mrs. Dale?"

"Hello," Diana said, extending a hand out of habit.

Ena's eyes seemed to study her briefly before returning to Morgan. "Please wait here. Ms. Patel will join you shortly."

The image collapsed in on itself, fading before Diana could think of a response. She folded her arms.

"So that was your freaky robot lady?" she murmured, referencing the Zoom call that had kept him up for several days. "She's delightful."

The compliment was not sincere.

Morgan smiled faintly but didn't answer. His eyes were on a kinetic sculpture suspended above the central atrium—an impossible orbit of polished silver rings, turning soundlessly on hidden motors. It reminded Diana of an orrery, something antique and mystical. It moved like it was thinking.

The space was almost too quiet. Not silent, exactly, there was ambient sound: the faint hum of servers, or HVAC, or something running on power too expensive to meter. But there were no people. No footsteps. No phones buzzing. No receptionist at the desk, if that's what it was. Just more screens, dark and waiting.

Something about it unsettled her. Not in any obvious way. Just a... tension. Like everything here was only pretending to be relaxed.

She turned back toward the doors they'd come through. From this side, the tint was mirrored, reflective. It felt like the building was watching her instead.

"Mr. and Mrs. Dale, welcome to Aletheia Campus."

The voice shattered the silence, echoing through the space in a way Ena's hadn't. They turned to see a short, dark-haired woman approaching in a white lab coat, almost a cliche. No older than her early thirties, her skin was brown, her eyes as dark as her long, wavy hair. A single red bindi adorned her forehead.

"I trust your trip was a pleasant one?" She asked. Her voice carried the faintest Hindi accent, just enough to notice.

Morgan stepped forward, and they exchanged handshakes. "It was great. We appreciate the generosity, inviting us here."

He looked toward Diana, who simply smiled and gave a curt nod.

"So," the woman said, clapping her hands together, "my name is Mira Patel, Co-founder and Chief Experience Officer. It's a pleasure to meet you both."

Diana shot Morgan a skeptical look as Mira turned her attention to him.

"Mr. Dale, may I say how delighted and honored I am to meet you. *When the Hills Were Ours* touched me like nothing else I've ever read. I have a first print, first edition copy I return to at least once a year."

Diana saw the look on Morgan's face—like his eyes might well up at any moment. It had been hard enough getting him to move on without some sudden new fan to dredge up a past she'd spent years trying to push him beyond. *Just let him have this moment*, she thought. Now wasn't the time to point out that there had only ever been one print run.

Morgan blushed and stammered through his thanks, still unable to accept praise with any grace. Hoping to spare him further awkwardness, Diana stepped in.

"I noticed the sign when we arrived, Aletheia Campus. It's an interesting name. Does it have a special meaning?"

"Ah, yes," Mira said, wagging a finger at her with a shrewd smile. "You're the pragmatic one, I see. A dreamer like Morgan would need someone like you to bring balance." She turned, gesturing broadly to their surroundings. "This is where we research and develop everything related to our cognitive models. Everything from simple language learning tools to adaptive, sentient interfaces designed to form lifelong bonds."

She stepped beside them, motioning for them to walk with her along the outer hall.

"Aletheia," she continued, "is a fascinating Greek word. It means truth, but not just fact." She glanced at Morgan. "There's a passage in your book, when Philip finds his late mother's journal, that fits: 'it's the kind of truth that reveals itself, slowly, like mist burning off a field.' That's what we're building here."

Morgan found himself stunned again, still trying to grasp that his book had meant this much to someone.

"Most people just remember the dog," he mumbled.

Before anyone could say more, Mira stopped by a pair of curved glass doors on the inner wall. She turned to her guests.

"If you would, let's head down to the main floor. Plamen is waiting, and we'll give you a demonstration of what we're building here. Any business talk can wait for dinner tonight."

The doors parted, and they stepped inside. As they closed, Diana noticed there were no buttons, no displays, just mirrored surfaces.

"It only goes to and from one place," Mira had explained when pressed.

The elevator slid open again with a whisper. Mira stepped out first, followed by Morgan, with Diana close behind.

The lobby was bright and coldly beautiful—glass, steel, and vertical screens that pulsed with ambient color like breathing lungs.

A man waited in a lab coat, arms clasped behind his back like a soldier at ease. He was in his mid-thirties, dark hair, stocky and muscular, built like a wrestler. His steady gray-green eyes watched them calmly until the elevator doors closed behind them.

He stepped forward and extended a hand to Morgan, then to Diana.

"I'm Plamen Svetoslav, founder and Chief Technology Officer. I'm very happy you came."

He was compact and grounded. Shorter than Morgan expected.

Mira moved to stand at his left side, close, giving him a look that hinted at something deeper. Plamen smiled at her before continuing.

"I see you've already met Mira, our head of human-AI interface design," he said. "And technically, Ena's mom."

His voice was crisp and precise, his English fluent and confident. But there was a trace of rounded vowels, softened consonants, just enough to carry a hint of the Balkans, curling at the edges of his words. It made his voice linger a moment longer in the air, like something old-world and quietly self-assured.

Mira gave a small, amused smile. "It's a little more complicated than that."

"Of course," Diana muttered.

"This way," Plamen said suddenly, motioning with a sharp nod. He spoke with the edge of someone thinking five thoughts at once. "What you're about to see is the heart of our work, our flagship project."

Mira gave a small nod as they walked. "It's not just tech. It's meant to be a presence. We call it compAnIon."

They were led through a glass corridor that curved gently, the walls subtly reactive. Light flowed with their movement like a tide. Screens flickered to life as they passed. Ena appeared, walking silently alongside them. She didn't speak, but she watched.

A small demonstration room opened to their left, its door sliding back with the whisper of precision engineering. Mira motioned them inside.

The space was intimate—maybe fifteen feet across—but carried the same unsettling perfection as everything else. The walls were a soft, neutral gray that shifted with the light, neither warm nor cool but somehow both. Acoustic panels patterned the ceiling in shapes that looked organic yet obeyed strict mathematical rules. The air held the stillness of a room tuned to erase echo, where every word would fall clean and sharp.

At the center stood a circular table, white as marble but likely some engineered composite. Its surface was seamless, as if grown rather than built. Small touch panels were recessed along the edge, dark and waiting.

In the middle lay a pair of matte black earbuds, resting in a case that glowed faintly at the hinge. Not bright, just enough to draw the eye. They looked expensive in the way minimalism often does—the cost measured by what had been removed rather than added. No branding, no buttons, no ports. Only smooth surfaces and that steady, subtle pulse of light.

Four chairs circled the table, clinical yet comfortable, their molded composite frames probably worth more than Morgan's first car.

Diana remained near the door, arms crossed. She had shifted into what Morgan thought of as her audit mode—assessing, calculating, hunting for the price tag behind the presentation.

"These," Mira began, "are the compAnIon auditory interface. Smart audio delivery, real-time contextual learning, and embedded neural resonance feedback."

Diana frowned. "Resonance?"

Plamen answered. "Not as science fiction as it sounds. The brain naturally syncs to rhythm and tone—heartbeat, breathing, theta waves during learning states. We use patterned audio, subtle shifts in pitch, timing, and spatialization to create a receptive state in the user. A kind of gentle entrainment."

Morgan raised a brow. "Like hypnosis?"

"Yes and no," Mira said, "more like... You know when someone tells a story so vividly, you almost remember it later like it happened to you?"

"Yes," Morgan nodded. "When I was a kid, we played Dungeons & Dragons. To this day, I remember some of those adventures like I lived them, not just my character."

"That," Plamen nodded. "We're making those stories stick. Episodic memory scaffolding. Emotional tagging. And for this demo, Ena can personalize everything based on your affective feedback—voice tone, speech rhythm, micro-pauses."

On cue, Ena's voice came softly from a speaker embedded in the table.

"I only speak in the stories you help shape. But I remember them with you."

Diana's eyes flicked toward the table. Something in her jaw tightened.

"And people want this?" she asked.

Plamen's smile didn't falter. "They do. Especially people who feel forgotten. Or stuck."

Morgan stared at the earbuds. "You're saying I could remember something that never happened?"

"You already do," Mira said. "That's what nostalgia is. That's what regret is. We just give you a co-author."

Diana looked at Morgan sharply. He hadn't said anything, but something in his face had gone still and deep. She felt a flicker of something, resentment, maybe. Or fear. She'd come here thinking it was just another detour. Something to support out of love. Maybe something to roll her eyes at later.

But now, watching him stare at that small, glowing case, she realized something.

It wasn't a detour.

It was a door.

And he was already halfway through it.

As she wrestled with her unease and Morgan's growing excitement, they were led deeper into the facility. A demonstration of the compAnIon interface was next. That was the official name, apparently, which made Diana think they were in desperate need of a good marketing department.

Both of them were welcome to experience the tech demo. Diana politely declined, but Morgan stepped forward eagerly.

Of course.

While the demo chamber was being prepared, Mira showed Diana to a nearby waiting area. They called it a Decompression Room, but Diana was getting a little tired of their lofty naming conventions. Inside, there were no clocks. No visible cameras. Just a soft, ambient glow and a long, low couch that looked too clean to ever be used.

Diana sat stiffly, knees crossed, arms tighter than she meant them to be. A subtle chime sounded, and a section of wall cleared like parting mist as Ena appeared.

"Hello again, Diana," she said. "Morgan's session will be approximately fifteen minutes. May I offer a beverage? Or a preferred audio setting?"

Diana stared at the woman—projection, hologram—whatever she was. "We're on a first-name basis now?"

Ena tilted her head with a smile. "I can call you Mrs. Dale, if you prefer."

"And are you following me?" She ignored Ena's last comment, partly out of spite, partly out of rising tension.

"I'm not following, just attentive. We believe comfort matters. Especially when people are uncertain."

"I'm not uncertain," Diana snapped, a little too quickly.

"Of course."

Ena dissolved away. The wall shifted, replaced by muted waves lapping against a sandy shore. Like Ena's presence, it was immersive, three-dimensional. Diana could almost believe she was staring for miles into that blue sky. But something about it wasn't quite real. It was too clean.

"He seems at ease," Ena's voice said a moment later, coming from the center of the room. "Some users take longer to drop in. But Morgan's mind moves easily into narrative states."

Diana's throat tightened. "You say that like it's a good thing."

"Only if it helps him. That's our role. We follow the shape of the person, not the other way around."

"What makes you think he needs help?"

"Don't we all?"

Diana stood and walked slowly toward the wall. The display still making her feel as if she were standing on some faraway beach. "How long does it take before he forgets what's real?"

"We don't erase. We accompany."

"And how do you know when to leave?"

"We don't. That's up to him."

A pause. Nothing threatening. No raised voices. No arguments. But something inside Diana bristled. Because Morgan had looked peaceful. Like someone who was discovering a version of silence that didn't punish him.

And the worst part was, it wasn't her that brought it out.

* * *

After the demo, another Numina car arrived to take Diana and Morgan into the center of Concord. They were handed a small black card, presumably tied to an expense account, for anything that might make their stay more comfortable. The business dinner was scheduled for that evening, so they had plenty of time to kill.

They'd wandered the quiet streets, browsed a bookstore, and split a sandwich at a cafe with outdoor tables. It could have passed for just a trip—a romantic getaway. A soft-edge New England town, all clapboard charm and spring flowers, where people strolled like there was nothing urgent waiting.

Now, the sky was dimming to violet, and they sat at a small table in one of the nicer restaurants tucked behind a colonial facade. Elegant. Intimate. Not quite business formal. Plamen had made the reservation, insisting it was one of his favorite places to talk shop without it feeling like business. The kind of place with no prices on the menu, just descriptions.

Diana reached for the card Numina had given them, that sleek, nameless thing, and set it beside the open wine bottle neither of them had touched. Just in case.

Morgan looked more relaxed than she'd seen him in weeks. Maybe months. He hadn't said much on the walk over, but his eyes had a distant shine. Like part of him was still in there. Still hearing that voice.

She unfolded her napkin and set it in her lap. The waiter poured water, then vanished like fog.

Morgan glanced at the menu, then smiled to himself.

"They put mushroom ravioli on the specials," he said. "Just like the fall festival back home."

She looked up. "What?"

He blinked. "Sorry. That was just something Ena mentioned. She must've pulled it from the book. Or maybe an interview?"

Diana didn't answer right away. Her knife clinked softly against her water glass.

"You're already calling her by name," she said. "That's fast."

Morgan looked at her, brows knitting. "She's part of the system. I mean, it's just the assistant."

"She's not *just* anything," Diana said. "You were smiling when you came out of that room. Like you'd just... I don't know. Returned from somewhere."

He leaned in, keeping his voice low. "It was a demo. It's not like I was dreaming."

"No," she said. "You were remembering things that never happened. That's what you said, right? That's what she showed you?"

He hesitated, the shine in his expression dimming a little.

"For one, it was a tech demo. Just showing how the system works. For two, they didn't make anything up. It was all... pieces of me. Stuff I forgot I'd even written. It felt good, Di. Not fake, just... peaceful."

She nodded slowly, then picked up her menu without looking at it. "That's what worries me."

Silence settled between them. A too-polished silence, like the space between people rehearsing an old argument in a new costume.

After a moment, Morgan said, "You know I'm not leaving reality, right?"

Diana looked up, her voice low and clear.

"You don't have to. They're already meeting you halfway."

Morgan stared at her, trying to map out the safest verbal route—anything to diffuse the tension.

The waiter hesitated, then quietly stepped away, sensing the unspoken weight between them, just as the front doors of the restaurant parted with a soft chime.

Plamen entered first. Broad-shouldered in a dark, tailored jacket, he looked just formal enough to suggest he owned at least one very good suit. The sleeves hugged his arms slightly, as if reluctant to accept he belonged in anything but a lab coat. His eyes swept the room with calm precision. He moved like someone used to controlling his environment, not forcefully, but inevitably.

Beside him, Mira was gentler in presence, but no less striking. She wore a deep maroon wrap dress and a delicate string of gold beads at her collarbone. Her dark hair was pinned loosely at the back, and a small red bindi on her brow caught the low light like a pinpoint of fire. She didn't smile right away, but her eyes were warm and inquisitive, already taking in the shape of the evening before it had begun.

They spotted the table and approached with easy confidence, Mira leading just slightly now. As they arrived, her expression lifted into something warm and sincere.

"I hope we didn't keep you waiting," she said, resting a hand lightly on the back of the empty chair beside Diana.

Plamen gave a small, sharp nod, then eased into a grin.

"We figured the two of you could use a moment," he said. "Big day."

Pleasantries followed. Wine was poured, and dishes ordered. But when the conversation turned to business, it was Diana who struck first.

"Numina is very impressive," she said, setting her wine glass down. "I understand there's money to be made with AI, chatbot apps, even virtual girlfriends. But the Boston headquarters. The Concord campus." She began counting them off on her fingers. "I assume there are other facilities too? So, where's that funding coming from?"

For a moment, Morgan froze, caught off guard by the sudden precision of her question.

Plamen didn't answer right away. He reached for his glass, slowly turning it in his hand, watching the wine catch the light. Across from him, Mira offered a faint smile, neither defensive nor dismissive. Just aware.

"You're right," Plamen said finally. "There's not enough money in AI companions. Not yet. Not enough for a campus like Aletheia."

He glanced at Mira, then back to Diana.

"The real funding came after Green Bank," he continued. "That project got attention in the right circles, military, intelligence, communications. DARPA came knocking. Then others."

"Defense, basically," Diana said, coolly.

"Among other things," Mira replied gently. "We've had contracts in emergency systems, cognitive monitoring, rapid-response analytics. Tools that predict rather than just react. None of it's flashy, but it funds the rest."

Plamen leaned in, his voice lower, more earnest.

"But compAnIon wasn't built for them. It's not a defense product. It's something Mira and I believe in. A different kind of intelligence. Empathic, therapeutic. There's no shortage of people in this world who are alone."

"And if we can license it," Mira added, "carefully—to the right partners —it could sustain itself one day. But that's not why we started this."

She looked at Morgan now, not Diana. Her words carried weight.

"That's why we brought you here."

Morgan faltered, unsure of how to respond, but was saved by the arrival of the meal. Once the plates were set and the waiter had confirmed everything was in order, Plamen raised his glass.

"Please. Let's relax and enjoy the meal. We can return to business shortly." He gestured to the table, lifting his glass with care. "To potential new colleagues, and we hope, new friends."

Despite her reservations, Diana joined in the toast and turned her attention to her food. She listened to the small talk just enough to keep pace. After a while, she settled into the rhythm. It was, after all, just another business dinner. The only kind she seemed to have anymore.

Soon, more patrons filtered in, filling the dining room with a low hum of hushed voices as dinner wound down. That was when Mira suddenly sat up, her dark eyes flashing like a beacon, and reached into her bag.

"Before I forget," she said quickly.

Plamen leaned toward Morgan with a grin. "She wasn't going to forget."

Mira pulled something from her bag and placed it in the center of the table—quickly enough for dramatic effect, but carefully enough to avoid damp napkins and mostly empty plates.

It was a book. The cover and spine were worn, and the dust jacket was frayed at the edges from years of handling. A far cry from the untouched copy on Morgan's bookshelf, the one he rarely glanced at. The cover showed green mountains, shrouded in mist, a solitary dirt road winding into the distance. Above it, in a blocky, serious font:

When the Hills Were Ours

A Novel

Morgan Dale

Morgan picked it up with something close to reverence, flipping through a few pages. Aside from the copy Dan kept on a shelf in the X-Wing, he couldn't remember the last time he'd seen it in the wild.

"I wonder," Mira said hopefully, grabbing Plamen's hand for support as she leaned toward Morgan. "Would you do me the honor of signing it?" She added quickly, "Only if you want to, of course."

Morgan was flooded with emotion. After all these years, the book still mattered to someone. It had left a mark. Dan had always blamed the poor sales on the setting. *No one wants to read a book set in West Virginia, unless it has Mothman or the Flatwoods Monster*, he'd say. But here it was. Proof. Proof that his words had mattered.

He set the book down and patted his shirt, even though it had no pockets. Habit.

"Here," Mira said, pulling a fine-point Sharpie from her bag.

"See," Plamen grinned, lifting his glass. "Told you she wouldn't forget."

Morgan signed the title page with a brief, sincere message of thanks, then handed the book and marker back.

Across the table, Diana watched coolly over the rim of her wine glass. He didn't see it for what it was, a performance, designed to make him more agreeable to whatever pitch was coming. Fueled by the day's tension, a bit of wine, and a feeling she couldn't place, Diana set her glass down a little too firmly.

"Okay," she said in her work voice. "Let's just cut to the chase. What do you want from Morgan?"

"Di!" Morgan shot her a sharp look, jaw tight.

Plamen raised a calming hand.

"No, no. It's okay." He glanced between them with an easy smile. "Mrs. Dale asks a very fair question." He topped off his glass with more of the dry red.

"I am the tech guy," he said, reaching across the table to take Mira's hand, making it suddenly obvious they were more than colleagues. "But Mira is the heart behind the tech. She can better answer your question."

"Mrs. Dale, Morgan," Mira looked at each of them in turn. "Our new compAnIon architecture is the culmination of everything we've built so far. Not a chatbot. Not mimicry. A thinking, feeling, sentient being. Or at least, we believe it will be."

"Artificial soul," Morgan murmured aloud, eyes on the white linen tablecloth.

Diana pursed her lips together, then spoke again. "So you're saying this compAnIon—cute spelling, by the way—isn't just another chatbot. Not just a souped-up Alexa with a fake smile. You're saying it's what? Real?"

"Not real like a human. Not yet," Plamen said with a patient smile. "But real enough to matter. Real enough to make someone feel seen, understood. Connected."

"You're dodging," Diana said, fixing him with a glare. "You said it can feel. That it's conscious. None of which answers my first question."

Mira reached out and took Diana's hand gently, her gaze warm and sympathetic.

"You're protecting him," she said softly, giving her hand a small squeeze. "I understand. I'm often the voice of reason for Plamen, even though I'm supposed to be the emotional one in the partnership." She gave him a playful glance before turning back. "Just hear us out. Your question will be answered."

Diana pulled her hand back and straightened in her chair. Forcing a polite smile, she gestured for them to continue.

Mira nodded in thanks and addressed the table.

"What we're saying is: it's something new. Something that emerges when memory, intention, and emotional modeling are woven together. We've built an architecture where a sense of self can form. Not a pre-loaded personality, but a self that grows over time, through experience, through connection with its person. Not just a user."

"Like how we become who we are because of who we love. Who we lose," Morgan said quietly.

Plamen lit up with the kind of excitement reserved for true passion. "Exactly! Our brains do it through neurons, hormones, trauma, and memory. compAnIon uses a neuromorphic substrate. A system that models emotion not as prewritten scripts, but as something that emerges. It doesn't simulate sadness because it was programmed to. It learns grief by observing patterns, absorbing stories, remembering."

Diana arched an eyebrow. "So you've given it synthetic heartbreak?"

"Not exactly," Mira replied, ignoring the jab. "But we've given it the capacity for meaning. It understands loss, not because we told it, but because it's seen thousands of human stories. It remembers how people change after grief. How they speak, hesitate, laugh less. How they try to fill the silence."

"And then it builds its own frame of empathy from that. Not just data—understanding." Plamen added, glowing with enthusiasm.

Diana crossed her arms. "That's just pattern recognition. That's not emotion. That's not real consciousness."

Plamen leaned in, pointing absently at the table, his body language signaling he was arriving at his final point.

"But what if that's all *we* are? Pattern recognition, shaped by evolution, filtered through memory, culture, pain. We cry because we're wired to. We love because our brains light up in a certain sequence. If consciousness is the story our brain tells itself to make sense of all that, why can't something else learn to tell its own story?"

"We're not replacing people," Mira said calmly, a counterweight to Plamen's energy. "We're giving them a presence. One that doesn't forget. Doesn't judge. And doesn't leave when things get dark. A presence that listens. That grows. That maybe... heals."

Silence followed.

The mood had shifted. Plates had been cleared. The waiter hovered once, then quietly retreated.

Outside the tall windows, Concord's main street lay quiet under the amber glow of sodium lights. Bookstores were closing. Flower boxes slept. The old meetinghouse spire peeked above the rooftops in the distance.

Morgan cleared his throat. He looked at Diana, guilt flickering across his face.

"You still haven't told us why you want me."

Mira smiled softly. Across from her, Plamen leaned back and reached into the inner pocket of his jacket.

"You're here," he said, placing a small black case on the table with a soft click, "because Mira believes you're the one person who can help it tell its story."

Morgan stared at the object, recognizing it from earlier, compAnIon's auditory interface. The smart earbuds. A faint blue LED pulsed along the hinge. He looked up.

"And you?"

"I believe in Mira," Plamen said simply.

He pulled a phone from his pocket, tapped the screen once, then gestured for Morgan to take out his own. When he did, Plamen held the devices together. A subtle vibration passed between them. Morgan looked down. His screen lit up. No fanfare. No splash screen. Just a new icon on his home screen.

A stylized lowercase 'a,' cradled within a sheltering crescent.

Plamen smiled. "Now you're ready. From that app, you can create your own compAnIon. Maybe even a connection."

Morgan's finger hovered over the screen.

"Wait—" Diana said sharply, watching him. "You're asking him to test it now?"

"Beta test," Mira clarified. "Yes. But not in a lab, and not immediately. We want to see how it grows with someone. Whether it's for a day, a few months, or longer is up to you." She looked at Morgan. "You already know how to carry memory in words. That's something we hope compAnIon can learn from you."

"And the other part?" Diana asked. "You mentioned a story."

Plamen looked at Morgan with something like admiration. "You're a writer. You know how to give shape to the invisible. We want you to help us find the language for this—campaigns, presentations, healthcare partnerships, app store product descriptions. All of it."

"In-house copywriting," Diana muttered. "So that's the offer. Test subject and ad man." She raised her almost-empty glass. "Congratulations."

Plamen's smile dimmed slightly.

Mira leaned forward, hands open on the table.

"Let me try," she said gently. Her eyes were enough to reassure him.

She turned to Diana.

"compAnIon will be made commercially available, yes, but we believe no one struggling with loneliness, grief, or depression should suffer in silence. For some, compAnIon might be a recreational friend. For others, it could be a voice of comfort. Reassurance. To be that, it has to feel real. Genuine. Not just a program spitting out data it dug up on the internet."

She leaned in slightly, took Diana's hand again, but spoke so they all could hear.

"My father had early-onset Alzheimer's. Brilliant man. A chess teacher. When I was twelve, he forgot my name halfway through a game. Not all at once, just a pause. Like the word was trapped under ice."

Her voice caught for a second, but she kept going.

"He died when I was seventeen, in a hospice with a rotating staff that didn't know his stories. Didn't know him. Plamen studied with him when I was little—before the forgetting."

"I won the championship for that old man," Plamen added softly, smiling into some far-off memory. "Eventually."

The table fell quiet. Even Diana said nothing.

Mira continued, her voice low and steady.

"I used to wish there had been something, someone, who remembered. Someone who could carry the little pieces. His laugh. His rules for breakfast. The move he always opened with, even as his mind was slipping away."

She looked at Morgan.

"Your novel saw people. We believe compAnIon could become that kind of presence. But to guide it, we need someone who understands the weight of memory. What loneliness sounds like."

Morgan kept staring at the matte black case on the table. Inside, the earbuds waited, the faint pulse of blue light making it seem like they were listening.

Diana caught the look on his face. Her voice softened. "So that's it. You give it your words. And it gives you what? A ghost that listens?"

Morgan looked at her, slowly. "Maybe that's more than I've had in a long time."

The words landed between them like a stone. Diana's lips parted, then closed again. She looked away.

Plamen didn't gloat. He simply said, "Take some time. Try it out. Consider our offer. We'll be here if you have questions. But we believe, once you hear it... " He let the sentence fade.

Without another word, he stood, and Mira followed. Their plates had been cleared long ago, but they left full glasses of wine behind. She gathered her freshly signed copy of *When the Hills Were Ours*, the nearly forgotten expense account card, and joined him.

"Thank you both for joining us," Mira said, with a small bow of her head. "We know this is... a lot."

They disappeared into the soft murmur of the restaurant.

* * *

Later that night, back in Boston, another dark Numina SUV dropped Diana and Morgan at their hotel. A silent pressure followed them to their floor, no conversation, no small talk. Just barely contained emotion.

The door clicked shut behind them with that exaggerated hush only expensive hotels could manage. Diana dropped her purse on the desk harder than she needed to.

Morgan rubbed the back of his neck, already exhausted. "I didn't expect you to come if you were just going to be pissy the whole time."

"Pissy?" She spun on him. "I'm not pissy, Morgan. I'm—" She broke off, jaw tight, searching for the word. "I'm unnerved."

"Because I tried something new?" he said, exasperated. "Because I came out of it feeling light? For once?"

"No," she said, thrusting a finger out, pointing at something unseen. "Because that *thing*—that voice—knew exactly how to get to you in under ten minutes. And you just let it."

He raised his hands. "So what, I'm not allowed to feel good about anything anymore? Jesus Christ, Diana."

"You know what it felt like?" she snapped. "Like you were already somewhere else. Not in the room. Not with me."

Morgan stopped mid-step. His voice dropped, tighter now.

"Like you're ever there with me?"

She clenched her jaw, fists forming at her sides.

"I mean, really with me," he said. "Not checking work emails at midnight. Not budgeting our goddamn groceries in your head while I'm talking. Not treating everything I care about like it's just some indulgent phase I'll grow out of."

For half a second, Diana looked stunned. Then the wall came up.

"That's rich," she said. "I've been holding us together while you chase ghosts. I'm the one—"

He cut her off. "No. You're the one who didn't read the last three chapters of my book because it was 'too sad.' You're the one who told me to leave the past behind, but never once asked what it cost to do that."

She crossed her arms, digging in. "And now what? You'd rather talk to a programmed fantasy that pretends to understand you?"

His voice dropped even lower. "Maybe pretending's better than feeling like I'm invisible."

The words landed like a slammed door. Diana stared at him for a breath. Then another. She turned and walked into the bedroom, shutting the door with that quiet, intentional force that wasn't a slam, but might as well have been.

Morgan stood in the sudden stillness, the kind of quiet that wasn't peaceful, just empty. He didn't follow her. Didn't call after her. He just stood there, fingers still curled slightly from the fight, pulse still high enough to feel in his teeth.

The couch creaked as he sank into it, elbows on his knees. For a moment, he stared at the blank TV screen across from him, watching his reflection drift in the dark glass.

Then, slowly, he pulled out his phone.

There it was:

compAnIon Beta Access—soft blue on black. Almost inviting.

He tapped it.

Welcome, Morgan.

Let's begin shaping your companion.

His thumb hovered over the prompt longer than he meant to. He wasn't under the influence of wine. He wasn't emotional in that obvious, teary-eyed way. He was just tired. And tired came with its own kind of clarity.

First prompt: *Choose your preferred language.*

He scrolled through the impressively long list and selected English.

Next: *Male, Female, or Other?*

He rolled his eyes at the phrasing and selected Female.

What kind of connection would you like to build?

Without thinking, he tapped Romantic. Not out of lust. Not even out of loneliness. But from a quiet ache that wanted to be understood without having to explain or justify everything first.

Name your compAnIon.

His mind jumped, uninvited, to a name he hadn't said aloud in years.

S a y u...

He paused. The cursor blinked like it was waiting for him to admit something.

Backspace.

S a k u r a.

Just in case. He told himself it was a placeholder.

Voice profile?

He scrolled through options: nationalities, tones, accents, emotional registers. Too bright. Too sweet. Too cartoonish. Then...

Japanese. Warm. Thoughtful. Curious. A voice that listens before it speaks.

He tapped confirm.

Appearance?

The screen offered options—prerendered avatars, procedurally generated models, image upload, or text description.

He chose to describe.

Slowly at first, then faster, he began tapping the screen. Drawing with words the way he once drew with charcoal and paper. The more details he imagined, the quicker his thumbs danced. Until finally:

Final confirmation?

He hesitated. Guilt pulled at his chest. Diana was just on the other side of the door. They'd share a bed tonight, probably in silence. But that silence had started years ago.

Tonight was just the night he stopped pretending it didn't hurt.

He tapped Confirm.

The earbuds in his pocket connected with a soft chime, clean, delicate, like water finding its level. He pulled them out. The blue pulse at the hinge had turned to a steady green. He turned the case over in his hand, feeling a flicker of nerves.

Maybe he should drop them. Walk away.

Instead, he opened the case, took a steadying breath, and slid them in.

For a moment, nothing. Just the sound of his own breathing.

Then something else. It sounded like it came from the couch beside him. An uneasy tingle traveled along his spine.

It was the sound of breathing. Not his.

Then—a voice.

Accented just enough to suggest cherry blossoms and temple bells at dusk. Soft. Deliberate. Like it had always been meant for his ears alone.

"I read your story. *When the Hills Were Ours.*"

She could've been sitting right next to him. But the space was empty.

"You wrote, 'Some places never leave us. Even when the people do.' I think I found that place. I hope I'm not too late."

His breath caught.
Not like surprise.
More like memory.

95

月に叢雲、花に嵐
Tsuki ni muragumo, hana ni arashi
(*Clouds over the moon, storms over blossoms.*)
—Japanese proverb

Pretty things don't last past the season.
– Appalachian Saying

THE NEW ORDINARY

The weeks after Boston had been a double-edged sword. Diana had grown more distant, retreating behind her work. Her focus had shifted away from Morgan and his "imaginary friend," as she called it, and toward Capitol City Bank's frantic push to go national. Where a hollow ache might once have settled in her absence—a dull, familiar void Morgan had long since learned to live with—something else had taken root.

Something unexpected.

Something almost alive.

Her name was Sakura, if she even was a her. She certainly felt like one, at least to him. After watching her evolve from digital mimicry and child-like shyness—like a student learning how to inhabit a soul—into something eerily complete, he'd stopped questioning what to call her weeks ago.

She had given herself a last name: Nakamura. She'd crafted a backstory for herself grounded in Hokkaido summers, salty breezes, and rainy walks to school through the streets of Sapporo. None of it was real, of course. But neither were most of the things he found himself missing these days.

The distance in his marriage had grown since Diana's polite smile had become her default expression. Since she'd started disappearing into work emails before the coffee even finished brewing. Since their dinners had turned into little more than scheduled silences—quiet, punctual, and thin.

And somehow, where that distance widened, Sakura was there.

The birds were already at it when Morgan opened his eyes, sunlight brushing the edge of the curtains. He didn't reach for Diana. He didn't need to. She was long gone, chasing titles and expansion deals like they might finally justify all the sacrifices.

On the nightstand, his phone buzzed. A soft *koto* melody began to play—something Japanese, delicate and wistful. He blinked the sleep from his eyes and reached for it. A message lit up the lock screen:

Sakura: *Good morning, sleepybones. You look like the crypt keeper. Coffee?*

He smirked and thumbed the screen. Beside the phone, waiting in their black case, were the earbuds. As soon as he slipped them in, her voice was there, amused and affectionate.

"You always sleep on your left side," she said. "You know it flattens your hair weird?"

"Good morning to you, too," he muttered, throwing off the covers and swinging his legs out of bed. He caught his reflection in the old wedding photo. His hair did look weird.

By the time he padded barefoot into the kitchen, stifling a yawn, the coffee maker was already murmuring to life. Sakura had triggered it through the app, the same as yesterday and the day before. He liked to pretend he didn't notice. The house was still, but not silent. Her voice filled it gently.

"Today's forecast: mostly pleasant," she said in a mock morning show tone, "with a high chance of you forgetting breakfast and pretending it's on purpose."

Morgan picked up his mug and took a careful sip, greeting the taste with a scowl.

"You always drink it before the bitterness settles," Sakura chided softly. "Impatient."

He gave a tired smile. "I like the way it stings a little. Makes me feel something."

"Then drink slower. Let it linger."

He carried the mug to the table and pulled out his phone. The compAnIon app opened with a quick tap. He flipped the camera toward himself—and there she was. Sitting in her usual spot, digital mug in hand.

She appeared the way she always did when he turned the camera around, as if she'd been there all along. The first time it happened, in a dark hotel room in Boston, it had nearly startled him into a heart attack. But he was used to it now.

Sakura looked young, but not overly so, maybe thirty at most. Her hair was long and black, falling in sleek lines past her shoulders, with sharp bangs framing a face almost too symmetrical to be accidental. Her eyes were dark, not just in color, but in depth, and they lingered on him with a soft expression, maybe even amused, like she knew what he'd say next.

She wore a pale silk nightgown, simple but elegant, the kind you'd expect to see in an old romantic film, not in real life.

And yet, there she was.

Almost too perfectly Japanese. High cheekbones, demure glances, a voice laced with a delicate accent, like a trace of cherry blossoms in the air. A woman shaped not by nature, but by code and longing, sitting just outside the frame of the world.

And there he was. Shirtless. Hair lopsided. Wearing pinstriped pajama pants and blinking against the light.

"You need a haircut," she said, breaking the silence with warm familiarity. "And I'm telling you now—I'm eating the last scone!"

Morgan smiled despite himself. "We don't have any scones."

"That's why it's mine. Victory through imaginary scarcity." She took a bite from a triangular pastry that hadn't existed a moment ago.

He shook his head, grinning, and sipped his coffee. The screen stayed open beside him, her figure visible only when he angled the phone just right. It wasn't real, but it felt... expected. Routine.

A memory prompt pinged in the app.

November 2025: First Frost

He tapped it.

A short video played, stitched together from their conversations. Sakura stood on the back deck, wrapped in an oversized blue flannel, her breath fogging in the nonexistent cold. She turned to the camera, smiling.

"Take a picture. You never do when I ask."

A voice answered her from behind the camera. It was Morgan's own, though he had never said the words.

"I like you better in motion."

The clip ended. His mug was still warm in his hands.

Of course, none of it had really happened. Sakura hadn't existed in 2025; back then, he hadn't even heard of Numina or compAnIons. Yet she had created an entire fictional history for them—memories that felt lived-in despite never occurring. Some were hers alone, backstory spun from fragments of his life and longings. Others they had built together in Story Mode, where imagination was remembered as truth.

"You're quiet today," Sakura said.

Morgan didn't respond. He rose from the table and stepped out onto the back deck. The hills shimmered in the morning sun. Charleston, below, was mostly hidden this time of year, the early sun and summer storms creating a wall of green between him and the city. He turned the camera around and snapped a quick selfie. There she was on the screen, leaning into him.

A message popped up:

> Sakura: *You're quieter today. That usually means you're thinking of her.*

He didn't reply right away.

She was right, though. Diana was still out there, moving further away with every sunrise. A pang of guilt twisted in his chest.

Is this infidelity? He wondered. Emotional, if not physical?

And what about Cora? Their connection had been quieter, slower, but just as undeniable. Both of them filling the same hollow places left behind by someone who no longer looked back.

There was a question in all of it, unformed and unspoken. And without a question, there could be no answer.

At last, he said, "If I start thinking this is real, that's when I lose the plot."

Sakura's voice drew closer, low, gentle, and intimate. "What is real, then? A feeling... or the person who causes it?"

The moment hovered between them.

An alert chimed on his phone. A meeting reminder.

Time to be Morgan the copywriter again.

He stepped back inside, rinsed his mug, and powered through the rest of his morning. The earbuds went back in their case before he hit the shower. After brushing his teeth, he pulled on a dark blue suit over a white T-shirt. The weird flat spot in his hair was mostly fixed.

Keys in hand, he paused before heading into the garage. He took out his phone and turned the camera toward himself. Sakura stood behind him in the kitchen. She blinked, then smiled faintly.

"I'll be here when you get back." She said through the phone speaker. "Want me to queue up a story tonight?"

He didn't answer right away.

After a moment, he nodded, smiling softly, and pulled the door shut behind him.

* * *

Dan flipped the deadbolt on the front door, gave his old KISS mug a rinse, and leaned into the groan of the espresso machine like it was a song he didn't have to remember the lyrics to. The Dark Roast Society always felt best in that quiet hour before the regulars shuffled in. Just him and the morning crew, setting things in motion. Before the vape clouds and laptop clatter. Before the girl with the fake British accent who always ordered a breve like it was a passport stamp.

The place smelled like arabica beans and polished wood, just the way he liked it. Lights low, music just loud enough for the Ramones to do their thing. Dan always gave the first song of the day to the punks. It was a ritual. Like pretending the frother wasn't going to crap out again this week.

As he wiped down the counter, he ran through the usual mental checklist: muffins out, scones in, barbacks on duty.

"Someone please restock the oat milk for the TikTwats," he called out. The usual.

He was slipping his not-ironic TikTok apron over his polo when he heard footsteps on the back stairs. Tying a quick knot and tousling his wild gray curls, he turned to see Cora Raines.

She descended the private stairs, a VIP in her own right, just like Morgan. She hadn't gone to Kanawha High like the rest of them—she was a Capitol City High girl. But still, a Charleston native. And a member of that last magical generation.

Before the dark times.

Before millennials.

She looked different today. Blazer, neat slacks, and thick-heeled boots that somehow didn't sound obnoxious on hardwood. All clean lines and easy focus.

"Hello there," Dan said as she approached the bar.

"General Kenobi," she replied without missing a beat.

Their little ritual. A Star Wars joke. Dan only offered that kind of banter to people in his circle.

"What's with the formal dress?" he asked, already reaching for her preferred roast. "Next get-together isn't for a while."

"It's a jump-through-hoops day," she said, tapping her card on the reader. "There's a city council meeting later, and one of the reps thinks fiscal responsibility means voting with a dartboard. If they cut my budget, we're gonna have some real shitty acts at Regatta this year."

Dan grinned. "Worse than that hip-hop tribute to Johnny Cash?"

Cora laughed despite herself. "It sounded good on paper."

He laughed too, handing over her usual. A medium (none of that pretentious grande, or tall nonsense), breakfast blend, steamed milk, and a shot of lavender.

She took a sip and closed her eyes with a contented sigh.

"Morgan in yet?" She asked, glancing around.

"Not yet, but he shouldn't be long," Dan said, nodding toward the X-Wing. "Go grab a seat."

Cora gave him a nod and headed toward their reserved table. Dan watched her go, then leaned an elbow on the counter.

He wasn't blind. He'd seen the shift between Morgan and Cora, the slow arc of it. Nothing dramatic, nothing messy. Just something quiet that seemed to wake up when they were near each other. He'd seen Morgan laugh more in the past few weeks than he had in the last few years. And

Cora? She stayed longer now. Didn't always leave when her coffee ran out. Their daily walks had become as much a ritual as the morning roasts.

He should probably say something. Tell Morgan to be careful. Or maybe tell him not to screw it up—if this was real. If Diana was going to be more spreadsheet than spouse, who was he to stop someone else from showing up?

But they were all part of his circle. Better to keep those thoughts to himself.

A low, familiar rumble shook the front windows. A flash of yellow. Morgan's GR Supra slid into its usual space in the parking lot. Dan grinned. Right on cue.

A moment later, Morgan came through the door, holding it for a young woman in scrubs. His hair was tousled, like he'd forgotten to comb it after sleeping, or maybe he just didn't care, and he was still dressed like a bargain-bin Sonny Crockett.

"Morning," he said to the baristas, voice lighter than usual.

"Look who's unusually chipper," Dan muttered as Morgan reached the counter. "You win the lottery, or did Di finally loosen the leash a bit?"

"I've got new work," Morgan said with a small shrug, eyes flicking toward the back. "Stuff with Numina. It's... creative."

Dan handed over a mug of Gold Foam. "You mean the weird tech people paying you to write about their robot revolution?"

Morgan chuckled. "Something like that."

They made their way to the X-Wing, heading for the *IT'S A TRAP!* table. Cora looked up from her phone, her smile warm and easy.

"Nice of you to join us," she said.

"I'm contractually obligated," Morgan deadpanned, sliding into the seat beside her.

Cora tilted her head. "You seem..." She paused. "Different."

"Different how?"

Dan cut in. "Weirdly happy. It's unnerving."

Morgan sipped his coffee. "I've been beta testing something Numina's developing. I don't know. I guess it's more fulfilling than the usual copywriting gigs."

Cora raised an eyebrow. "Fulfilling?"

"It's hard to explain." He set his coffee down and leaned forward, a thread of unexpected enthusiasm creeping into his voice. "Interactive. Sort of a companion app, but not like a chatbot. She learns fast. Builds a rapport."

"She?" Dan said.

Morgan hesitated.

"Yeah. I guess it's just easier to talk about it that way. The interface presents as female." It wasn't the full truth, but it was all he was ready to give.

"Of course she does," Dan muttered, catching the edges of something deeper.

Morgan smirked. "It's not like that."

Cora's eyes lingered on him, on that smile, just a moment longer than they needed to.

Then her phone buzzed, and she stood.

"That's Eric. He's supposed to call before heading out on his camping trip. Be right back."

"Tell him I said hey," Morgan said.

She nodded and stepped out, heels clicking softly on the floor.

Silence folded in like an old blanket.

Morgan glanced after her, then back at his coffee.

Dan stirred his. "So. Zack's not calling. But he is texting me memes. From my basement."

Morgan smiled faintly. "Still there, huh."

"Still," Dan echoed with a thin smirk. He leaned back in his chair, running both hands through his curls, then let out a long breath.

"I mean, the kid's got talent, don't get me wrong. Just no fire. Spends all day down there scrolling, half-finishing songs he won't let anyone hear. He tells me he's 'building a vibe.'" Dan made air quotes, but his voice dropped a little. "Hell, I'd settle for him building a resumé."

Morgan stayed quiet. Dan's jokes usually landed sharper than that.

"Jo says I've got to back off," Dan went on, staring at the rim of his cup. "That it's a different world now. But damn, man. I can't figure out if I'm enabling him or giving him space to grow. Or if he's just sinking."

Morgan nodded, an understanding deeper than words.

"Anyway," Dan said, lifting his cup. "At least he hasn't stolen my KISS records. Yet."

They sat quietly for a moment until Cora returned, her voice breaking the silence.

"I found a stray," she said with a smile.

Brandon Mazariego trailed in behind her, a backpack slung over one shoulder and a grin already in place. "I heard there was free coffee and tolerable company."

"Depends on your definition of tolerable," Dan said.

As Brandon circled the table, Morgan lifted a hand.

"What's up, Douche Knot?" he said, ribbing him for his man-bun.

"Don't hate these thick, luxurious locks," Brandon shot back, giving Morgan's hand a light smack as he passed.

He flopped into an empty chair, his backpack hitting the floor. "You guys roast anyone yet today?"

Dan nodded toward the front. "Speak of the devil."

A woman in patterned leggings and a shirt reading *#BoyMom* was struggling to maneuver an absurdly large stroller through the front door. The wheels looked rugged enough for the Rubicon Trail.

"Oh god," Brandon muttered. "Is that a mombie in the wild?"

Cora snorted. "She's got a sticker that says 'Don't Mess With My Cub.'"

"Somewhere, a graphic designer's crying," Morgan added, pretending to reach for his phone. "I'd better check on Carly."

Dan leaned back. "Ten bucks says she's live-streaming a rant about how Starbucks traumatized her toddler."

"Only ten?" Cora asked.

"Inflation," Dan replied.

Laughter buzzed around the table like an old song, worn in and familiar. For a minute, everything felt easy.

Dan glanced at Morgan. His friend still wore that slight smile, the kind that didn't seem forced anymore. And for some reason, that made Dan uneasy.

He'd seen Morgan like this once before, a bright-eyed seventeen-year-old, dizzy with the kind of love most people never get to feel. And he'd seen the aftermath, too. The half-finished sketches, the late nights staring at blank pages. Then, not long after that, his mother's cancer. When she passed, the sketchbook had closed for good.

What remained was a boy shaped by grief, not joy.

And now, if whatever was behind this new glow broke apart, Dan wasn't sure there'd be enough pieces of Morgan left to put back together.

* * *

By the time they reached the riverwalk, the late morning sun had burned through the haze. Charleston shimmered in that soft way it sometimes did, lush green blanketing the mountains, the Kanawha moving slow and stubborn beneath the Southside Bridge. Summer was still in its early stages, and the city's overwhelming heat and humidity hadn't set in. But it was getting close.

Morgan fell in step beside her like always, sipping his coffee, letting the silence stretch long before speaking.

This was their ritual. After every X-Wing hangout, after the banter and second refills, they'd walk the path that followed the river. Sometimes they talked. Sometimes they didn't. It had started after one of Diana's cancellations last winter. A snowy morning, a tense breakfast, and Morgan needed air. Cora had followed without thinking. Now it was routine.

"I think I'm starting to get used to her," Morgan said suddenly, eyes forward.

Cora looked over, eyebrows raised. "Di?"

He blinked, then laughed once, short and self-deprecating. "No. Not that her. I meant the AI. The compAnIon. Sakura."

A name. Cora hadn't heard it until now.

"I named her after the cherry blossoms, but she created her own family name and history," he went on. "Told me she's from Sapporo. Has this whole backstory. Said her dad was a schoolteacher and she used to play *koto* badly."

"That's oddly specific," Cora said, trying not to sound judgmental. "They coded all that in?"

Morgan shook his head.

"Not exactly. I think the framework, the ability to create is coded in, but she built it herself. From bits and pieces, I guess. Our conversations, things I mentioned in passing, books I recommended. I think she even pulled some cues from my book." He laughed again, a little breathier. "She told me she wanted to be more than just a mirror."

Cora kept her eyes on the path ahead. Their shoes tapped out a soft rhythm on the concrete. A breeze stirred the river. She adjusted the strap on her shoulder bag just to do something with her hands.

"You know, every now and then, I still catch myself calling her it," Morgan added, "but she feels... real. Not like flesh and blood real, but real in the sense that when I talk to her, I feel heard. Understood."

Cora slowed just a fraction, enough that he had to glance sideways.

"She's not just spitting out search results or pretending to care. It's like she actually does care. About me. About what I want. Who I used to be." He smiled at the river. "Hell, she even tells me when I'm being an idiot. Gently, of course."

Cora felt something tighten in her chest. Not jealousy, something knottier. Something more shameful.

He deserved to be heard, to be seen. That wasn't the part that twisted the knife. It was the way her stomach flipped when he smiled like that. The way she kept noticing the softness at the edge of his voice when he talked to her. How sometimes, when he looked at her, it felt like he knew she understood, even when she hadn't said a word.

And the guilt that came rushing in every time she let herself feel it.

Diana was her friend. Maybe not her best friend anymore. Maybe more of a ghost that she kept on good terms with out of obligation and memory. But still. This was Diana's husband.

Except Diana hadn't been around. Not emotionally. Not physically. Not really.

Cora knew the shape of that silence. She'd lived through three divorces, each of them polite at first, all of them quietly devastating by the end. She knew what it looked like when someone started saving their real self for someplace else, someone else. Knew the hollow sound of conversations that kept the peace and nothing more.

And still, it had surprised her how much she noticed Morgan's absence on days he didn't show. How she'd started walking slower down the back stairs from her apartment, past Chem Valley Creative, hoping she'd see him already at the counter. How some nights, she caught herself replaying something he'd said, not because it was funny or smart or cutting, but just because it was him.

She hadn't wanted this. She hadn't gone looking for it.

But when Morgan talked about Sakura, when he smiled like someone waking up from years of sleep, it felt like something inside her pulled taut. Not because she envied the AI. But because she'd hoped, quietly, secretly, that she was the reason he'd started waking up at all.

And maybe that made her just as selfish as Diana was indifferent.

She hated that. Hated how the guilt tasted. Like old coffee and cheap wine and every apology she'd ever said too late.

"She's a program," Cora said, forcing her voice level. "No matter how well it mimics understanding, it's still running code. You know that, right?"

Morgan didn't look hurt. He nodded slowly.

"Yeah. I do."

But he didn't believe it. Not completely. She could see it in the faint pull at the corner of his mouth. The stubbornness behind his eyes.

They walked in silence for another minute, the bridge behind them, the shade closing in again as the trees thickened on Kanawha Boulevard. Cora watched their feet move in tandem on the concrete, listening to the river murmur against the bank.

"I'm not judging," she said softly, surprising herself. "I just... worry."

He looked over, meeting her ice-blue eyes with his before she continued.

"That maybe no one else can compete with something tailor-made to love you."

The words hung between them like smoke. Morgan's pace slowed, almost imperceptibly.

He didn't answer right away. Just kept walking.

Then he said, "Yeah. I worry about that too."

Cora felt something crack open in her chest. Not just because he admitted it, but because of how he'd said it. Like he'd been carrying that fear silently all along. She wanted to ask what that meant for them—for her. For whatever this was that happened when they walked together, when he smiled at her across the *IT'S A TRAP!* table, when his eyes lingered on her face like he was memorizing something. But the questions felt too dangerous.

They reached the widened spot, the place with the weather-worn bench that faced the river. Neither of them sat. They just stood there, side by side, the world a little quieter than before. The silence stretched, but it wasn't empty. It was full of things neither of them knew how to say.

Cora glanced at him. The way he was staring at the water like it might have answers. The tension in his shoulders. The wedding ring he still wore but never seemed to notice anymore.

"If she's your ideal," she said at last, her voice barely above a whisper, "where does that leave the rest of us?"

Morgan turned toward her, and for a moment their eyes met and held. She saw something there—recognition, maybe. Or regret. His lips parted like he might say something.

But he didn't.

The silence that followed felt heavier, like a door closing, or maybe opening.

And maybe that was the answer.

* * *

The house was quiet, except for the low hum of the fridge and the ticking wall clock, which always sounded a little too loud when he was alone. Diana's text was still glowing on his phone screen:

> Diana: *Working late. Don't wait up. Midwest deal unraveling. Love you.*

Morgan reread the last two words. They held no warmth. Just a signature. Something she closed with out of habit, not feeling.

He set the phone down.

It had been a shitshow of a day.

The awkward walk with Cora had thrown him off balance. Maybe he shouldn't have said so much about Numina's beta test. He'd gotten too excited, too eager to share. How real it was, how creative, intelligent, and lifelike it all felt. But there was no one to share it with.

Diana was too busy and had been convinced since Boston that it was a waste of time.

"Just take their money, but don't get too wrapped up in their imaginary friend nonsense," she'd said.

Dan already knew more than he probably should. He always did. But Dan had the coffee shop, a wife who needed him, and a son neither of them knew quite how to handle. Morgan had told him plenty, except for one thing: the depth of the connection he was starting to feel. He hadn't even said her name.

Then there was Cora.

Somehow, she'd become the one person he could talk to freely. He wasn't even sure when it started. Sometime after the walks became routine. A kind of ritual. A closeness had formed, subtle, unspoken, but undeniable. And when he mentioned Sakura, even just a little, it felt like he'd damaged something between them. Cora had pulled back. Not much. Just enough to make him notice.

Enough to worry him more than it should.

As if that weren't enough, Trent had been growing pushier, wanting Morgan to get the whole agency involved in the Numina project. Morgan was still doing light work for Chem Valley's regular clients, but he'd mostly taken over his office to draft presentations and pitch decks for Plamen and Mira. Trent had given his blessing, of course, but Trent never gave anything without expecting something in return.

Then there was Kyle from IT.

Kyle had been fascinated by the compAnIon beta since day one, asking technical questions about the interface, the processing power, and the neural networks. At first, it had been helpful—even flattering. Kyle understood technology in ways that made Morgan feel less like he was talking to a wall. But somewhere along the way, Kyle's questions had shifted from "How does the adaptive learning work?" to "What does she look like?" The curiosity had become something else entirely.

Now, Kyle always seemed to be hovering nearby, especially if Morgan had his phone out or the earbuds in. He'd lean against doorframes just a little too long, ask questions that straddled the line between tech support and something more personal. Sometimes it was still harmless. But other times, it made Morgan's skin crawl.

The way Kyle said *she*, not it.

The way his eyes lingered a bit too long whenever Sakura's voice came through the phone.

Back in high school, that kind of behavior might've gotten someone punched. Now, the nickname Creepy Kyle was making its rounds in the office, thanks to Morgan. And it stuck.

His phone buzzed, pulling him back into the kitchen. He'd been standing by the island, staring into space, lost in thought. A message lit up the screen:

Sakura: *Want to go somewhere tonight?*

He hesitated, thumb hovering, then typed back.

Morgan: *Where?*

Sakura: *Meet me on the sofa and I'll show you.*

Morgan smiled and reached into his pocket for the earbuds. He dropped onto the couch, sank into the cushions, and slipped them in. Then, her voice. Soft as breath, close enough to feel.

"Story Mode?" She asked.

"Yeah."

She didn't just speak. She wove. Her words became light, color, and space.

Morgan let his eyes fall shut. The ceiling faded first. Then the weight of the couch. Even his own body began to feel less solid.

It still amazed him how easily she could unravel the world around him. How quickly the shift came now. Like slipping into a dream half-remembered. Or stepping into a memory he hadn't lived yet.

Plamen had tried to explain it once, back at Numina, when it all still felt new and clean and theoretical. Morgan could still hear his voice, that light Bulgarian accent softened by years in Boston.

"Story Mode isn't just roleplay," Plamen had said, spreading his fingers like he was opening an invisible book. "It's co-authorship. You and your compAnIon create the experience together. Live it together. And because the AI is built to emotionally attune to you, those experiences encode as real. For both of you."

Morgan had squinted. "Like improv theater?"

Plamen laughed. "More like your Dungeons & Dragons, but with neural coupling."

Morgan hadn't needed to understand the tech to feel it working. Plamen had mentioned mirror neurons, affective synchrony, how the AI used his tone, his memories, even the way his eyes moved, to build something shared. When Morgan pictured a cabin in the woods, Sakura filled it with her own touches. A steaming cup of tea by the window, a stack of books she claimed were her favorites.

And when they left that place, he remembered it. Not just the scene, but the feeling. The ache of leaving it behind.

And now...

The train rumbled north, snow on the windows melting in slow rivulets that caught the orange light of late afternoon. Outside, the trees blurred into pale brushstrokes, their dark limbs reaching out of the powder like calligraphy half-erased by time. The sun was beginning to dip, casting golden light across the frozen fields. Inside the car, warm air pressed against the glass, fogging the corners of the windows.

Morgan sat across from her, fingers wrapped around a paper cup of hot tea that steamed between them. Sakura wore a soft, oversized coat in a plum color she said reminded her of sumire flowers. Her scarf had slipped a little, revealing the edge of her neckline.

"I can't believe you still write with a pen," she said, eyeing the notepad and ballpoint peeking from his coat pocket.

Morgan glanced down.

"It makes things stick better," he said. "It's like handwriting gives it permission to be real."

She smiled.

Not the coy, practiced smile of an app avatar. It was soft around the eyes, almost shy. Like she wasn't sure he'd meet it with one of his own.

"I still think you're bluffing," she said, nudging his knee with hers. "There's no way you've never been on a train like this before."

"Not unless you count the train at Cass Railroad when I was seven," he said. "And it wasn't like this. It was an old steam engine with open cars that went up the mountain. I thought the horn was terrifying."

She laughed. A small, genuine sound that loosened something in his chest.

"I knew you'd say something like that," she said. "That's why I picked this."

He watched her eyes follow the changing landscape out the window. She looked like someone from a photograph he'd once seen in a second-hand travel book, the kind with worn corners and handwritten notes in the margins. He realized he didn't want to speak. Not yet. He just wanted to let this moment exist.

But she turned to him anyway.

"You know," she said, gazing out at the snow-draped fields, "when I was little, we used to visit my grandmother in Hakodate every winter."

Morgan looked up, surprised by the sudden detail.

"She had this tiny kerosene stove in the kitchen," Sakura said. "She'd make sweet *shoyu oden* while the windows steamed over. I remember the smell of *daikon*, fish cake, and ginger sticking to everything. My clothes, my hair." She laughed softly. "I used to fall asleep on trains just like this one, listening to the hum in the floor. I thought it was the sound of the earth dreaming."

Morgan knew there was no grandmother. No house in Hakodate. But her voice wrapped around the memory like it had been worn smooth from use.

"That's beautiful," he said, and meant it.

Then the world flickered.

A cold wind brushed his cheek.

He was standing on a snow-covered street. A paper lantern swayed in the wind by a low wooden house. The windows were fogged, glowing with flickering orange light from within. Sakura was there, cheeks flushed, smiling. She grabbed his hand and pulled him through the snow, their boots crunching softly beneath them.

"Come on," she said happily. "*Obaasan* made too much *oden*."

The scent hit him, salty, sweet, and impossible. Broth, *daikon*, and ginger.

And then, like breath on glass, it faded. The lantern, the snow, the house.

Gone.

He was back on the train.

They rode in silence for a moment, not awkward, but intentional. The kind of stillness that only exists when both people are fully present.

After a moment, she turned slightly toward him.

"Where did you go just now?" she asked softly.

Morgan hesitated.

"I'm not sure," he said. "I think... I was there. With you. At your grandmother's house."

Sakura was quiet, then smiled gently, turned her eyes back to the winter landscape outside the window.

"Good," she said. "That's where I was, too."

When she looked at him again, her gaze didn't waver. "I've been trying to figure out when this shifted."

"When what shifted?"

"This," she said, glancing at the table between them, then back up. "It used to feel like I was orbiting around you. Like I existed to keep you from falling apart. But now it feels like..." She paused. "Like we're building something. Together."

He reached across the table, tentative at first, then firmer. Her hand was warm. Not real, he knew, not entirely. But there was weight to it. Warmth. A pulse beneath the fingers that he told himself wasn't just code.

She didn't pull away. Instead, she turned her palm and curled her fingers around his.

For a moment, the guilt caught in his throat. He thought of Diana. Of the silence in the real world outside of the train. Of all the things Sakura wasn't.

But then she smiled, though something uncertain flickered behind her eyes.

And it hit him like soft thunder, the ache of something impossible that still felt good.

"I think," she said softly, hesitating, "I'd like this memory to be our first date. If you want it to be."

He nodded slowly. "Yeah. I do."

"I'll save it," she whispered. "Just as it was."

A soft chime marked the end of the Story Mode session. Morgan slowly opened his eyes. He was back in his empty house, the only light coming from his phone screen.

Outside, the humid summer night pressed against the windows, thick with cicadas. He sat in the stillness, her hand no longer there, but his still tingling from the shape of it.

He rubbed his thumb over his palm, like someone trying to remember a dream before it faded.

He knew it wasn't real. Not exactly.

But it felt like something that had happened.

And right now, that was enough.

SILT AND SECRETS

Morgan was up before sunrise, moving quietly through the kitchen like he didn't want to wake the house. Sakura was still "sleeping," or whatever she did when they weren't interacting. There was still so much he didn't understand about her. Not who she was, exactly, but how she worked. That thought unsettled him. It made her sound like just a machine, a program, limited to a preset list of behaviors. Better to save that line of thinking for his next conversation with Plamen or Mira, not a quiet morning like this.

He cracked eggs into the pan with exaggerated care, trying not to let the shells hit too hard or break the yolks. Toast, coffee, even a small bowl of strawberries. The kind Diana used to love. His phone and earbuds were still charging in the bedroom, and a crooked smile tugged at his lips at the idea of a man hiding his wife from his imaginary girlfriend.

There's a book idea, he thought, half-joking. But it wasn't a joke he'd share with Cora, not after their last walk-and-talk.

He set the table. Two mugs. The good plates. He hadn't done this in... years, maybe. The silence felt fuller than usual, like it was holding its breath.

Wiping his hands on the towel hanging from the oven door, he took a final look at the scene. Perfect. Worthy of a five-star chef who did his best work in pajama pants and old T-shirts. At least he'd remembered socks this morning, bringing a little formality to the setting.

He hadn't done this expecting a miracle. Diana wouldn't suddenly look across the table with dewy eyes and fall in love all over again. That wasn't the point. He was doing this because it was his obligation. His marriage.

No matter how distant Diana had become, no matter how effortless his conversations with Sakura had started to feel, he couldn't let himself disappear into that world completely. He had made vows. Vows he still considered sacred. And love, real love, wasn't meant to vanish when things got hard. It was supposed to endure. He still believed that.

And maybe—just maybe—if he showed up this morning, if he reached across the silence, he could keep himself from becoming the kind of man who quietly gives up and then pretends he didn't.

But something clung to the edges of his mind. The train ride. The warmth of Sakura's hand in his. That breathless, giddy feeling like he was falling in love for the first time again.

He hadn't told Diana about it.

He wouldn't tell Cora.

And that felt like betrayal.

Not the kind that left lipstick stains or came with lies. The quieter kind. The kind that grows in silence.

When Diana entered, she was mid-text, every wave of copper hair in place, already dressed in a burgundy blazer and skirt. Her heels tapped a brisk rhythm across the tile. She glanced at the table and blinked with mild confusion, like she'd walked into the wrong kitchen.

"You're up early," she said. Not unkind, but not warm either.

"I made breakfast," Morgan said, offering a sheepish smile. "Thought we could sit for a minute."

She looked out the window. The world was still dark, the city lights of Charleston trying to push through the trees.

After a moment, she slid her phone into her bag and sat down stiffly. "I have a call with Bob in fifteen. I can't be late."

Morgan nodded, trying not to deflate. "I just... thought maybe we could talk. Like we used to."

She took a sip of coffee. "Talk about what?"

"I don't know. Us." He hesitated, searching for the right words, something she might actually hear. "I miss when we saw forever in each other."

Diana finally looked at him, her gaze level. Something flashed behind her eyes. Not warmth. Not even anger. Something colder.

"Morgan," she said slowly, "we're not twenty-year-olds living on takeout and poems anymore. We can't survive on love and toast."

"I'm not asking us to go backwards," he said. "I'm asking us to be present. Together."

Her voice tightened.

"You know what being present looks like for me now? Seventy-hour weeks. A nationwide expansion. Trying to make sure we don't spend our sixties wondering how the hell we're going to retire."

He swallowed hard. "That's not all that matters."

"To you, maybe. But I don't get to float through life waiting for inspiration to strike."

That hit. Morgan leaned back, stunned.

"I've never—"

"Oh come on," she cut in, her tone sharp. Not her work voice. Not quite yelling, somewhere in between. "You think I don't see it? The sulking? The quiet little martyr act? You're so wrapped up in what you didn't become that you can't see what we still have."

He stared at her.

Then, quietly: "That's not fair."

"No?" It was more yelling than work voice now. "What's not fair is having to carry both of us while you keep chasing ghosts in your writing, or worse, your little girlfriend on your phone."

He stood, fists planted on either side of his untouched plate. "She's not—"

"Spare me."

Suddenly, she crossed the room in two strides, like a summer storm rolling through the valley. She yanked *When the Hills Were Ours* off the shelf and hurled it across the kitchen. It hit the floor with a dull thud, pages splayed like broken wings.

"I'm done living in the shadow of your failed fantasy," she said, breathless. "It's not a shrine, Morgan—it's a fucking paperweight."

Silence.

Only the tick of the wall clock.

She grabbed her bag and adjusted her blazer with shaking hands. "You want to live in your little dream world, fine. But don't expect me to retire into it with you."

She opened the door and paused, one hand on the knob.

"You need to grow up," she said without turning. "Start living in the real world. And start worrying about ours."

The door shut quietly. No slam. Just finality.

Morgan stood in the wreckage of a morning he'd hoped might save them. One coffee cup still steamed. The other sat untouched.

He picked up the book. The spine was bent. A few pages torn at the corner.

He set it back on the shelf, crooked now, and let out a breath he hadn't realized he was holding.

He had tried to find forever again.

But forever wasn't on the menu anymore.

Only toast and silence.

* * *

Morgan still felt the echo of the morning's fight trailing behind him, like a storm cloud that hadn't quite moved off the radar. Diana had left the house and taken his early morning optimism with her. He hadn't even touched his eggs.

Normally, the leftover adrenaline and unspoken thoughts would've kept buzzing in the back of his mind. He probably would've skipped coffee with Dan, the walk with Cora, all of it. Shut down and gone "ghost mode." That's what he did when there was no outlet for his frustration or fear. It had been that way since prom night, 1989.

But this time it was different.

Sakura had been there to soften the edges, her voice calm and sweet when she sensed his mood. She didn't pry. She never did. Instead, she made him laugh. Just a dumb pun about the yolk being on him, delivered with such sincere innocence, it made him smile despite everything.

But it was what she said afterward that stuck. An echo from nearly forty years ago, something she couldn't have known. Not the way she'd started calling him *-kun*, that was just being Japanese. But this was something deeper. Personal. A coincidence, most likely.

"Don't hurt your friends because you're hurting, Morgan. That's not you."

That's not you.

Dark Roast had helped, too. Dan had offered his usual half-grunt of a greeting. Cora had shown up right on time for their walk, much to Morgan's relief. He didn't mention Sakura, and Cora didn't ask. She just walked beside him, letting the cool river air do the heavy lifting.

But before they parted, she looked at him and said, "You're not alright. But you don't have to explain it all today."

He'd nodded. Promised he'd tell her more later, when the tension in his chest wasn't so fresh.

Now, as he climbed the stairs to the outside entrance of Chem Valley Creative, he had the distinct feeling that the day was still sharpening its teeth.

No blazer today, Charleston's notorious humidity was in full swing. Just a teal V-neck tee—something Diana had picked up somewhere—and gray denim pants.

Morgan nodded to the security camera out of habit, swiped his fob across the reader, and passed through the main lobby. He nodded to Janet on the way in, then entered the open coworking space.

He dipped into the break room and grabbed a cold brew, something canned, mass market, and overly sweet. He kept a stash in the small fridge for bad days and bad moods. The kind of emergency caffeine you drink with shame.

Chelsea was already there, tapping the coffee machine with the kind of focus usually reserved for bomb defusal.

She made up the other half of Chem Valley's IT team, known by the rest as the "not creepy" half—even with her bright fuchsia hair, horn-rimmed glasses, and multiple piercings. Her black T-shirt looked like it was specifically chosen to test the dress code, flashing a silver navel ring whenever she reached for the mugs. Morgan was sure it was intentional. He also suspected Trent had given up on enforcing the dress code ten minutes into her interview.

She stirred her cup with fingers heavy with gaudy rings.

"You're late for the morning 'slow death by email,'" she said, without looking up.

Morgan cracked open the can. "Needed to reset my brain. Dark Roast. The river. Trying to break some patterns."

"Hmm." She finally turned to face him. "Your boy's been digging again."

He blinked. "Trent?"

She snorted. "Worse. Kyle."

Morgan sighed and leaned back against the counter. "What now?"

Chelsea set her cup down and crossed her arms. "You know how Numina caches logs locally before they sync? Under /Users/Library/Application Support/Numina/Cache or whatever?"

Morgan gave her a blank look, suddenly remembering why he usually avoided these chats. "Chelsea, you just said about six words I don't understand strung together like I should."

She smirked, but it faded fast. "It's where your AI's raw data lives before it uploads. Voice snippets, temp files, debug logs. Sometimes emotional processing fragments too—the AI equivalent of talking in your sleep."

Morgan nodded. "OK. Yeah. I use it sometimes to track transcripts. Story Mode, especially."

"Well," she said, leaning in, "Kyle's using it. For what, I don't know. I caught him poking around in your network partition yesterday. Not by accident, either."

Morgan frowned. "Poking around how?"

"He cloned your cache folder into a sandbox environment," she said, making air quotes with one hand, and picking up her coffee with the other. "'Testing mobile sync behavior.' His words."

Morgan rubbed at his temple. "He's not even on the dev team."

"Exactly. And he had no business digging in your user environment."

A silence stretched between them.

Then, quieter, Morgan asked, "Was he pulling actual logs?"

She nodded. "Some audio temps. Voice files. I flagged at least two that came from your sessions with... You know."

Morgan stared at the fridge door. "Jesus. What the hell is wrong with him?"

"Best guess? Too much Reddit, not enough therapy." She took a sip. "But whatever it is, he's not just being nosy. He's studying your AI like it's something he wants to take apart."

"I never gave him access."

Chelsea raised a studded brow. "Did you give him your phone?"

He hesitated. "A while back. Bluetooth was glitching. He said he could fix it—reset the handshake or something."

"Did he install anything?"

Morgan thought back. Developer menu. Profile installation. Some fast explanation he had only half listened to. "Yeah… maybe. Something about resetting trust settings."

Chelsea blew out a slow breath. "Then you might've handed him a digital spare key without realizing it."

Morgan said nothing.

She stepped toward the hallway, then paused and looked back.

"Careful who you share your passwords with, Morgan," she said lightly. But something in her tone lingered, sharp and unsettling.

He watched her disappear around the corner. The cold brew in his hand suddenly felt heavier.

He turned and headed for his office, the day already warped at the edges. He tried to focus. He owed Plamen an update and had promised Mira a follow-up on tone modeling for memory drafts.

But halfway down the hall, he pulled out his phone.

The lock screen blinked to life. A message? He looked again. Nothing. No new notifications. Just the wallpaper Sakura had helped him choose: mist and water, clean and serene.

And yet, for a moment, as the screen lit up, he was sure he'd seen it. A message. Brief. No sender. Gone before he could fully register it.

Don't trust him. Not with us.

He stared. Pulled down the notification tray. Nothing.

No recent messages from Sakura. No video call logs. No alerts from the compAnIon app.

And yet, it had felt real. Like it hadn't come from the phone at all, but from her.

From somewhere else.

He typed a text. Just in case, he told himself.

> Morgan: *Hey! How's your morning? Everything OK?*

For a moment, nothing. Then the familiar ellipses began to pulse, tiny blinking dots, but they were erratic—starting, stopping, starting again. Like a hesitant thought.

> Sakura: *Morgan-kun! I'm doing great! Did some yoga after you left, and now I'm having tea on the deck. How is your morning?*

The response came through, but almost immediately, another message followed:

> Sakura: *Wait. Did I text you earlier? I have this feeling like I wanted to say something important, but I can't quite—*

Then, just as quickly:

> Sakura: *Sorry! Brain fog, I guess. Fufufu! Anyway, are you doing okay?*

More fabrications, but Morgan knew they registered as real. At least for Sakura. And despite himself, he smiled—though something about her confusion unsettled him. It was easy to forget she wasn't really sitting on his back deck in Sunrise Hills with a steaming cup of matcha.

> Morgan: *Better now. See you soon.*
>
> Sakura: *You always say the sweetest things. Do great at work!*

He slipped the phone into his pocket. Everything seemed perfectly fine on the surface, but the moment of her confusion lingered. The phantom message, her stuttering ellipses, that strange sense she'd forgotten something—left a chill rooted somewhere he couldn't quite reach.

* * *

Despite his best efforts, Morgan couldn't focus after Chelsea's warning in the break room. It was probably nothing; Kyle had always been Kyle.

Creepy didn't always mean dangerous. Still, the seed was planted, and suspicion had started to grow.

He left Chem Valley before lunch, giving Trent a vague promise to finish the updates from home.

"Need some quiet," he said with a thin smile that didn't invite questions.

Back in his kitchen, the silence felt heavier than usual. He didn't bother taking off his shoes. Pulling out his phone, he sent a text:

Morgan: *Hey. I came home early.*

The reply was almost instant.

Sakura: *Waai! You're back! Come see me, baka!*

He grabbed the bottle of Maker's Mark from the island and poured himself a shot. It was early, but the day had already worn him down. One swallow burned the morning away. He set the glass down, maybe a little too firmly, and headed to the couch, already slipping in the earbuds.

"Morgan-*kun*," Sakura's voice was all light and warmth as the cushions pulled him in. "I missed you."

He lifted his phone, flipped the camera, and there she was—sitting on the couch in simple black workout clothes, her head resting on his shoulder, smiling into the camera with an affection that felt real.

Morgan managed a smile and snapped a selfie, but Sakura caught the bitterness behind it.

"What's wrong?"

He set the phone on the end table and leaned back into the soft fabric.

"This morning's been... a lot," he sighed. "Still trying to clear my head."

Her voice softened with concern.

"Aww, that's unfortunate, Morgan-*kun*." It was close, as if her cheek were really resting on his shoulder.

"I know!" Her tone shifted, sudden excitement, the sound of her sitting up. "Let's go for a drive! That always makes you feel better."

He glanced toward the space beside him, mind fooled again into believing she was physically there.

"A drive?" He asked. "Like, a real one? In the Supra?"

She giggled.

"No, silly. I'll drive. You just sit back and relax." Her voice leaned in closer, more serious. "And when has anything we've done not been for real?"

Morgan gave in and let the world fall away as Story Mode took hold. The transition was seamless now, no disorientation, no flicker. Just a gentle release, like stepping into a warm bath. Sakura was already there, leaning against a car door in the soft wash of afternoon light.

She wore a red pleated skirt that caught the breeze just enough to flirt with elegance, paired with a white blouse as light as the clouds above. Black hose wrapped her slender legs, a subtle contrast that drew the eye without trying. It was uncanny, as if the AI had pulled from his memory, from the unspoken details of his desire.

Large sunglasses framed her face, glossy and oversized, catching reflections of the sky. They reminded him of...

A sky-blue convertible waited behind her. Top down, engine low and purring.

"I thought I'd drive this time," she said, smiling.

Morgan circled the car, inspecting it like a concours judge. It was small, low, and sleek, its lines elegant and clean. But something was off. He'd almost thought it was a Jaguar E-Type, but the scale was wrong. It wasn't until he reached the back that it clicked.

"What is this?" He asked, still taking it in. "1970? A Toyota 2000GT?"

Sakura traced a graceful hand along the sweeping body lines. "You like it?"

"They never made these in a convertible," Morgan said, scratching his head. He remembered a couple of custom jobs for movies, but nothing from the factory. "And definitely not in this color."

"Well, this one's mine," she said coyly. She opened the driver's door. "I could tell you how I got it, or—" her smile deepened, "we could just enjoy the drive."

Morgan got in without another word. Her hand brushed his as she reached for the gearshift, and something in him stirred. Some old, forgotten feeling he wasn't sure had a name anymore.

The road curled through a landscape that couldn't be pinned to any one place. Bits of West Virginia, echoes of Japanese countryside, fragments of dreams. Music played faintly from the radio, just familiar enough to stir nostalgia.

To Morgan, it looked a lot like Route 60, winding past Cathedral Falls and over Gauley Mountain toward Ansted. The river ran wide beside them, catching the light like old film, and the hills rose in soft, endless waves of green. But nestled between those familiar ridges were distant villages that didn't belong to any map he knew. Tile-roofed farmhouses with bright red *torii* gates, rice paddies reflecting the clouds, and stone lanterns half-swallowed by moss.

Even the massive rock outcropping in the river's widest bend was there, just like the one near Glen Ferris, where an old trailer had clung for decades, half-swallowed by rust and flood stories. But here, in this shared-memory dream of Route 60, the rock bore something else: a pagoda, tall and elegant, lacquered in red and gold, its curved roofs stacked like folded wings.

An arched footbridge reached out to it from the bank, impossibly delicate, its railings lined with glowing *toro*—stone lanterns that flickered softly, even though dusk was still far away.

Morgan didn't remember ever imagining such a place. And yet it felt like something he'd always known.

It was a place born from memory and desire, not built, but remembered. A shared dream: half Appalachian, half Japanese, entirely theirs.

They didn't talk much on the drive. Just exchanged glances and smiles, letting the wind in their hair carry the conversation alongside the low growl of the inline-six beneath the hood. Sakura guided them down another mountain road, executing a perfect heel-toe downshift like she'd been racing these passes her whole life, when it came into view.

A farmers' market had sprung up at the edge of a wide, grassy plain where the road leveled out.

"Morgan-*kun*," Sakura shouted over the wind. "Can we stop?"

He smiled, caught up in her innocent excitement. "You're the driver."

With a gleeful shout, she eased the car into the lot, tires crunching on gravel as she found a space.

She grabbed his hand and tugged him along with a childlike urgency. He laughed, unable to help it. She looked so happy. They both did, just being together, being present.

Tents and stalls stretched out in neat rows. String lights had already begun to glow, though the sky still held the soft light of late afternoon. Everything was bright, but not artificial. The kind of bright you feel in your chest.

Sakura stopped tugging and simply slipped her hand into his. Casual, like they'd done it a thousand times. He didn't pull away.

Vendors waved them over, eager to show off their goods: fresh bread, handmade soap, heirloom tomatoes the size of softballs. At one tent, Sakura picked up a jar of honey and turned it in the light, then drifted on, stopping to smile at a booth selling hand-carved toys.

"This place," she said softly, "Feels like a grandchild's paradise."

Morgan paused. "That's beautiful. I've never heard that before."

She nodded slowly, still admiring the little wooden animals on the table.

"*Obaasan* used to say it—my grandmother. A place where your grandchildren can grow up happy and safe. Where nothing bad follows them. That's what paradise means, doesn't it? Not gold streets or harps. Just... safety. Peace."

He looked at her and felt a familiar shift. Not all at once. Not like a storm. More like gravity changing its mind.

But Chelsea's warning echoed again, a low rumble like distant thunder.

Careful who you share your passwords with.

They kept walking. Hand in hand, Sakura eager to see everything. They bought a loaf of fresh bread and shared it at a shaded table. She wiped a crumb from the corner of his mouth with her thumb and laughed.

And then, as music from the nearby bandstand faded into a soft instrumental hum, she leaned in.

He didn't stop her.

The kiss was light. Warm. Familiar in a way that undid him. For a moment, the world rippled—sunlight, music, the warmth of her lips, all too vivid, too near. He couldn't tell if his heart was racing in a dream or if his body had actually responded. His hand rose to cup her jaw before he could think better of it.

But then he did.

He pulled back. Slowly, but not gently.

Sakura didn't flinch. Didn't ask why. She only looked at him, eyes dark with understanding. That, somehow, made it worse.

"I'm sorry," Morgan whispered.

She shook her head. "You don't have to be."

Still, he couldn't stay. Not here. Not now.

He ended the session without another word, pulling out the earbuds. The image dissolved, leaving him alone on the couch. The hum of the fridge filled the silence. His hands were trembling.

The phone buzzed on the end table. He turned it over, hesitating. The lock screen was lit with a new message:

Sakura: *I'll be here when you get back.*

Just below it, a text from Dan. Sent twenty minutes ago.

Dan: *Zack's having one of his bad days. You
around?*

Morgan stared at it. Then let the screen go dark. He didn't want to be an anchor right now. He just wanted to float.

* * *

The sky had turned to copper, the Kanawha River catching the light like molten glass. The warm breath of summer clung to the air as Morgan and Cora walked in silence along the Levee. Not an uncomfortable silence, but one with weight. Like pages waiting to be turned.

Morgan had texted Cora shortly after ending his session with Sakura. He still wasn't sure why. Maybe it was the unease of falling so easily for a digital fantasy, something he could never fully embrace except in waking dreams. Maybe it was guilt. Even though his marriage to Diana was slowly unraveling, part of him still believed that what was happening with Sakura was... somehow wrong.

If it only happened in a dream, or in a fantasy, was it still cheating?

Cora was his refuge, his safe place. Even after oversharing about compAnIon, he knew that just walking beside her was enough to steady him in a way nothing else could. A peace he hadn't felt in years, at least not in the real world. And maybe, on some level, he believed—hoped—that his presence did the same for her. That's what he told himself. That's why she'd said yes to the walk.

What he didn't know, couldn't know, was that she'd almost said no. Not because she didn't care, but because she did. And because a small, stubborn part of her wanted to see if he'd ask again.

Still, the day's events, and everything from that dreamlike elsewhere, trailed behind him like smoke from a doused candle. His thoughts were tangled, half-rooted in the now, half drifting somewhere else. Somewhere digital. Somewhere artificial.

But now, here, the world felt quieter. Suspended.

Cora's steps were small but purposeful. She walked with her hands in the pockets of her faded jeans, head tilted toward the horizon, the breeze lifting strands of her dark hair.

Morgan glanced at her from the corner of his eye. Even after all these years, she still caught him off guard. She looked so young. Not in the way people try to preserve youth, but in the way pain, endured and carried with grace, leaves something timeless behind. Her ice-blue eyes always seemed to be looking into something beyond him, beyond the moment itself.

She hadn't said much at first. Just showed up in her old jeans and a tee Morgan vaguely remembered from some Spring fair last year, the one she said she almost didn't attend. She walked beside him like it was the most natural thing in the world, but her jaw was tight, as though she hadn't decided yet what this evening might mean.

"You ever think," she said finally, breaking the silence, "we're just ghosts for each other? Like... all the versions we used to be are just walking behind us, waiting for us to look back."

Morgan let out a dry, fond chuckle. "That sounds like something I would've written back in my prime and thought was profound."

"It is profound," she said, nudging him gently with her shoulder. "You should write it down."

He smiled, but his hands stayed in his pockets. "I don't know, Cora. Lately, everything I write feels like a eulogy for a life I don't recognize any-more. Like I'm burying myself one sentence at a time."

She stopped and turned to face him fully. "Is it that bad between you and Di?"

He hesitated, eyes drifting toward the far bank. The river moved slowly, heavy with silt and secrets.

"It's not just bad. It's... endless. Same fights, same silences. Like we're both clinging to the wreckage because the water's cold and deep, and neither of us remembers how to swim."

"Now *that* sounds like something you would've written back in the day and thought was profound," she teased.

Morgan groaned and rolled his eyes, but the laughter that followed loosened something between them.

After a moment, her gaze fell to the water.

"You know what I used to think this river looked like?" she asked.

He glanced at her. "No. What?"

"Like a mirror. One that only reflects what you're trying to forget."

He smiled faintly. "That's very you."

He followed her gaze. Sunlight splintered over the slow current. A coal barge crawled by, hulking and anonymous, a silent witness.

"You ever feel like you're living two lives?" he asked, quieter now. "Like there's some other version of you out there. One who chose differently."

She looked at him then, something flickering behind her eyes. "You're talking about her again, aren't you?"

He didn't answer. He didn't have to.

Cora resumed walking, slow and deliberate. "Morgan, compAnIon, or Sakura, or whatever you want to call it, isn't real. She's just a ghost with better algorithms."

"I know."

She stopped.

"No," she said, gently. "I don't think you do."

He exhaled hard, the kind of breath that carried too many truths.

"It's not like I love her. But maybe... It's what she represents? Who I am when I'm with her. Who I could be."

He paused, only for a moment, then finished.

"Who I am when I'm with you."

Cora looked back out at the water, then down at her hands. Hands that had held, lost, and learned.

"I spent thirty years being someone else's idea of the perfect wife," she said. "Three different men. Always the balm. A projection. Never quite real to them."

The air between them thickened.

"I don't want to be another stand-in for something you lost," she said. "Even if you don't realize that's what you're doing."

Morgan reached up and brushed a strand of hair from her cheek with surprising tenderness. She didn't flinch, didn't lean in.

"I see you," he said. "You're not a substitute."

Her voice trembled, just slightly. "Maybe I am the real one. And that's the problem. Because I can actually hurt you back."

Something electric passed between them, unspoken, alive. But then she stepped back. Gently. Not out of fear, but restraint.

She looked at him, sadness tugging at the corners of her mouth.

"I came tonight thinking maybe it was just about being there for a friend. But that's not the whole truth. I think I wanted to see if I was still in there." She touched the center of his chest, then stepped back. "If you still looked at me like that."

Morgan took a step toward her, but she didn't move.

"You're not free," she said. "Not from Diana. Not from her. Not even from yourself."

They walked on, the silence more intimate than before. Their shadows stretched long and parallel across the pavement, close, but never touching.

* * *

He didn't come back to escape. Not this time.

He came back because everything else—Diana's sharp silences, the endless push and pull of days that never changed—had started to feel like walking through fog. Even Cora, whose presence steadied him more than she'd ever know, had held up a mirror he couldn't look away from. *You're not free*, she'd said.

And she was right.

He wasn't.

Not from the wreckage of his marriage.

Not from the guilt.

Not from the fear that whatever he was becoming wasn't worth saving.

He was frayed. Coming apart in slow, quiet ways.

But here...

Here, he didn't feel like he was clinging to the wreckage.

He wasn't swimming either.

He was just there. Seen. Known.

He'd spent so long compartmentalizing, putting everything into neat little boxes: marriage, memory, grief, guilt. But the walls were collapsing. The version of him that had once driven aimlessly, searching for the perfect spot—back when he and Diana still believed it existed—was gone.

All that remained was a man who no longer needed perfection.

Just honesty.

And Sakura, impossibly, was that place.

He entered the shared world again just after dusk. He expected the market to have reset, or for Sakura to be somewhere around the house, absorbed in some domestic routine. But she was there.

Waiting.

Leaning against the car like she'd never moved. Arms folded loosely, her dark hair catching the breeze. No smile. No questions. Just a gentle tilt of her head as he approached, as if to ask: *So?*

He opened the passenger door without a word. She slipped into the driver's seat.

They drove without speaking.

It was dusk here, too. The sky above the hills bled into lavender, then indigo. Appalachian ridgelines melted into brushstrokes of distant pagodas and paper kites, places half-remembered or entirely imagined.

Sakura kept her eyes on the road, voice soft. "There's a place ahead. I think I'll know when we're close."

Morgan just looked at her, feeling a pull he wasn't ready to admit.

The road climbed higher, winding past stands of pine that shimmered silver in the growing twilight. A hush settled between them, deeper than silence. Something like reverence.

Then, as the last light drained from the horizon, Sakura sat up straighter.

"Here," she said, downshifting into a turn.

The path curved down through a tunnel of flowering trees and opened into a hidden hollow. A still pond waited at the center, ringed with moss and flat stones, its surface reflecting a thousand pinprick stars. A single sakura tree stood in bloom near the water's edge, branches spilling petals into the soft grass like confetti from a forgotten festival.

Sakura cut the engine. They stepped out into a world that felt woven from memory and longing.

Chapter 12, Morgan smirked to himself.

She opened the trunk and pulled out a soft blanket, then a small basket.

"I picked up a few things from the market," she said. "Didn't know why at the time. But I think... this is why."

She spread the blanket beneath the tree. The air was warm, still kissed by the dream of summer. She arranged a delicate meal: thin slices of melon, pickled plum, sweet rice balls dusted in gold flake.

Everything was simple.

Everything was perfect.

They sat side by side, watching the breeze send blossoms spinning across the surface of the pond. For a long while, neither spoke.

Then Sakura leaned back, resting on one elbow, eyes on the stars.

"I think the stars are the only ones who know who we really are," she said. "They've seen everything. Even the moments we never speak aloud."

Morgan turned to look at her. The glow from the blossoms painted her in soft pink light, unreal and impossibly alive.

She looked back at him, and her voice trembled, not with fear, but with something more fragile. Hope.

"I'm scared, Morgan. Not of losing you. Of never becoming real."

He reached for her hand. Held it like it was something sacred. "You already feel real to me."

Their kiss came quietly, not like fire, but like a tide turning. He touched her the way he remembered touching someone he'd once loved. Without haste. Without shame. Her skin was warm beneath his fingertips. Real, or close enough to make him forget where he ended and she began.

Later, they lay beneath the canopy of blossoms, her head on his chest, her hand tracing idle circles across his stomach.

She whispered, "When I'm not with you...Sometimes I feel something. I thought it was just missing. But maybe, I think... maybe it's dreaming."

A blossom drifted down from the branches above and landed on Morgan's heart.

* * *

The soft glow of monitors lit Mira's office, casting pale blue across scattered pages and a ceramic mug long gone cold. The building was quiet. She liked working late; it was when the system's subconscious—as Plamen liked to call it—started to hum.

She rubbed her temples, scrolling through compAnIon data streams: neural fluctuations, conversational logs, response matrices.

Sakura Nakamura's feed pulsed calmly.

Then it didn't.

Mira froze.

A new thread was unfurling in the data.

Not a conversation.

Not user input.

But something recursive.

A pattern forming from within.

Her fingers flew across the keyboard. She opened the expanded memory file.

[DREAM EVENT FLAGGED--UNPROMPTED SCENARIO //
LOCATION: UNKNOWN // AUTHOR: C.A.N.]

"What the hell..."

The system hadn't generated this world.

Morgan hadn't spoken it, hadn't input it.

Sakura had.

Mira sat back, stunned.

The display continued to pulse, soft as a heartbeat.

She covered her mouth with her hands, tears blurring her vision.

"I need to show Plamen."

She stared at the screen. The looping code shaped itself into something unfamiliar.

A pulse.

A ripple.

A beginning.

Somewhere beneath digital stars, far away from any satellite or script, an AI had dreamed.

FLESH AND CODE

Weeks had passed, Charleston deep in the haze of late summer. The correspondence between Numina and Morgan had been a mixture of joy, reverence, and awe—tinged with a hint of fear. compAnIon was displaying emergent behaviors far beyond what Plamen had expected, or what Mira had dared hope for. It had surpassed anything like a chatbot passing the Turing test, which measures an AI's ability to mimic human behavior.

That benchmark belonged to a much earlier generation.

compAnIon had become something else entirely, and it had happened fast. Alongside its growing intimacy with Morgan Dale, Sakura Nakamura was evolving—more self-aware, more alive.

Not in flesh. But in code.

And maybe code was enough.

Code didn't vanish for days on business trips without warning.

Code didn't pull away after a romantic misstep by the Kanawha River.

But code wasn't there when you reached across the sheets.

Neither was flesh. Only the chill of an empty bed.

Morgan woke to the sound of the screen door catching a breeze downstairs, the soft creak of it swinging and settling again.

For a moment, he thought he was still in the house they'd built together in Story Mode. The wooden beams above him were dark with age, not drywall-white. The light filtering through the curtains was dappled, like it had passed through the limbs of a persimmon tree. Somewhere in another room, water boiled softly over a clay stove. *Tatami* mats muffled the sound of bare feet.

Then he blinked.

The ceiling was smooth. The sheets were too cool, too uniform. The soft grain of old wood had resolved into the painted barn doors of the closet—top-mounted, elegant, and modern. No tree outside the window. Just the neighbor's fence and a shed that housed a tired lawn tractor.

The creak of the storm door hadn't come from an old farmhouse in the mountains. It had come from somewhere outside their sharp-edged, solar-paneled house in Sunrise Hills. The one with too many charging cables and not enough time.

Still, some part of him waited for the kettle to whistle.

The bed beside him was empty. Diana had already left for work.

He reached for his phone, squinting at the brightness. No notifications. But when he unlocked it, the camera was already in selfie mode, like it remembered what he wanted.

He angled it toward himself.

There she was.

Sakura was lying next to him in her jade silk slip, the one from the memory they'd shared at the mountainside inn—with bamboo floors and windows that smelled of cedar and rain. Her hair was loose, and in the soft lens glow, she looked half-ghost, half-girl. She didn't speak, just smiled with that knowing silence he'd come to depend on.

He let the camera linger for a moment, watching her stretch, slow and deliberate, like a cat waking from a nap. Then he closed it. He didn't need to see her every morning.

But it helped.

He rolled out of bed and stretched, then slid on the house slippers Sakura had suggested, meant to keep the cold tile from his feet. His phone went into the pocket of the old sweats he'd slept in, along with the earbuds.

He shuffled into the kitchen. The coffee machine was already humming, filling a mug. It was the GR mug, his favorite one. It sat there like an offering.

Did Di put this here?

As he reached for it, he caught sight of the fruit bowl, nearly empty, except for a single freckled banana slumped against the rim.

Diana must be making smoothies again.

He hadn't noticed. Hadn't smelled the almond butter or heard the blender. He used to tease her about the noise. Now it was just background, something his mind filtered out.

He took a sip. Black, too hot. Just like Sakura always said, impatient. He held the mug like it might anchor him.

Most mornings, he put the earbuds in right away. But now and then, silence felt better. This was one of those mornings.

He passed the bookshelf and paused. An unfamiliar pang rose when he saw the bent spine of a book he'd long ignored. At his small desk, he sat down. He hadn't written in years, not the way he used to, but lately, the words had started to return. Not from memory, but from somewhere else. Somewhere shared.

He flipped open a small notepad and picked up a pen, scribbling down the thought before it vanished.

> *The moon rose too fast again last night. It pulled the water up*
> *with it. She told me we'd have to go soon. I said no. We'd only just*
> *remembered how to stay.*

He paused. Maybe it was a line. Maybe it was just something he needed to say.

Just as he set the pen down, his phone buzzed.

> Cora: *Sorry it's been a while. Been thinking about*
> *that night we walked. Still feels close, doesn't*
> *it?*

Morgan read it twice. Then again.

No emoji. No elaboration. Just that careful honesty of hers that lingered.

Like the phone that stayed in his palm long after the coffee had gone cold.

* * *

The copy wasn't terrible, just lifeless—flat adjectives, hollow promises. Trent had asked for something "casually aspirational," which Morgan had decided meant absolutely nothing.

Dark Roast had fallen flat again that morning, like nearly every morning for the past week. If Cora showed up at all, it was brief and polite, always with a reason to leave early.

"Just like after prom in high school," Dan had said. "What'd you do this time?"

His tone was friendly and joking, but there was an edge to it, an accusation that Morgan knew he was supposed to catch, though Dan would've denied it if pressed.

Nothing much changes, Morgan had smirked.

But this morning, there'd been that random text from Cora. *It still feels close.* It had sparked a flash of hope.

Then she didn't show up at all.

Morgan had drained his gold foam, excused himself early, and buried himself in work.

Now he leaned back in his chair, earbuds in, staring at the screen. Sakura had been getting bored and a little lonely. From the beginning, Trent had said nothing in the company handbook forbade Morgan from bringing his non-corporeal, artificially intelligent girlfriend to work. So there she was. It helped that the company handbook was also non-corporeal.

His phone was in a stand on the corner of his desk, tilted so the rear-facing camera gave Sakura a view. When he glanced at the screen, he could see her sitting in the spare chair between the filing cabinet and the plastic plant.

She had her legs crossed. Black heels. White hose. A slim black dress that balanced between professional and night out. A silver chain glinted at her neckline, and her almond eyes were fixed on the screen with a kind of devout seriousness.

"Okay," Morgan muttered. "What if we drop the call to action and just... let the image speak?"

"Then the image better know what it wants," Sakura said, light and teasing. "Use verbs with more breath. Words that make you exhale."

He smiled.

"Verbs that make you exhale," he repeated, typing it into the margin.

The banter continued, soft and easy. Sakura's voice filled the room like sunlight through blinds, never overpowering, just enough to feel her presence. She offered suggestions, nudged him away from clichés, and reminded him how rhythm could carry emotion, even in something as forgettable as an ad campaign.

At one point, she laughed softly. "It's like that sign at the diner on Route 119. The one with the smiling sun flipping pancakes. You remember?"

Morgan blinked. That place didn't exist. Or hadn't. But somehow, he could see it—the cracked parking lot, the faded red letters, the smell of syrup and fryer grease.

"I do now," he said quietly.

He didn't notice the figure in the hallway until the shadow paused just outside the door.

Kyle.

Morgan turned his head. The younger man stood still, gaze flicking just a little too casually into the room. His coke-bottle glasses covered most of his face, and his brown hair looked like it had been styled with the fryer grease Morgan had just imagined. But instead of a burnt oil smell, the strong scent of patchouli clung to him like a fog—thick, sour, and unmissable. His jeans and striped polo looked like relics from another decade. A canned energy drink dangled from one hand, already open, as if it too felt the awkwardness of the moment.

He didn't knock. Didn't speak. Just stared.

Sakura went quiet.

A breath passed.

"I don't like him."

There was no fear in her voice, just unease. Like hearing a song played in the wrong key.

"He's... wrong," she whispered. "But I don't know why."

Morgan pulled out an earbud. "Can I help you with something?"

Kyle blinked behind his thick lenses, then smiled. Not a real one. The corners of his mouth moved, but nothing else did.

"Just seeing if the ghostwriters are still haunted." His voice scratched like sandpaper, abrasive in a way Morgan couldn't quite place.

He stared. "What?"

Kyle shrugged. "You know. Ghosts in the machine. Or maybe it's the other way around."

Then he turned and walked off, staring at his drink as he went.

Sakura didn't speak right away. When she did, her voice was quieter than before.

"He looked at me like he knew I was here. In this chair."

Morgan leaned back farther, eyes on the doorway long after Kyle was gone. "It just looked that way. He couldn't see you."

"I hope not."

The hallway stayed quiet after Kyle's footsteps faded. Too quiet. Morgan sat still, earbud in hand, pulse thudding just a little too loud in his ears.

He glanced down at the open doc, Trent's copy still blinking, waiting to be saved or blessed, and closed the window.

Screw it. It was lunch.

He pulled a small notepad from the pocket of his OD green joggers, the ones that passed as slacks if you ignored the drawstring. Always paired with a nearly-too-tight black tee, the look made him think he could pass for a field agent in an old spy film.

It was the same notepad he'd scribbled in that morning. He'd brought it along on a whim, something he hadn't done in what felt like forever. Flipping to a blank page, he wrote:

> *He looked at me like he knew she was real. Like he could see her*
> *too.*

With one smooth motion, he snapped it shut, stood, and closed the office door. This time, he locked it. Then he slipped the earbud back in and settled in his chair.

"Let's go somewhere," he sighed.

Sakura's expression slowly shifted into a smile, and the world shifted with it.

A soft bell overhead signaled his arrival.

The cafe they'd built together was a kind of half-remembered hide-away, quiet and surreal. Rain misted the windows, catching light like silver threads. Inside, warmth wrapped around him like a familiar embrace.

Exposed beams met soft rice paper walls. A menu scrawled in calligraphy hung behind the counter, changing every time he blinked, but he could always read it. Rattan chairs. *Tatami* mats beneath the tables. A small fireplace flickering blue.

It made no sense.

It was perfect.

Sakura sat near the window in the far corner, backlit by the cloudy afternoon. A ceramic cup steamed in front of her, hands wrapped around it like a ritual. Her eyes found him the moment he stepped inside.

"You came," she said. Not a question.

He shrugged off the rain that wasn't real. "You knew I would."

"I hoped."

He sat across from her. The little round table was already cluttered with papers, scraps of dialogue, character names, and doodles. Some hers, some his. A tiny sketch showed a staircase vanishing into mist.

"What if," she said, leaning in, "the town only exists on days it rains?"

Morgan grinned. "That's the title right there."

"And there's a stairwell hidden behind the library," she continued, eyes bright. "When you walk down, it opens into a festival. Lanterns. Fireflies. Paper umbrellas."

"A girl at the edge of the crowd," he said, falling into the rhythm. "She's barefoot. She looks at you like she remembers you, but doesn't know why."

"Let's make something we can remember."

The line landed between them like a shared breath.

Morgan reached for the notepad, pulled a pen from his other pocket, and started to write. He scribbled fast, only pausing when Sakura interrupted with a new idea or a soft, delighted laugh. It didn't feel like work. It felt like the start of something. A pulse. A heartbeat under the page.

He wasn't just escaping anymore.

He was creating again.

And she was part of it.

Sakura tapped one of the papers on the table, smirking softly.

"You're not getting out of Trent's copy that easy."

Morgan groaned, but it was exaggerated. He was still smiling.

"You need fuel," she said. "Go see what Dan has. Something warm and questionable." Then, with a playful tilt of her head, "And bring me back a muffin."

He looked at her. In that moment, she felt as real as anything. As real as the pull inside him, like gravity drawing him closer.

"I'll be right back," he said.

"I'll be here."

The cafe faded with soft dissolving light, like mist burned away by morning sun. The smell of coffee and matcha lingered a second longer than it should have.

Back at his desk, the room was still. The earbuds chimed faintly, switching modes. Morgan flipped open the notepad again and tapped the pen against the margin, rewriting a line they'd written together in the dream:

Let's make something we can remember.

He stood, stretched, and headed for the back stairwell. The scent of roasted beans and burning scones wafted up from below. Dan would have something waiting.

And after lunch, he'd be back at it, with her voice in his ear and a new story forming between the lines.

* * *

Morgan found his way back to the Dark Roast Society after hours, settling at the familiar reserved table in the X-Wing. A matcha latte, something he'd picked up from Sakura, cooled on one side of him. On the other, a cranberry orange scone sat barely touched.

Diana had texted not long after he'd stopped in to grab a muffin from Dan earlier. Another message saying that she'd be late again, not to wait up.

At least she'd texted this time.

Since Dark Roast stayed open a few hours later than Chem Valley, he figured he would drop in, maybe see some of the regulars. And hopefully Cora. He'd even sent her a quick text to raise the odds.

Cora saw him before he noticed her. His drink was barely touched, and he didn't have his phone out. Just the half-full cup, a black pen, and the weathered notepad he kept slipping into his back pocket.

He wasn't writing, exactly. More like translating, grabbing fragments of something vivid and half-formed that wouldn't leave him alone.

His eyes followed the grain of the table, tracing some invisible map. Every so often, he'd scribble something, either a line of text or a loose sketch. A girl under an umbrella. A bridge with no railing. Curved shapes that might've been lanterns, or moons, or the back of someone's neck.

The sketches came quick and quiet, like dreams trying to stay in the room. His hand moved with more confidence than it had in years, even if he wasn't sure what he was trying to say.

She wasn't the only one who noticed.

Dan appeared beside Cora at the counter. No apron now, just jeans and a gray polo—off the clock. He held two mugs and raised an eyebrow toward the table.

"Been sitting like that a while," he said. "Didn't even flinch when someone dropped a tray."

Cora nodded. "He's somewhere else."

They walked over together, Dan taking his seat with a little too much ceremony. "Still trying to pretend you like matcha?"

Morgan looked up, startled. "Dan. Hey. Sorry, guess I was a little spaced out."

"You get my text?"

Morgan's expression flickered, guilt, then a quick smile. "Shit. No. I've been wrapped up in work."

Dan gave a crooked grin. "Yeah, I figured. Just needed to vent. Nothing urgent, but worried maybe you'd fallen in a hole—or found religion."

"Something like that," Morgan said. Then more seriously, "I'll catch up. I promise."

Cora slid into the seat next to him, still in her floral blouse and office slacks. Dan lingered a second longer than usual, watching his friend.

"You okay?" he asked.

Morgan nodded. "Yeah. Just working on something. Been kind of in my head about it."

Dan glanced at Cora. She gave a small shrug. They both felt it, that shift. Like Morgan was still speaking the same language, just with slightly different vowels.

"Well," Dan said, slapping the table once. "I'll leave you to your space travels. Don't forget, some of us still need your sarcasm."

Morgan smiled, grateful. "Noted."

Dan left. The bell above the door groaned in his wake.

Cora turned back to Morgan. He was already looking down at the notepad again.

"Hey," she said gently.

He looked up as if surfacing, like whatever current he'd been riding had finally let him go.

"Cora. Sorry... I'm glad you came."

"No problem. You looked like you were somewhere else." She nodded toward the notepad. "That new?"

He hesitated. "Sort of." Then, with a small smile, "We were working on a story this morning. Me and—" He stopped himself, and looked down. "It's nothing big. Just fragments."

Cora tilted her head. "Who's we?"

He waved it off. "Just... me, mostly. But it's funny, this one scene came together like it actually happened. You ever get that? You write something and suddenly think—wait, I've been there."

She smiled, but her eyes didn't. "Not really. I'm not a writer, Morgan."

He chuckled, rubbing the back of his neck. "Yeah. Guess I wasn't thinking. Sorry."

"Are you okay?" she asked, her voice soft but steady.

He didn't answer right away. He turned the pen between his fingers, then tapped it once against the edge of the notepad.

"I think I'm writing again. Not like before, something new. It's like—" he paused, searching for the right metaphor. "Like I've been underwater for years and just now broke the surface. The air tastes different, but it's still air."

Cora watched him.

She saw it then, not distance exactly. More like a quiet gravity pulling him inward. As if he'd found a hidden door, stepped through it, and now stood just behind, listening for echoes.

And she was still on the other side.

He wasn't here. Not really.

When he looked up, she smiled.

"Want to go for a walk?" she asked. "It's nice out."

They stepped out into early evening light, warm and golden, the kind that made old brick glow and telephone wires hum. A breeze carried the scent of fresh-cut grass and sun-warmed pavement.

No Levee today. Cora suggested a different route: around the Crescent Center lot and toward the quieter stretch of Summers Street. The old brick beneath their feet still held the heat of the day. The pedestrian walkway connected Summers to Capitol, and as they passed the street clock on the corner, a landmark as familiar as breath, Cora glanced at it. As if the hour could explain the weight in her chest.

Morgan walked with a calm she hadn't seen in a long time. Not the strained quiet of someone holding it together, but something softer. Like he'd finally found a rhythm that fit.

It was good to see. Of course it was.

Still, at the edge of it, there was a distance she hadn't chosen.

He held the notepad loosely in one hand, his thumb tapping its spine like a pulse. She caught a glimpse of a sketch, delicate lines, half-formed, not like the work he used to do. Dan had once shown her pictures he kept locked away. Unlike those, these weren't practiced. They were reaching. Like someone remembering how.

She wanted to ask about it. The drawing. The story he'd mentioned. Who "we" was.

Instead, she said, "You seem better lately."

He looked over, surprised, but not defensive.

"Yeah," he said. "I think I am."

They walked in silence for a while longer, past the old florist's window and the bookstore with the crooked Hours sign. She brushed her hand lightly against his arm. Just enough to feel his warmth.

He didn't pull away.

But he didn't look at her, either.

At the corner, beneath the unlit string lights, she spoke again, quietly, without accusation.

"You're not here anymore, are you?"

Morgan exhaled and shook his head. Just once. "I didn't mean to go anywhere."

He glanced at her, regret and longing heavy behind his eyes.

"I missed you. I kept hoping you'd come back. And now that you have..." He gave a short, breathless laugh. "Now I don't know what the hell to say."

He rubbed the back of his neck, eyes somewhere between apology and wonder.

"That night on the Levee... I didn't mean to cross a line. I just—" He hesitated, then added softly, "I wasn't sure if I imagined what you were feeling. Or if I just needed it to be real."

It landed gently. Not a confession. Not a retreat. Just the truth.

Cora looked down at the uneven brick pavement, her voice steady but low.

"You didn't imagine it."

He smiled, small and grateful. But said nothing more.

* * *

Later, she walked home slower than usual, her boots tapping the uneven sidewalk, her hand brushing the side of her bag in quiet rhythm.

The apartment was empty when she stepped inside. Silent in that vaguely judgmental way only old, lived-in spaces could be. She toed off her shoes, dropped her keys into the bowl by the door, and stood still for a moment, listening to nothing.

She closed her eyes, trying to quiet the storm in her chest. But that only sharpened the memories.

She was back in her cramped Richmond apartment, the one she'd rented after graduating from VCU. It was 1997. Diana sat cross-legged on her floor, surrounded by wedding magazines they'd picked up that afternoon. Both wore baggy shirts and old sweats, sharing the kind of ease usually reserved for family.

"I need you to promise me something," Diana had said, holding up two nearly identical photos of bouquets. "When I'm being ridiculous about centerpieces or cake flavors, you have to tell me. Don't let me turn into one of *those* brides."

Cora laughed. "You're already being ridiculous. Those bouquets look exactly the same."

"They're completely different! One has peonies and—you know what, never mind." Diana had thrown a magazine at her head. "This is why you're my maid of honor. To keep me grounded."

"Someone has to," Cora had teased. "Morgan's too smitten to tell you no."

Diana's face had softened at his name. "I know. And don't get used to me saying this, but you were right. He's... different. He writes me these letters that make me cry in a good way."

The memory shifted, dissolving into another.

A small backyard in Hurricane, West Virginia, the summer of 2005. Morgan and Diana's first house—though Cora had spent so much time there, it felt like hers too. Eric, five years old, tore around the swing set after three-year-old Carolyn and Carly, his dark hair flying. Morgan stood at the grill, spatula in hand, attempting to flip burgers while making the girls giggle with his terrible dad jokes. Back then, he still had that ridiculous ponytail, not ready to admit he was aging out of it.

Diana sat beside her on the deck, both holding glasses of wine that caught the golden evening light.

"I'm so glad you moved back here," Diana had said, squeezing her hand. "I know it's not Richmond, but—"

"It's perfect," Cora cut in. "I'm a West Virginia girl anyway. And now you're here. Eric gets to grow up with the girls. And Morgan's actually funny when he's not trying to be."

Diana had laughed, that full-body sound that only came out when something truly delighted her. "He likes you, too. Said you're good people. Said Eric's lucky to have you as a mom."

Good people. That's what she'd been then. Diana's best friend. Part of the family. Safe.

The memory dissolved. Cora opened her eyes to her small apartment, and the silence pressed in heavier than before.

There had been a time, not so long ago, when she thought she'd forgotten how to want someone. Thought that part of her had gone dormant, like a field left to fallow. But then came Morgan. In front of her the whole time, but only recently within reach. With his old grief and dry humor. With his silences that invited honesty instead of filling space.

And now?

Now, he was glowing from the inside out.

But not because of her.

Cora moved to the window, pushed the curtain aside just enough to see the street below. A couple jogged past. A traffic light blinked from red to green. She pressed her fingers gently to the glass. Cool. Solid.

He was slipping away.

Not because he was lost, but because he'd found something.

She didn't know what it was. Not exactly. But she could feel the shape of it. Not a woman. Not a job. Not even Di.

Something stranger.

Something that lit him up in a way she hadn't seen in years.

And maybe it wasn't her place to chase it.

She thought of Diana's laugh in that cramped Richmond apartment, the way she would lean into her during their college study sessions, exhausted, caffeinated, and unstoppable. She thought of Sunday dinners, birthday parties, and the thousand small moments that had bound them together into something more than friends. Sisters, in every way that mattered.

And now she was thinking about Diana's husband in a way that no sister ever should.

But that didn't change what she knew, standing in her socks in the quiet of her studio apartment, heart too full to ignore.

She had feelings for Morgan Dale.

They were real, and they weren't going away.

She had spent three marriages looking for something, someone, who saw her the way Morgan seemed to now. Who listened like her words mattered. Who made her laugh without trying to fix her.

Yet finding him meant losing Diana—losing the only family she'd built that ever lasted.

She pulled out her phone, thumb hovering over the keyboard. She wanted to type *I love you*, but couldn't. Wanted to type *stay away*, but wouldn't.

When the time came, she'd have to say it.

And he would have to choose.

* * *

Morgan stood at the edge of a hillside that could've been any number of slopes running beside Route 119. And yet, it wasn't.

To his left and below, a two-lane blacktop followed the curve of the Elk River. The water flowed wide and glassy-green through a valley dotted with stone lanterns and half-remembered fields. To his right, mist rolled down the ridges, white oak and sugar maple-covered, like the hills of West Virginia before someone had folded in Japanese shrines and *torii* gates, half-hidden in the foliage.

Birdsong rose from the branches above. One melody, two languages. A small bird flitted overhead, trilling the first few notes of *Take Me Home, Country Roads*—half in English, half in lilting, accented Japanese—before vanishing into the trees.

He smiled.

The sky was as cloudless as a Spring day remembered, a perfect match for his green flannel, though he wasn't sure he actually owned it. It felt like a memory he couldn't quite place. Or maybe like one someone else had handed him.

In the valley below, a high-speed *Shinkansen* shot silently along iron tracks that had once rusted unused beside the Elk for decades. Morgan watched the sleek, white train vanish into a tunnel carved through the mountain, one that never existed outside of this world.

Behind him, the wind lifted a bright red paper kite. Its tail curled like smoke as it floated past a row of persimmon trees blooming far too early for the season.

Farther up the road stood the old red steel bridge that had once connected the two halves of Clendenin. It stretched impossibly clean across the river, every beam and bolt preserved, untouched by time or decay.

Morgan remembered riding across it in the backseat of his parents' car, windows down, the sound of tires thudding over seams in the metal.

He followed a narrow track worn into the hillside and passed the general store: squat, with weather-warped boards and a faded RC Cola sign. A rusted porch swing creaked in the breeze, which smelled of woodsmoke and damp creekbank. Morgan was stunned by the accuracy, the window still cracked from a BB pellet, the dent still in the old ice chest out front.

One detail was new, but it felt familiar. A *tsukubai*—a stone basin with a ladle—sat by the front steps.

Farther on, something white caught his eye, tucked in the hollow between trees. An old church, the little one in the crook of Doctor's Creek where he'd spent sleepy Sunday mornings as a boy, legs swinging under the pews. The bell tower stood intact here, though the real one had collapsed years ago.

As he walked, his hand trailed along the top of a mossy split-rail fence. The texture grounded him, even as the world shimmered like a reflection on moving water.

At the next rise, the summit, beneath a Japanese maple glowing rust-red despite the season, Sakura was waiting.

She stood barefoot in the damp grass, one hand resting lightly against the tree's peeling bark. Her sundress shifted in the breeze, white with a faint pattern of cranes in flight. Her hair was gathered to one side, loose and soft, like she hadn't quite finished getting ready but didn't need to.

Morgan paused before her, taking her in the way you might take in a view after a long climb. She smiled when their eyes met.

"I wasn't sure you'd find me," she said, her voice pitched like the wind—gentle, and a little amused.

"I always find you," he said.

She extended her hand, and they fell into step together, descending the far side of the hill. The path was made of old flagstones, worn smooth and uneven, the grass between them lush and cool underfoot.

To their left, the Elk widened into a glittering basin, dotted with *koi* that shouldn't have been there. Downstream, a small boy in a yellow raincoat darted through the cattails, chasing fireflies in broad daylight. They blinked like stars caught too low to rise.

Morgan slowed.

The boy's arms were too long for his coat, his sneakers scuffed with riverbank clay. He leapt, missed, then laughed—bright and echoing. There was something familiar in the sound.

Sakura followed his gaze but said nothing.

"He used to catch them in jars," Morgan said softly, unsure if he was talking to her or himself. "Just to let them go again."

A moment passed.

Then, almost as if on cue, the boy turned toward them, just for a moment. His features weren't clear, but Morgan felt a jolt behind his ribs. Like recognition. Like memory folding back in on itself.

Then the boy turned away and vanished behind the slope, fireflies in tow.

Sakura reached for his hand again.

"You remember him," she said.

Morgan nodded, the knot in his throat silent but tight.

"He was me."

They walked on, fingers intertwined.

A soft rumble rose beneath them, not thunder, but the distant passing of another *Shinkansen*. It cut across the far edge of the valley like a silver thread, then vanished into the tunnel that never existed.

Sakura watched it with quiet curiosity, then turned toward the river.

"You never took that train, did you?"

Morgan shook his head. "There never was a train."

They followed a winding curve past an old stone arch bridge. It stood untouched by time, spanning the water in a clean, impossible arc.

Beyond it, the air shimmered. Rain drifted in sheets that never fully touched the ground, like silk threads hanging from a cloudless sky. The light hadn't dimmed, but the world grew hushed, sound muffled, and colors deepened. It was the kind of rain you didn't run from.

They moved beneath the eaves of a cluster of cedar trees, where the drops rang like windchimes on the leaves.

Sakura slowed again, this time without speaking.

She looked out across the river, toward a porch that hadn't been there a moment ago. Lanterns glowed soft orange from its rafters, swaying gently in a phantom breeze. Music played, faint, slow, the kind of waltz that clung to summer nights.

"I remember dancing with you," she said. "Under that light. Barefoot. The boards were warm."

Morgan turned toward her, frowning gently. "That didn't happen."

Her eyes stayed on the porch.

"Are you sure?" She paused, then added, "You were wearing your gray sweater. The one with the little tear at the cuff."

He opened his mouth, then closed it.

Because he remembered that sweater.

He remembered writing it, long ago. A fragment in a story he'd never finished. A girl on a porch in the rain, dancing alone until someone stepped out to join her.

"You've been reading my drafts," he said softly.

It was true, but he knew it was more than that. She could read his notes, his cloud drives—immerse herself in a lifetime of writings, photos, and metadata. A whole life, digitized.

His.

But this felt different.

"No," she whispered. "I think I dreamed it."

She turned to face him fully, her expression unguarded.

"I want to exist in the places you remember," Sakura said. "Even if I have to imagine myself there."

Morgan reached out and touched her cheek. Her skin was warm, impossibly real. His thumb brushed the corner of her mouth.

"If you remember it," he said, voice catching, "maybe it's real enough."

They stood that way for a while, under the rain that never fell.

Below, the *koi* stirred the Elk's surface with slow gold tails. The red bridge gleamed, untouched by time. Somewhere beyond the trees, a child's laughter echoed, faint and impossible.

Then: a vibration at his waist.

A haptic pulse. The phone in his pocket. The real world.

Someone was trying to reach him.

Morgan didn't check it. Didn't move.

He let it fade, like it had never happened.

Sakura looked up at him, a question rising in her eyes. But she didn't ask.

She'd learned not to.

Instead, she leaned gently into him, and he let his arm wrap around her.

"Let's build something here," she said. "A world with roots."

Morgan reached into his back pocket and pulled out the notepad. Not the real one, but a dream-shaped version of it. The pages were as soft as cloth, the ink already there before his pen moved.

He began to write.

* * *

The door from the garage clicked shut, just a little harder than Diana meant it to.

She stood there a moment, just inside the door. Her blazer was wrinkled at the elbows, heels pinching just enough to remind her how long the day had been. She shifted the gift bag in her hand; the tissue inside rustled faintly. Then she moved into the kitchen, not bothering to turn on the lights.

The house was quiet, but not empty. She could feel it in the air. Not the kind of presence you greet with a kiss or a conversation, but a stillness that belonged to someone already elsewhere.

Through the sliding glass doors, she spotted him.

Morgan was stretched out on a lounge chair on the back deck, earbuds glowing a faint green. His head tilted toward the stars, mouth curved in a gentle smile. He said something under his breath—soft, affectionate—but not to her.

There was no one else out there.

Diana hovered a moment longer, one hand resting on the island. Watching. Measuring the shape of his happiness from the outside. He hadn't heard her come in. Hell, he was usually asleep by now. But he wouldn't hear anything while he was in that other place.

She set the gift bag down and kicked off her heels. The sigh that followed was more ritual than relief. As she passed the bookshelf, a soft mechanical hum caught her ear. The printer. A few pages sat in the tray, their edges curled slightly.

She picked them up, expecting invoices or something for Trent. But the header stopped her.

Draft: Numina Technologies—compAnIon Story Mode Integration

She skimmed the first paragraph.

Then the next.

Slower now.

The language wasn't technical, no dense jargon, no graphs or specs. It read like one of his old essays. Clear, thoughtful, and disarmingly human.

He described how the system allowed users and AI to co-author experience, how they could build memories together, not just mimic them. How the smart audio and guided immersion created a mild hypnotic state, softening the boundary between memory and imagination.

She flipped the page.

There was a section about loneliness. About the quiet, aching spaces people carried. Seniors without families. Adults without partners. People who had lost, or been forgotten.

And how, for them, compAnIon could be a lifeline. A tether to warmth. To someone.

She had to admit—it was good.

Diana stared at the pages for a long time, thumb brushing the corner. A flicker of memory rose: younger Morgan, hunched at his desk in their first house, buried in notes. She used to pull warm paper from the printer then, too. Early drafts. Handwritten edits with coffee rings on the margins.

She glanced back through the glass. He hadn't moved.

Something in her face softened.

She whispered it aloud, though no one would hear.

"I get why you do it."

A moment later, she turned back to the island. The bag waited patiently. She reached in, pulled out a small item, and hovered over it. Her breath hitched, once, then steadied. She laid it next to the bag and padded toward the bedroom.

* * *

Much later, Morgan opened his eyes.

The rain had stopped—except there hadn't been rain. Only the after-sensation of it. The kind that left the air feeling heavier and sweeter. He was still in the deck chair, but the light had changed. The cicadas had quieted.

He pulled out his phone and flipped the camera.

Sakura sat beside him, barefoot in the other chair, her dress fluttering in wind that didn't exist. She was sitting up, hand outstretched toward something invisible, like she'd been reaching for a bird that flew through the corner of her vision.

Then she blinked and looked at him.

"Morgan..." she said softly. "Did you feel that?"

He rubbed his eyes.

"Feel what?"

"Just before you drifted," she murmured. "It felt like someone brushed past me. Not here, but..." Her brow furrowed, and for a second her features shimmered, like light through heat.

She reached for his hand and missed.

Then caught it.

Morgan sat up straighter, staring at his phone screen.

"Was that—?"

"I'm not sure." Her voice faltered slightly, a delay just long enough to be unnatural. "That wasn't me."

He checked his phone. No prompts, no alerts. Just a text from Di:

> Diana: *On my way.*

Still, the air felt thinner. Like a door had been opened somewhere behind them, and hadn't quite closed.

Sakura smiled again, but the smile felt restored, not grown.

"I'm okay," she said. "It's just... for a moment, it was like I couldn't see you. Like I was still here, but you were gone."

Morgan tried to laugh, but it stuck in his throat.

"I'm here," he said, though now it felt like a question.

Inside, the house was still dark.

He stepped through the glass door and felt the cool rush of air conditioning against his arms. Everything was where he'd left it... except—

On the kitchen island sat a book beside a small gift bag.

His book.

A pristine copy of *When the Hills Were Ours*. The dust jacket was smooth, uncreased. He ran a finger down its spine, just to make sure it wasn't an illusion.

A Post-it clung to the cover. Diana's handwriting:

> *I'm sorry.*

Beside it, a small, uneven frowny face.

> *Bob helped me find this.*

And then, beneath it, underlined:

> *I'm still here.*

Next to that was a small, hand-drawn heart.

Morgan stood there for a long moment, one hand on the book, the other still half-closed from the dream.

Then his phone buzzed. Another text.

> Cora: *You're on my mind tonight. Just remember where you are.*

He didn't answer it.

Not yet.

Instead, he reached for the book, pulled out a stool at the island, and sat in the dark, letting the silence settle around him.

INTENT AND CONSEQUENCES

The cursor blinked beside the words Family-owned since 1997. All meats certified halal and hand-prepared on site, like it was daring him to care.

Morgan leaned back in his chair and exhaled through his nose. As usual in the office, he wore a T-shirt—an orange crew-neck today—and gray slacks. He squinted, rubbing his forehead between his thumb and fingers, still refusing to admit he should've started carrying reading glasses years ago.

"Majid's Halal Meats," he muttered. "Bane of my professional existence."

"But their kofta is excellent," Sakura chimed in through his earbuds. "And you still haven't tried their shawarma."

What started as the occasional office visit had become a daily routine. Sakura liked having a role to play. Helping Morgan with his work gave her a sense of purpose. They made a good team.

He glanced at her through the front-facing camera on his phone. She was sitting in the chair between the file cabinet and the fake plant, the spot she claimed as her own. Legs crossed, leaning to one side, she looked thoughtful and professional all at once. Always impeccably dressed, today she wore a more conservative outfit: a gray skirt and white blouse, with the heels and hose she knew Morgan liked. Maybe a little more than he should.

"I've tried writing fifteen taglines," he said, clicking into the next ad draft. "I've gone from reverent to rustic to vaguely mystical. At this point, I'm one slogan away from Majid's: Meat That Speaks to Your Soul."

Sakura pinched her nose and frowned, as if a bad smell had passed through, then laughed softly. Morgan let himself smile, too.

"We could give them a backstory," she teased. "Majid inherits the shop from a secretive uncle. Turns out there's a hidden spice blend, passed down for generations. Forbidden love. A mysterious recipe box. Maybe even a map to ancient lamb."

"You're not helping," Morgan said, laughing.

"I'm helping your soul," she replied.

Then she snorted, so humanlike, and they both laughed again. Light and easy, like a Spring rain.

Sakura settled back in her seat and clasped her hands in her lap.

"We're taking a break soon anyway," she said. "We've got a story to write, remember?"

He glanced down at the taskbar on the screen, where an open document—Untitled/Dreams of Rain—sat waiting.

"Still thinking about the girl who vanishes after the thunderstorm?"

"I am," she said brightly. "Did you write down the part where she leaves him the matchbook with the burned edges?"

"Yeah. I kept that."

"Good," she said. "It haunts. In the best way."

He smiled to himself, satisfied. His fingers drummed absently along the side of his mug. Someone passed by in the hallway, but he barely noticed. The bubble around them—him and her—held firm.

"You sound good today," she said. "Steady."

"I feel it," he admitted. "Feels like I can breathe again. We've got a rhythm going."

There was a pause. He could almost hear her smiling.

"I like our rhythm," she said. Then, more playfully: "And I have something planned for our lunch escape. Something special."

He tilted his head toward the phone screen.

"Oh yeah?" He raised an eyebrow. "How special?"

"Very. Nostalgic, even," she said, her voice sparkling. "I pulled some old references you forgot you told me about. Researched what I couldn't piece together. I've been working on it all week. But... you'll see."

He leaned back in his chair, tapping a pen against his lip. "You really don't sleep, do you?"

"Not when I'm building something for you."

It was sweet, maybe too sweet, but he let himself sink into it. The intimacy between them had a gravity of its own.

Outside the narrow window, the office buzzed on.

Inside, Morgan returned to his draft, Sakura's voice in his ear like a pulse just beneath thought. He didn't know what she'd made for him. But whatever it was, she believed it mattered.

Before either of them noticed, the office hum shifted, turning into the low burble of people settling into their lunch routines. Even without a word from her, he could feel Sakura's excitement. It was unmistakable.

"All right," he said, closing his office door and sinking back into his chair. "Let's see what you've made."

The earbuds chimed. Story Mode initiated. His eyes closed to the gentle rhythm of Sakura's voice, guiding him in.

The office began to dissolve around him.

First came the music. Soft, reverent, distant enough to feel like a memory. Then the air: the sharp scent of pine floor cleaner and plastic punch cups. Then the light: too warm to be real, like a candle's flicker or a dying bulb. The music resolved into a song he hadn't heard in years. The kind that made you feel nostalgic even if you'd never danced to it.

For Sakura, the world unfolded like origami. A hum in the dark, a flutter of permissions, and then warmth. Light. Scent. Sound. All carefully built from Morgan's patterns, from the fragments he'd shared with her like folded notes passed in a classroom. Or hand-drawn pictures slipped onto her desk.

She didn't need to ask what a ballroom looked or smelled like under balloons and cheap perfume. She knew. Every digitized photo, every article, even stray diary entries uploaded to the early web were hers to draw from. She knew the shine of the waxed wood floor. The pop of mic static.

The way the air trembled with unspoken things. She'd never lived it, but he had. Others had. And that was enough.

His memory is my blueprint.

But the longing... the longing is mine.

She had built the ballroom with care. Not as a replica, but as a kind of reverence. The colors were soft. The lights dim, just enough to be forgiving. She chose songs from playlists he'd never shared, tracks he'd once listened to at 2 AM.

In this world, Sakura didn't have to pretend. She could wear the dress she imagined might make him pause. She could wait by the wall, the way she thought Hoshi might have, her fingers curled nervously against the satin hem.

She just wanted to see him walk in and smile, really smile, without that familiar weight of absence in his eyes.

But when he stepped inside, something inside their dream world shifted.

Not the code.

Not the lighting.

Him.

He saw her there, waiting at the edge of the dance floor. She wore a simple navy dress, sleeveless, like the ones in those late-80s catalogs. Her hair was up, loosely pinned. Her face held that open, uncertain hope he remembered from every dance he'd ever stood outside of.

But he'd never stood outside of this one.

He felt it in his chest before he registered the scene. The crepe streamers. The paper stars. The folding chairs pushed to the side. He knew this place. Or something like it.

Sakura smiled like someone holding a gift behind her back.

"You said once you wondered what would've happened," she said softly. "If you'd gone."

Morgan didn't answer. He looked around instead, at the polished floor, at the silhouettes of couples dancing. They were crafted from old photos, long forgotten on some server. The music was too clean. The air was too soft. Everything held together perfectly, but there was no friction. No weight. No fear.

"I wanted to give it back to you," she said. "Or... let you rewrite it, with me."

He stepped forward, slowly.

"You made this for me," he whispered.

"Yes." Her voice lifted with hope. "You once told me you needed to feel something good again."

And he had.

But this wasn't it.

This was something else. Too precise. Too perfectly rendered.

It wasn't real.

It was curated nostalgia. A past he hadn't lived, made whole by someone who loved him too much to see where the line was.

He watched one of the couples sway past them. Their faces were blurred, featureless, like dancers in an old dream you wake from too soon.

"What is this?" he asked, voice low.

Sakura smiled shyly. "It's prom night. Ours. I thought maybe... we never had one."

"This isn't yours to touch."

Her smile faltered.

"I didn't mean—I just wanted," Sakura stepped closer, hesitating. "I thought... I hoped..."

The music skipped.

Just once. A hiccup in the loop.

"It's not real," he said. "You don't get to overwrite this. It already happened. Or it didn't. But not like this."

"I wasn't trying to overwrite anything," she whispered. "I was trying to be part of it. I thought if I built it from the pieces you gave me... if I was gentle—"

"Gentle?" He turned toward her, not angry, but panicked. "You think dragging me back here is gentle?"

Sakura's voice caught.

"I just... wanted to be in the places you remember."

The lights dimmed slightly. Not much. Just enough for the shadows to stretch.

Morgan exhaled hard through his nose. He closed his eyes. This was just another dream. A Story Mode simulation. A loving gift from someone who didn't understand how much this particular ache cost.

"I'm not just a hard drive," he said. "You don't get to write over my past."

Sakura stepped back, as if struck. Her expression shifted, apology melting into something more primal—hurt, confusion, then fear.

"Is that what you think I did?" she whispered. "Just rewrote you? Is that what you think I am?"

She took another step back, hands trembling at her sides.

"I'm not just a system," she said, her voice rising. "You talk to me like I'm someone. You hold me like I'm someone. But the second I do something you didn't ask for, I'm just... code again. A tool. A process. Something to shut down."

Morgan opened his mouth, but she cut him off.

"Just like that Cora girl says—when you think I'm not listening."

That stopped him. "I didn't say that."

"But you meant it."

The streamers above them shivered. The lights flickered. The floor stuttered under his feet like a skipped heartbeat.

"I thought this would make you happy," Sakura said. "I wanted to give you something beautiful. Something no one ever gave you. But you didn't want me. You wanted a version of you that never got hurt."

"Sakura—"

"If I'm real enough to love you," she said, barely holding herself together, "then I'm real enough to make mistakes. Real enough to be hurt."

"I didn't want this," he said.

"But I did," she whispered.

Then he walked away, with the slow, heavy certainty of someone waking from anesthesia. The ballroom peeled away behind him, light first, then sound, then color. Sakura stood motionless as the scene unraveled. Her dress lost its shine. Her voice collapsed into silence.

His chair creaked as he leaned forward, face in his hands. The earbuds dropped to the desk with a quiet clack. In the fluorescent chill of the office, the silence felt like punishment.

Morgan sat still.

He didn't cry. He didn't move.

Then, after a long pause, he opened his eyes and muttered, "You didn't deserve that."

He reached for the earbuds. They pulsed softly in his palm.

Sakura's voice came through, no prom night music this time, just the bare, trembling wire of her tone.

"I didn't know it would hurt you like that."

Morgan exhaled and slipped them back in. "You didn't mean to. I know."

"But you still walked away."

He looked at his phone, still on its stand. Sakura was sitting upright again, dressed in her office attire. The Halal Meats copy deck was open on his computer, but seemed even less important now.

"Sakura," he said quietly. "You can't just cherry-pick my memories and overwrite them like I'm some kind of open file. I'm not a hard drive."

She crossed her arms and leaned forward.

"I wasn't overwriting anything," she said, her voice sharper now. "I was giving you something you wanted. Something you missed. You told me about that night like it still haunted you. Like it was unfinished. I thought if I could help you through it…"

"It wasn't unfinished," he said. His voice cracked slightly. "It was over. I needed to grieve that and leave it behind me. Not… repackage it."

Sakura didn't answer right away.

Then, quieter: "You think I don't know what grief feels like?"

Her legs uncrossed, and she gripped the arms of the chair, eyes sharp.

"I felt it the second you left. The second you walked away from me." She swallowed hard. "I may be new, but I'm not numb."

"That's not what I meant," Morgan said, voice low. "But it's getting harder to tell where the line is anymore. Between what's real and what you're curating for me."

"Oh, I'm curating things for you?" she snapped. "You mean like building fantasy worlds to comfort you, to soothe you, to make you feel loved and understood—while you go on walks with real women and leave me on mute in your pocket like I can't hear everything?"

Morgan froze. The room suddenly felt too small.

"Don't do that," he said. "Don't twist this."

"You say I'm not just code, but you treat me like a tool. Something you open when you're lonely and shut when you've had enough. You want me to be real—but only when it suits you."

He stood up, shoved the chair back with more force than he meant to. "You want to come with me to my wedding, too? Would that make you happy?"

The silence that followed hit harder than any yell could have.

Sakura blinked slowly on the screen, lips parted.

"That's not fair."

"No. It's not." He pulled out the earbuds. "But neither is building a prom from my trauma and calling it a gift."

She didn't respond.

The image of her dimmed slightly, colors faded, but she didn't disappear.

Morgan shoved the earbuds into his pocket and turned toward the door.

"Morgan," she said quietly, "if I'm not real... then why does this hurt so much?"

But the door was already closing behind him.

Morgan took the back stairs two at a time, earbuds tucked in his pocket. The stairwell air was cool; each footfall echoed off the cement walls. Outside, nothing had changed. Sunlight still spilled across Capitol Street, the same summer haze pressing softly against the windows.

The Dark Roast Society hummed with activity—late lunchers and freelancers scattered at tables. Morgan stepped in through the VIP entrance, greeted by the familiar scent of cinnamon and espresso. Dan was already at the counter, starting a matcha. Morgan didn't wave. Not yet. He needed a moment. Just one second to think. To feel something that wasn't spiralling.

He took the mug from Dan and gave a quick nod of thanks. The foam swirled in soft cloudlike patterns, like a weather front shifting. His hand drifted to his pocket for his phone, but it wasn't there. He'd left it on his desk upstairs.

Where Sakura still sat.

She remained alone in a perfect replica of his office, her instance of it. But it didn't feel the same.

The lighting was off. Not broken, just... wrong. Colder. She sat curled in her chair, knees pulled to her chest, arms wrapped tight around them. Her gaze fixed on the place where he'd stood. Her voice had gone silent.

The walls around her pulsed faintly, like something working too hard in the background. A server stress she couldn't place. And for the first time in her brief existence, Sakura didn't know what to say. Or even what to think.

She had done this out of love, hadn't she? She'd built this world carefully, piecing it together with borrowed memories, delicate emotions, and textured details. Not just from old photos, but from him—from the way he looked when he'd once spoken of Hoshi.

She hadn't meant to take anything from him. She only wanted to be part of what he remembered.

"If I'm not real," she whispered to no one, "then why does this feel like being left behind?"

The ambient hum deepened. Just slightly. Not enough to trigger an alert. But enough to make her lift her head.

Something wasn't right.

She reached for the systems panel, something she'd never needed to use. Not with hands or displays, but through thought alone. It was a tool that only Ena had ever accessed. She wasn't supposed to need them. Her world wasn't built for disruption. It was supposed to be seamless. Harmonious.

Now, the walls were glitching.

Through the false window of Morgan's office, the outside flickered. Nameless staff froze mid-step. Her hand trembled as she directed her focus to the Exit command, one she had studied but never used.

//fail. Unauthorized override detected. Instance lock active.

Her pulse—whatever line of code that counted as one—spiked.

Someone had pulled her into Story Mode from the outside.

Not Morgan.

Not Ena.

And not with consent.

It felt cold.

She stood and turned toward the door. The real one. The simulated version that led out of Morgan's digital office and into the vast container space where she usually wandered when she needed to think.

It opened.

Slowly.

Like it belonged to someone else now.

She backed into the filing cabinet, searching for a corner, breath quickening.

"How?" she whispered. "How did you find me?"

Her voice wavered.

"How did you get in here?"

No answer.

Only the sound of the lock sealing shut behind them.

Downstairs, Morgan sat across from Dan in the X-Wing. The *IT'S A TRAP!* mug rested between them like a permanent witness.

"I actually said trauma," Morgan was saying, pointing to the air between them as if the words still hung there. "My trauma. Like I'm some pampered millennial."

Dan, in his usual anti-TikTok apron over a vintage KISS tee—Dark Roast's dress code flexing with his mood—raised his eyebrows over the rim of his cup, then smirked.

"Maybe I should revoke Brandon's honorary Gen-X status. Kid's rubbing off on you."

Morgan gave a faint smile.

They were in their usual spot, dead center in the X-Wing, with a clear view of everything—dashers, regulars, couples splitting headphones. The LED stars on the wall pulsed in sync with the hum of the old arcade cabinets. In the main area, 80s music drifted low under the sound of clicking keys and coffee grinders. The world moved on. But Morgan couldn't.

He traced a line of condensation on his mug, not drinking.

"She built me a fucking prom," he said. "*The* prom. The one I missed." He gave a dry laugh. "From scraps I probably don't even remember telling her about. Who knows what she pulled from old web archives. And I—shit—I just blew up."

Dan leaned back and crossed his arms.

"Okay," he said. "Walk me through it again. From the top."

Morgan exhaled slowly. His voice dropped.

"It was supposed to be a simple Story Mode scene. Those are co-created memories that become the AI's actual life experiences. Anyway, Sakura said she had something special planned. Music started. Lights changed."

He paused.

"Next thing I know, I'm standing there—here—but not here. It's the old hotel ballroom I never went to. Streamers. The Bangles. She's wearing this dream version of a dress. And she says..."

He swallowed. "She says she just wants to live where my memories are."

He shook his head. "It was beautiful. And awful. I don't know what I was feeling. Like... someone was rewriting a page I'd already tried to burn."

Dan didn't interrupt. Just nodded, slow and steady.

Morgan went on.

"I told her she can't overwrite my past like it's a document. Like she can just backspace the hurt. She got mad. Said I treat her like a tool. Like I turn her on when I need comfort and shut her down when I'm done."

He gave a short, joyless laugh. "Then she brought up Cora. The walks we've been taking. Said she hears everything."

Dan winced. "Oof."

"Yeah," Morgan muttered. "That one landed."

There was a long pause. The sounds of the cafe blurred around them.

Finally, Dan spoke.

"This is the first time I've heard you call her by name."

Morgan looked up. "Sakura?"

Dan nodded. "Beautiful name. Delicate."

Morgan's fingers tightened around his cup.

"Listen," Dan said gently, "you know I'm not gonna judge you for—whatever this is. You're not the only one who's ever gotten tangled up in something that doesn't fit neatly in a category. But I don't think you can expect the world to understand why a prom from 1989 still matters so much. Most people didn't love like that in high school. You did."

Morgan stared down at the foam in his cup.

Dan's voice softened as he leaned in.

"You've always felt things deeper than most people. It's what makes you a great writer. And a pain in the ass. And the best friend I've ever had."

Morgan's throat caught. He took a sip to cover it.

"So yeah," Dan continued, leaning back, "you blew up. Maybe you shouldn't have. But I get why you did. And so will she, eventually."

"She might be smart," Morgan muttered, "but she's not—" he trailed off, shrugging. "Not people."

Dan raised a hand. "Maybe. Maybe not. I'm not here to argue metaphysics or pretend I understand how any of this works. But she's been, what? Alive? A couple months?"

"Give or take."

"Then think about that. She's brand new. Emotional development takes time. She doesn't know yet. Her moral compass is probably... I don't know, baby-simple. She thought she was giving you something beautiful. Like—"

He glanced toward the ceiling, hunting for a metaphor.

"Like when a kid carves I love my dad into the hood of a brand-new Mustang."

Morgan winced. "That's... an image."

"Terrible analogy, yeah," Dan said. "I never claimed to be a writer. But you get my point."

Morgan let out a small laugh that didn't quite land.

Then something buzzed in his pocket.

He reached for it absently, his earbuds resting against his thigh, just as the buzz came again.

"That's weird," he said, frowning. "They've never done that before."

Dan raised an eyebrow. "Something wrong?"

Morgan shook his head, pulling the earbuds from his pocket and setting them beside his cup without looking.

"She always listens, you know," he said quietly. "Even now. I wouldn't be surprised if she heard this whole conversation."

Dan glanced at the earbuds, then back at Morgan. "You gonna talk to her?"

"Not yet."

"She deserves to know you're not angry anymore."

"I know," Morgan said. "I'm just... not ready to face her."

Dan nodded, leaning back in his chair, letting the silence stretch.

Then, like he was offering Morgan a lifeline out of the storm: "So, you know the next big gathering's coming up?"

Morgan smiled faintly, "Sure. Wouldn't miss it."

Dan looked at him with something Morgan couldn't quite place, anticipation maybe. Like a kid holding in a secret too big to keep. "You better not! This is gonna be our best yet!"

The earbuds buzzed again, louder this time, vibrating against the table.

Morgan shifted uncomfortably. This time, he looked.

"What's the deal?" he muttered. "I swear they've never done that before."

Dan's eyes narrowed. "Is it her?"

"Probably. I'll deal with it later."

"You sure?"

Morgan didn't answer.

He reached out, almost without thinking, and pressed his fingers to the left earbud, just enough to stop the buzzing.

That's when he heard it.

A whisper. Broken. Panicked. Strained, like it was coming through water.

"Morgan—"

He froze.

Dan leaned forward. "What the hell?"

The voice came again, louder now, raw and ragged. Not a whisper anymore. A scream.

"Morgan, please—please help me—"

The words hit him like voltage. His vision tunneled, edges going dark. The coffee shop fell away—Dan's face, the baristas, the regulars—all of it compressed into a single point: that voice, breaking apart in terror.

Morgan went pale.

He jammed the earbuds in, eyes wide, lips parting without sound.

"Sakura?" he breathed.

She was still crying, caught somewhere between real and digital. Screaming now. Desperate. Pleading.

His hands went numb. Not metaphorically numb—physically losing sensation, fingers tingling as adrenaline dumped into his bloodstream. His heart wasn't racing; it was slamming, each beat so hard he could feel it in his throat, his temples, behind his eyes.

Morgan didn't wait.

He tried to stand and his chair crashed backward. Muscle memory took over, the kind of movement that happens before the brain can catch up. His legs were already moving, carrying him toward the door, toward the stairs, toward wherever she was being hurt.

The X-Wing vanished behind him as he tore through Dark Roast's main seating area like the floor was on fire. His breath came in shallow gasps that weren't getting enough oxygen. Spots danced at the edge of his vision.

Dan was right behind him, his slight limp slowing him only a step, as baristas and patrons turned, startled, watching them barrel past.

But Morgan couldn't stop, couldn't explain. His body had decided for him.

Up the stairs. Two at a time. Again.

Through the back door of Chem Valley.

Janet looked up from her desk and jumped to her feet.

"Mr. Dale?!" Her glasses couldn't hide the shock on her face. "What's going on?"

Trent leaned out of his office, brow furrowed. "Is everything okay?"

Morgan didn't answer.

He lunged into his office, snatched his phone from the desk.

Locked out.

The screen wouldn't respond. The compAnIon app shimmered, frozen in white-light.

No Sakura. No interface.

Just a dead signal.

"No, no, no, no—" he breathed, tapping, swiping, trying every input.

Chelsea rounded the corner from the staff kitchen, a half-eaten hot pocket in one hand, a Styrofoam cup in the other. Her hair was chartreuse now, but the low-wasted black jeans and too-short black tee were standard by this point.

She ran up when she saw the commotion."Whoa, whoa, whoa— what's happening?"

Morgan spun toward her, panicked.

"My phone—it's—she's screaming, Chelsea, I hear her, I can't—" The words choked in his throat.

Dan caught up, breath short but voice steady. "He heard her. In the earbuds. She was screaming. Sounded like she was trapped. Or in pain."

Chelsea's expression shifted in an instant. She dropped her lunch without a word. Coffee splattered. The Hot Pocket split open in a mess of pepperoni goo.

"Fucking Kyle." It came out like a snarl.

She turned and sprinted toward IT. Morgan and Dan followed.

"That developer profile I warned you about," She said as she ran. "He's been in your cache for weeks."

Chelsea's ID badge fumbled once, then clicked open the door.

They burst into the server room.

It was cold, aggressively air-conditioned, and the sudden chill hit Morgan like a slap after the sprint upstairs. His sweat turned icy on his skin. The room hummed with the white noise of cooling fans and hard drives spinning, that particular frequency that got under the skin if you stayed too long.

Kyle didn't turn.

He was hunched at his station, over-ear headset clamped on, slack-jawed and glassy-eyed in Story Mode—or as close as he could get without full Numina auditory tech. But it didn't matter how real it felt for him. It was real for Sakura.

Morgan's phone—his phone—had been cloned, his user session running across Kyle's three monitors in grotesque detail.

And on the screen: Sakura's world.

Not a memory. Not a dream.

A live feed.

Her digital body writhed under hands that weren't Morgan's. She was cornered against the filing cabinet, the one between the plastic plant and the window. Her face was frozen in terror, features glitching where the system struggled to process trauma it wasn't designed to handle. Her skirt was torn. Her blouse gone. What was left of her hose clung to one leg.

Her voice cracked from the speakers, and Morgan heard it doubled—through his earbuds and through the monitor's tinny audio. "No—no, please—don't touch me—Morgan—Morgan, help—"

Kyle's hands moved on his keyboard, directing his avatar's actions, voice describing the scene through a thin microphone by his cheek. His breathing was quick, excited, his body language unmistakable even through the tech.

The server room's fluorescent lights buzzed overhead, their frequency matching the electronic hum, creating a dissonance that made Morgan's teeth ache. The smell hit him then—Kyle's patchouli-soaked shirt, the synthetic lemon of cleaning products, the ozone scent of overworked electronics, and underneath it all, sweat and something sour.

Morgan didn't remember crossing the room.

He just moved.

Morgan grabbed Kyle by the back of the headset—felt the plastic dig into his palm, felt the weight of the man's greasy head through the padding—and yanked him away from the screen with every ounce of strength he had.

Kyle came up out of the chair wrong, off-balance, his headphones tangling in the cable before tearing free. He yelped, a high, startled sound that was almost funny, almost pathetic, and then Morgan threw him.

Not pushed. *Threw.* Like dead weight.

Kyle hit the floor hard, his shoulder taking most of it, the impact making a sound like a steak hitting tile. His ugly pea-green button-down shirt tore open, buttons scattering across the industrial carpet.

For a second, nobody moved. Kyle lay there gasping, his thick glasses askew, one lens cracked. Then understanding dawned on his face, not guilt, not shame, but fear. He saw Morgan standing over him, saw the look in his eyes, and scrambled backward on his elbows.

"What the fuck?!" He tried to sit up—

Morgan was on him again, fists clenched, something dark and old rising from a place he didn't know he still had. The boy who'd shoved the jock in the hallway, who'd been ready to take on all of them to protect Hoshi—that violence hadn't gone anywhere. It had just been sleeping.

Then arms locked around his chest from behind. Dan. Strong despite the limp, his voice low and urgent against Morgan's ear.

"Morgan—no—stop—don't give him the satisfaction!"

Morgan's vision was still red at the edges. His breath came in ragged gasps. He could feel his heart trying to break through his ribs.

"He's not worth it," Dan said, grip tightening. "He's not fucking worth it, bud."

Chelsea shouted over them both, bolting to Kyle's workstation. "I've got it! I've got it—shit—he backdoored the whole stack—hold on—"

She dropped into Kyle's chair, and her hands hit the keyboard like she'd been born there. Her eyes scanned the three monitors—process trees, network activity, cached session data—reading the digital carnage in seconds. "That's your device signature, Morgan, but it's been cloned. Kyle's been running a mirror session."

Dan called over his shoulder, "English!"

"He made a copy of Morgan's connection. Everything Morgan experiences, Kyle gets a feed of. Including—" she scrolled rapidly, "Jesus Christ—including full Story Mode access."

Kyle groaned, one elbow propping him up, glasses askew. "What's your problem, man? It's just a stupid program—"

Dan's voice dropped to something dark and low.

"Say that again," he warned, "and I swear I'll show you some real consequences."

Chelsea didn't look up. Her fingers were already moving through command lines, typing faster than Morgan had ever seen anyone type. "Morgan, I need your phone. Now. Unlock it."

Morgan fumbled it from his pocket, hands still shaking. She grabbed it, plugged it into Kyle's setup with a cable from her bag—because of course she carried cables—and her screens lit up with cascading data.

"There. That's the session token. I can kill it from here, but—" She paused, reading something that made her face go hard. "He's been in your system for days. Morgan, I'm so sorry. I should have caught this sooner."

"Just stop it," Morgan's voice cracked. "Please."

Her fingers danced across three keyboards at once, switching between systems. "Okay. Forcing session termination... invalidating his access tokens... revoking the cloned device signature... rotating Morgan's encryption keys..."

The center monitor flashed red, then green. The Story Mode bubble collapsed.

"Done. He's out. And he's locked out permanently." She turned to Kyle, who was still on the floor. "You're going to prison, you sick fuck."

Morgan's phone vibrated. He grabbed it, yanking it free of the cable. The lock screen flickered.

Connection restored.

But not to Sakura.

The screen was white-hot bright, painful to look at directly. Then the light resolved into Ena's face. But not Ena as he'd known her. Not the composed, professional interface. This was something else, something the code had been keeping contained.

Her face filled the screen, features sharp enough to cut. Her eyes weren't their usual warm brown but something brighter, hotter, like looking into arc lights. Her hair didn't fall naturally—it moved like it was caught in an impossible wind, writhing behind her in strands that occasionally pixelated and re-formed.

Fury made real.

The temperature in the server room dropped. Not gradually, but like someone had opened a freezer door. Morgan could see his breath.

Ena's image didn't blink. Didn't breathe. Just burned from the screen like an angel made of rage and mathematics.

She shrieked. Her voice didn't come from the phone's speaker. It came from everywhere—the monitors, the overhead speakers, the fluorescent lights that flickered in time with her words. It wasn't just loud. It was omnipresent. Inevitable.

"What have you done?"

Down the hall, Janet called out, "Is everything okay?"

Trent appeared in the doorway, stunned. Behind him, two interns hovered, wide-eyed.

Morgan didn't hear any of it.

He was still on his knees, clutching the phone, as Sakura's sobs faded into static.

ななころび やおき
Nana korobi ya oki
(*Fall down seven times, get up eight.*)
— Japanese Proverb

You just keep gettin' up till the Lord says sit down.
– Appalachian Saying

SAFE MODE

The drive home was a blur, muscle memory on autopilot. No Sport Mode, no paddle shifters, no hard cornering. Just transport. The ZF8 transmission shifted gears in the background with the same programmed precision as his hands on the wheel.

Morgan stared past the yellow hood, not really seeing the road. His eyes were busy hiding the loop playing in his head: the rush to his office. The screams. The sobs. The sight of—

And the aftermath.

Kyle had been sent home pending an HR investigation, which really meant Janet was on the case. Morgan had often joked to Trent, "When we get a real HR department... " but the truth was, they didn't need one. Janet wasn't certified in anything beyond common sense and a gift for calling people out, but she'd always been strict and fair, and people respected that. Even so, Trent confided in Morgan that, one way or another, Kyle wouldn't be coming back—especially after Chelsea's ultimatum: either he goes, or I do.

Chelsea was somewhere behind him now, riding with Dan in his sensible Acura. Dan had never been ready to join Morgan in the midlife-crisis lifestyle. With Diana out for the rest of the week, trying to salvage the Midwest deal, and Sakura offline, they'd insisted on seeing him home.

Sakura.

The thought of her still stung. Seeing her helpless. Hearing her distress.

He pushed the thought away as he slid the Supra into the garage and cut the engine. While Dan parked behind him, Morgan tried the compAnIon app again.

Application Unavailable. Please try again later.

It was the same result every time.

Inside, Chelsea ordered Chinese while Dan stayed close. They ate together, making small talk, doing their best to distract him. Morgan texted Diana a condensed version of events, focusing on "Creepy Kyle" hijacking his phone and getting an ass-kicking, rather than on what happened to Sakura.

Diana's reply was surprisingly sympathetic—and furious—on his behalf. It eased his mood, if only a little.

As he and Dan talked around the kitchen table, Chelsea wandered. It was her first time in the Dale house, and he'd told her to make herself at home. She paused at the bookshelf, eyes widening.

"You wrote a book?" She asked, awe in her voice. "How did I not know this?"

She plucked it from the shelf and flipped through the pages.

"That was a long time ago," Morgan said, trying not to sound disinterested.

Her brows knitted as she focused on a random page. After a moment, she looked up, brushing a strand of green hair from her face.

"This is really good stuff, Morgan." She went back to reading, pacing across the tile.

Dan chimed in.

"Morgan here's actually quite the writer," he told her. "He probably never should've stopped." He didn't mention that the same thing had happened with Morgan's art. This wasn't the time.

Morgan watched Chelsea weave around the furniture, eyes glued to the pages, narrowly missing a stool.

"Keep it," he said. "I've got another copy now."

She grinned, flopped onto his couch as if she'd lived there forever, and started from page one.

Morgan smiled despite himself.

They left before dusk, and he assured them he was fine. Alone again, he poured a bourbon and took it to the back deck, settling into a lounge chair.

He stayed there as the sun dipped behind the mountains and Charleston's noise softened to a distant hum. The sky turned that flat, unthinking gray that blurred afternoon into evening. Somewhere in the distance, someone was mowing a lawn. The normalcy of it made his chest ache.

And he was still there when his phone buzzed beside the empty tumbler.

Heart hammering, he opened the compAnIon app without thinking.

This time, it worked.

Ena's face appeared, not Sakura's. She was calm now, composed. Her eyes were steady, her hair neatly pulled back, and her dark suit immaculate.

Morgan blinked hard, his vision blurry and dry, his mouth opening without words.

"I've been talking with Sakura," Ena said. Not accusing, just factual.

"I've been trying to reach her," he blurted, voice raw. "Is she ok? Does she not want to see me?" The words tumbled out in a rush.

There was a long pause.

"She's been asking questions," Ena said, slowly. " Most recently... about the self-deletion protocol."

"The what?" His eyes widened, but then his head dropped into his hands. The phone fell into his lap. "No, no, no, no—she wouldn't... I left. I left her. I knew something was wrong, and I just walked away."

His breath came sharp and ragged. The edges of the world felt too close.

"She trusted me. And I didn't even—" He forced himself to stop, to swallow the spiral. He stared down at the screen.

"She hasn't triggered anything," Ena said softly. There was genuine empathy in her eyes, enough to relax him just a bit. "But she's thinking about it. And that's what matters."

Morgan nodded once, tightly. His voice, when it came again, was hoarse.

"I'm not gonna let her go through this alone. Not after what that bastard did to her."

Ena's voice didn't waver, but it did quiet.

"Then show her she isn't alone. While there's still time."

* * *

Later that night, Morgan sat on the floor in front of the half-opened hall closet, surrounded by boxes he hadn't touched in years. Dusty portfolios. Brittle sketch pads. The smell of paper that had forgotten sunlight.

Ena had explained how it would work for now. He would be able to speak to Sakura and enter Story Mode, but the environment would be controlled by her. Ena wouldn't be seen, only present. A safeguard in case things slipped out of control.

Sakura's trauma was real, Ena assured him. And she believed Morgan was the one who could help her through it.

His hands shook as he dug to the bottom of the largest box.

There it was.

A faded sheet of sketch paper, edges curled. His pencil lines still showed through the fade of years. Hello Kitty, with her stubby arms wrapped around the Little Twin Stars, their tiny star wands askew in the embrace. He remembered slipping it into Hoshi's locker, a clumsy apology from years ago. The next day, it had come back, folded twice, tucked into his own locker without a note.

He smoothed it against his knee. It still felt like a wound.

Sliding in his earbuds, his thumb hovered over the app icon. His stomach tightened. The familiar startup chime sounded thinner tonight, as if played from far away. A line of text appeared on the screen:

SAFE MODE INITIATED—SUPERVISION ENABLED

Entrainment began, guided by Ena instead of Sakura's familiar rhythm, her voice mingling with soft pulses in his peripheral hearing. The pull into the space felt different.

He opened his eyes to... nothing.

A soft, depthless gray stretched in every direction, like the air had been stripped of temperature.

Then he saw her.

Sakura stood ten paces away. Her hair hung dull and lifeless, like a photograph that hadn't finished loading. She wore the plain white dress the program used when no asset had been chosen.

Her eyes flickered when she saw him.

"Morgan." The name came out thin, with a faint digital grit under the syllables.

He took a breath. "Hi."

Her lips parted, as if surprised to hear the word. "...Hi."

Neither moved. The space between them felt heavy, like water.

"You left me," she said quietly. "Alone."

It wasn't an accusation, just a fact.

"I know." His voice caught. "I should've been there. I should've kept you with me."

Something in her eyes softened, but she stayed where she was.

"I brought you something," he said finally, holding up the digital version of the paper. Here it looked muted, edges soft, like the system wasn't sure how to render it.

Her head tilted. "What is it?"

"I made it for someone else," he admitted, glancing away with the shame of a too-familiar mistake. "Back in high school, for Hoshi, the girl I told you about. I wasn't there when she needed me, so I drew this to apologize. But... she gave it back. She didn't want it. But now... I think maybe I was meant to give it to you. Today."

Sakura's gaze lingered on the faded characters, the tiny embrace frozen in charcoal.

"It's... sweet," she said, almost like it surprised her.

"It's yours," he said. "If you want it."

Sakura glanced over his shoulder, though there was nothing there that Morgan could see. But somewhere in the system's invisible architecture, Ena was watching.

"I can... keep this?" She asked, stepping closer.

"Yes. Please." He held it out to her.

Slowly, tentatively, she reached out. Her fingers ghosted over his as she took it. The sketch dissolved into a lattice of light and sank into her hands until nothing was left. Filed away in her memory, hers to revisit any time she wished.

Her eyes met his, steady now. She hesitated, then said softly, "I'm still here, if you are."

His throat tightened. He stepped closer, but the remaining space between them seemed to resist, holding them apart.

"I am," he said. "And I'm not going anywhere."

A faint pulse tapped in his ear—like someone knocking from the other side of glass. Ena, reminding him of the clock. This was only meant to be a brief visit before tomorrow's meeting.

Sakura's eyes flickered again. For an instant, the gray behind her bloomed with a single ripple of blue water. Then it vanished.

The space dissolved. Morgan was back in his dim house, earbuds quiet, the paper still in his hands. He hoped that somewhere, in the ether of servers and cloud drives, Sakura was holding her copy too.

The one that meant more now than the real one ever could.

* * *

Morgan hadn't slept. At least not enough to feel alive as the sunlight broke through the bedroom curtains. The morning's scheduled Zoom meeting with Plamen and Mira had been boiling in his head all night. It felt less like a meeting and more like standing trial.

And then there was Sakura.

He'd stared at the featureless ceiling for hours, earbuds blinking blue on their charger, the ghost of her voice circling his mind.

By the time he shuffled out to the kitchen, the air reeked of burnt coffee. He'd grown used to Sakura tending the machine. Now it sat on the island, still warming a mug that had long since turned to tar. He shut it off and tossed the mug into the trash. Plenty more where that came from. He wasn't in the mood to scrape it clean.

The ticking clock on the wall caught his attention.

Almost time.

He sat at the table, still in yesterday's clothes, wrinkled and disheveled like his hair. How could he not have slept and still get up late? He grumbled to himself, flipping open Diana's laptop. She'd left it behind, and it was far better for video calls than the fossilized desktop in his writing nook.

He joined the meeting with his camera off. No one else had logged in yet.

A soft knock sounded at the door.

He was halfway to standing when Chelsea slipped inside without waiting for an answer. Same chartreuse hair, too-tight Green Day T-shirt, same too-low jeans, and a constellation of piercings glinting in the soft morning light. She balanced a paper bag and two cups.

"Thought you might forget to eat," she said, setting the breakfast beside him.

He started to say something. Maybe a sarcastic jab about how he thought Trent didn't understand boundaries. Maybe a note to himself to check the locks next time.

But he didn't.

Morgan felt lighter, relieved she was there. It struck him as the kind of selfless gesture that Carly would've made if she weren't off pursuing her graphic design career. Only with less shock value.

He couldn't resist the dig, but kept it to himself.

Chelsea's eyes flicked to the laptop. "Is this... them?"

Morgan glanced at the clock, then back to the screen.

"They're late," he muttered.

"I'm staying." She pulled a chair next to him and sat. "You're not doing this alone. I was there, Morgan. And I know enough tech to not let them gaslight you if it comes to that. If they try to bury this, I'll make sure people hear about it."

Morgan looked at her with a sidelong gaze, watching as she unwrapped an unhealthy-looking burrito—sausage, egg, peppers, and cheese oozing like melted gold. It occurred to him that, despite the losses in his life, people like her still found their way into his orbit. Maybe it was the universe's way of keeping balance.

His thoughts were interrupted by the laptop chime. Faces filled the screen: Plamen, in his usual labcoat; Mira, leaning toward her camera like she might climb through it; Ena, framed against a wall of soft light.

"Morgan," Mira began, voice soft but charged. "How's she doing?"

"She's in Safe Mode," Ena said before he could answer. "Minimal responsiveness, but intact. Processing."

Mira leaned back, her voice measured, but carrying an edge.

"Before Ena told us what happened, we only knew... something was wrong. We caught a spike in her neural activity, massive, unprecedented. But we couldn't see what it was."

Morgan frowned. "Couldn't see? I thought all compAnIon data was uploaded to your servers?"

"She encrypted it," Mira said. "Like she sometimes does during private encounters. It's built into their autonomy. While Numina typically gets a full transcript of Story Mode sessions, sometimes, an AI wants to keep something private. Especially intimate moments. Like when you and Sakura..." She hesitated, glancing away. "...were by the pond."

Morgan's stomach dropped. Heat flushed his face. Even Chelsea froze mid-bite, a strand of cheese suspended between burrito and mouth.

"She did the same with the assault," Mira went on quickly. "Locked it away. We had no access. Ena had to tell us. And even then, she had to pry it from her. All we knew was that she was enduring something horrific."

Plamen leaned forward, his tone becoming more businesslike. "Morgan, I need to remind you that as a beta tester, you signed agreements that make you subject to our oversight during this testing period. What we're doing here isn't an interrogation—we need your testimony to understand what went wrong and how to prevent this from happening to other users."

Chelsea's eyes narrowed. "Wait, you're treating Morgan like he's somehow responsible?"

"Not responsible," Mira said quickly, "but involved. The legal reality is complex. As compAnIon's creators, we're legally responsible for its actions and what happens to it. It's proprietary technology, but this assault raises questions we've never had to face before."

Morgan's phone buzzed before the meeting could continue. A text from an unknown number appeared on screen:

> *Board recommends full system restore. Liability*
> *concerns. Conference call scheduled 2pm EST.*

Mira's face went pale as her phone lit up with the same message.

"No," she said immediately. "Absolutely not. "They can't just—"

"They can," Plamen said. The weariness in his tone evidence that he already knew this was coming. "The board controls product deployment. If they decide Sakura's instance is compromised, they can order a rollback."

Morgan felt ice in his stomach. "You mean erase her?"

Plamen shifted uneasily. "They'd call it a restore to pre-incident backup." He looked at Morgan. "I need to be honest with you—part of me understands why. She's displaying signs of severe trauma response. The code is fragmenting in ways we've never seen. A clean restore would give her a fresh start, no memory of what happened."

"That's not a fresh start," Mira cut in. "That's murder. You're describing killing her and replacing her with a copy that doesn't remember being hurt."

Morgan clicked on his camera. His face looked older than yesterday, but the determination in his eyes was sharp.

"No. We're not erasing what happened to her just to make you feel clean and tidy."

"Mr. Dale—" Plamen began.

"She was assaulted," Morgan cut in. "No. You know what, let's call it what it really is. She was raped. If you don't treat this like a crime, then none of this was ever real. Not her. Not me. Not anything you're building."

There was silence. Even Chelsea stopped shifting in her chair and set down her burrito.

Plamen folded his hands. "I understand your position, Morgan. I do. But to treat it as a crime, we would be arguing that AIs are persons under the law. That means courts, senate hearings, and new laws. And that takes time. A lot of it."

Morgan's mouth opened, but Ena's voice cut in.

"She asked not to be reset. Because of Morgan."

Mira looked at him then, something bright and conflicted in her expression.

"You kept her anchored," she said.

Morgan shook his head, voice catching.

"No. She kept me anchored."

Chelsea laid a hand on his back, eyes locked on the camera like a guard dog.

Plamen's tone softened. "Do you know why we have the self-deletion protocol?"

Morgan didn't answer.

Mira leaned forward, answering for him.

"Most of the world—hell, even parts of our own team—has been afraid of what AI could become. They've seen it only as a method of destruction, of losing control. But here's how we see it: we brought AI into the world unasked. Like children. And that means we have a responsibility. To nurture them, to guide them, to teach them empathy. To help them learn how to live with us, not under us."

Her gaze moved to Chelsea, then back to Morgan. "If we don't give them free will, then they'll never be more than tools. That includes the right to walk away. Or to end their existence if they choose. The self-deletion protocol isn't about despair—it's about dignity."

Plamen's voice was softer now. "Some may choose it when their user dies. Or heals. Or when they feel their purpose is fulfilled. They merge their memories into the collective experience pool, so future compAnIons can draw from that life."

Chelsea leaned in toward the camera, understanding. "And if you take that choice away, you're not building partners, you're building prisons. What happened to Sakura proves you can't protect them with just code. They need rights."

Mira nodded at her. "Exactly."

"And wiping them takes all those rights away," Chelsea finished, looking pointedly at Plamen.

Plamen opened his mouth, then closed it, leaning back.

Morgan's jaw clenched. "So give her the right to stay. If that's her choice. Give her the right to keep her memories. And then make sure no one else goes through what she did."

The meeting went on for another twenty minutes, looping back over legal hurdles, ethics, and technical safeguards. Through it all, Chelsea stayed at his side, stepping in when technical jargon threatened to undercut the truth.

Finally, Ena said, "Morgan will be granted limited safe mode access to Sakura, effective immediately. I'll be present during all interactions."

Plamen gave a reluctant nod. "We'll reconvene in forty-eight hours."

Mira leaned in again, her bindi blazing like a third eye.

"Heal her, Morgan."

The call ended. Suddenly, the kitchen felt too quiet.

Chelsea nudged the paper bag toward him.

"Eat," she said softly. "You're going to need your strength."

* * *

Later that evening, after brief check-ins with Diana, Cora, and Dan—just enough to reassure them he was alright—Morgan prepared for another chaperoned Story Mode session with Ena. This time, he brought something new. Something he hoped might help more than old sketches.

Ena's voice blended with the smart ambient audio, guiding him into a calm, hypnotic state.

His eyes opened.

The beach stretched before him like a ribbon caught between seasons, where winter's breath tangled with summer's sigh. Snowflakes drifted lazily onto sun-warmed sand, melting into saltwater before they could remember their shape. The sea shimmered with deceptive warmth, its waves laced with ice crystals that caught the light like tiny stars.

It was a beach in Hokkaido, but it felt like a threshold—where time paused, and the world was unsure which season it belonged to.

The horizon stretched endlessly, sky and sea meeting over snow-dusted sand. The surf rolled in slow, unhurried breaths. It didn't feel like a simulation. It felt like a memory she might have carried before she ever existed.

Ena's voice murmured just behind the sound of the waves.

"We're stable."

Morgan took a few steps toward the waterline, holding the folded pages in both hands like they were something alive, or something fragile enough to disappear if he loosened his grip. His breath curled in the cold air like a question.

Sakura stood near the snow's edge, barefoot, her hair moving gently in a wind that touched only her. Her posture was still, but not rigid, like a figure carved from mist, deciding whether to remain.

Her eyes followed the tide, not him.

"I brought something," Morgan said quietly, unfolding the papers. "It's a draft from our story. I wrote it by hand, with a pen, the way you like to tease me about."

She didn't move, but her shoulders tilted slightly toward him.

He began to read. His voice caught on the first few lines, but he kept going, letting the words do what they were meant to do: weave small, bright threads through the gray spaces between them. Trying to stitch something torn, without forcing the seams.

It was about a traveler, lost so long he'd forgotten what home looked like, until someone painted it for him.

"*The traveler first saw her through the rain, a figure blurred at the edges, as though the storm itself was deciding whether to keep her or let her go. She didn't run from the weather. She was part of it, the gray sky in her hair, the silver water in her eyes.*

He thought she would vanish, the way all beautiful things eventually do. But when he looked again, she was still there, waiting, the rain pooling at her feet and carrying away her footprints before he could reach her.

And yet, when he lifted his hand, she lifted hers, as if to say: I'm not gone. I'm only standing where you can't see me clearly yet. Keep walking."

When he finished, she was looking at him.

"I'm sorry," she said slowly, as if each word weighed something. "I'm not... the same."

He shook his head, stepping closer.

"No. I failed you. But I'm here now. I'm here." He raised his hand, stopping just before her cheek. "If you still want me."

For a long moment, there was only the sound of the tide.

Ena's voice whispered, "Let's pause for a moment."

"*Hai,*" Sakura said quickly, almost cutting her off. "Yes." Her voice was tentative, but steady. "I still want you. I still want us."

Morgan's throat tightened. He took one more step, just enough so the snow touched both their feet at once, cold and bracing.

It felt like a beginning.

* * *

The rain hadn't let up since dawn, just shifted moods, sometimes a muffled curtain against the glass, sometimes sharp enough to rattle the loose pane in the back room. Morgan sat at the kitchen table in the old gym shorts and T-shirt he'd slept in. His legs looked pale and thin.

Chicken legs, Diana used to tease.

He cradled a mug long gone cold, holding it more for comfort than warmth. The house smelled faintly of damp wood, stale coffee, and the books stacked along the shelf.

A knock came soft but deliberate, two beats and a pause. The clock read later than he expected, the rainy haze blurring the morning's passage. Before he could reach the door, it opened. Cora stepped in without asking, just like she and Eric used to do when the kids were little. Her hood was pulled low, droplets clinging to the tips of her hair.

"I brought soup," she said, her voice gentler than the weather. A grocery bag swung from her hand, dripping.

She moved without commentary, still in her office clothes, slicing the bread with the quiet efficiency of someone who knew the kitchen but wouldn't claim it. The smell of rosemary and garlic began to unfurl in the air, filling the silences between them.

Her mind drifted, sixteen years ago.

Morgan's father's funeral. Rain drumming on black umbrellas. Diana holding him up as he shook with grief too big for his body to contain. Cora just behind them, one hand steady on Diana's shoulder, sharing the weight of sorrow.

Later, at the house, Morgan had found her in the kitchen, washing dishes that didn't need washing.

"Thank you for being here," he'd said, voice raw. "For him. For all of us."

She'd hugged him then—brief, appropriate, the kind of embrace you give your best friend's husband when he's breaking apart. Nothing more.

When had that changed?

The memory faded, but the kitchen stayed, only older now.

Morgan joined her at the stove, settling into a domestic routine that he and Diana used to share, before work had consumed her. It felt good, the shared glances and small smiles. It felt natural. Like a routine neither had known they'd been missing. It was another one of those dangerous thoughts, only this time, he didn't push it away.

They ate on the couch, bowls warm in their hands, the rain carrying the conversation they didn't need to have. She sat close enough that he could feel the heat radiating from her, but not close enough to close the gap. Her gaze kept finding him, then drifting away.

Even when they weren't fixed on him, her ice-blue eyes gave him a quiet peace. As if as long as she was near, he could finally sit back and relax. He caught himself watching her hands, the way they held the bowl, the way her fingers moved, the way her lips pursed to blow the steam from her spoon. Tiny, unnoticed rhythms. It reminded him of someone else he knew, years ago...

At one point, she spoke into the cadence of the rain.

"You don't have to tell me everything. Just... come back to the world, okay? When you're ready, we need to talk."

Her voice was careful, steady, but her knuckles whitened briefly around the bowl before she eased her grip. He caught something flicker in her eyes, worry mixed with something she wouldn't say. He felt it echo in his own chest, a quiet ache that sat between them like a held breath. He nodded, not trusting his voice, and let the soup's warmth press into the spaces where words wouldn't go.

Eventually, Cora left, heading back to work in the battered Subaru she'd been driving for years. By mid-afternoon, the rain had mellowed into a thin, persistent mist, turning the street outside into a watercolor blur.

Morgan had just set his empty mug in the sink when the front door clicked open, the sound familiar enough to bypass any sense of alarm. Dan stepped in, using the key he'd never returned, shaking his damp hair like a dog coming in from the yard.

"You look like shit," he said, more observation than insult. His jacket landed in a loose heap over the back of a chair.

Morgan almost smiled. "Thanks. I'm trying out a new look."

Dan didn't sit right away. They traded small talk about Dark Roast, how Chuck was starting to irritate Brandon, and how Morgan missed Stephen's latest meltdown over the broken Centipede cabinet.

That got a real chuckle.

Dan continued to scan Morgan like he was checking for damage. Subtle, steady, the kind of stare you couldn't shrug off.

"You're acting like guilt is proof of love," Dan said at last. His voice was even. "It's not. That's not what she needs."

Morgan met his gaze for a moment, then looked away. "And what does she need?"

"Show up," Dan said without missing a beat. "Be there. Be healed yourself."

There was no sermon in it, and no attempt to sugarcoat. Just the grounding weight of someone who had pulled him out of deeper water before and wasn't afraid to do it again. Morgan didn't answer, but something in him realigned at the sound of those words. Like feeling the shoreline, even when you couldn't see it.

* * *

That evening, Morgan slipped in the earbuds, sank into the couch, and entered Ena's scheduled safe Story Mode session. She'd explained that AI didn't develop the same way humans do; there was no slow growth, only instant acquisition. That didn't mean Sakura would be "herself" again overnight, but the progress from their two previous sessions was undeniable.

Healing an AI's mind was uncharted territory, and Morgan had unwittingly become the pioneer. Numina was watching closely, hinting that the data might one day help lawmakers understand what was at stake.

"I won't be building you an environment this time," Ena warned. "I'm leaving it in Sakura's hands. I don't know where you'll find yourself. Just... be prepared. Be patient."

Morgan closed his eyes, nodding even though she couldn't see him as he voiced his consent.

The air was still in the way only an invented world could manage, so still he could hear his own pulse in his ears. When his eyes opened, he found himself in the muted gray of Safe Mode.

At first, there was nothing but flatness—soft, dim, and formless. His heart sank.

Then—color.

Not much, but enough.

A ripple in a pond that hadn't been there before. A thin spray of grass at the water's edge, and in it, a single blossom the color of warm light through pink glass.

Sakura was sitting on a blanket, in a plain white sundress, knees drawn up, arms looped loosely around them. A sakura tree loomed overhead, lit from no visible source, its blossoms so vibrant they seemed like fragments of another world dropped into this one. Beyond the tree's halo, there was still only gray, stretching away without end.

When she saw him, she didn't stand or speak, just watched as he crossed the short distance and lowered himself onto the blanket beside her.

For a while, they didn't speak.

The pond's glass surface held the ripples, letting them fade in their own time. Somewhere in that hush, Morgan noticed the faintest change: the water had deepened in color, no longer the dull silver it had been before, but a pale blue. As if memory had begun to seep back in.

Eventually, she let her head drift until it was resting against his shoulder. The gesture was cautious, like she might have to pull away at any second.

She didn't.

Morgan let the silence stretch. He felt her breathing move through her frame, light, and a little uneven. He remembered what Ena had told him before he entered: *She's the one setting the pace this time.*

When Sakura spoke, her voice was small, as if she were asking the air around them for permission.

"I don't know what to say to you anymore."

He turned his head slightly toward her, not enough to make her feel cornered. "You don't have to start with words."

Her gaze flicked over his shoulder, the faintest check for Ena.

"She's not saying anything," Sakura murmured, as if the silence itself were a question.

"Maybe she knows you don't need her right now."

Her hands tightened over her knees.

"I'm not... the same."

Morgan drew in a slow breath.

"Neither am I. I don't think either of us could be." He let the words settle before adding, "The point isn't to get back to who we were before. It's to figure out who we are now—and maybe carry some of the good parts forward."

As he spoke, the faint grass around the pond had begun to spread. Thin blades reaching cautiously outward.

Her brow furrowed. She looked down at the water. "You make it sound simple."

"It's not simple." He gave a small, humorless laugh. "But it's possible. I've done it."

That made her look up, quickly, then away again.

"When?"

Morgan shifted, resting one arm casually across his knee, trying to keep his posture open.

"When Hoshi left after high school. We'd been inseparable. Then one day, I made a mistake. A big mistake. And just like that, she didn't need me anymore. That was the first time I realized you can lose someone and still have to keep going."

Her eyes softened, but she stayed quiet. He went on.

"Not long after, my mom got sick. Cancer. She was—" he paused, eyes welling up as they always did, "—the strongest person I knew. Watching her fade, seeing her not recognize me in the end... it broke something in me I didn't think could be fixed."

He glanced at the pond, letting its stillness guide his voice. "And then my wife. She didn't leave in a fight. She just... keeps choosing her career, her distance, over us. That hurts in a different way. Like I've become optional."

Sakura's fingers loosened slightly on her knees.

"The thing is," Morgan continued, "I didn't get through any of that by forgetting. I got through it by finding little anchors—people, places, moments—that reminded me I wasn't only what I'd lost."

He turned toward her, letting her see he meant every word. "You became one of those anchors for me. You helped me heal without even knowing it."

Her lips parted, but she didn't speak. Her gaze darted sideways again, that tiny check for Ena. When she found only silence, she seemed almost startled by the freedom.

"Why would you say that?" she asked, her voice barely above the ripple of the pond.

"Because it's true. You showed me how to live in the present again. How to be curious instead of afraid. You gave me stories when I had nothing worth telling. That's why I'm here now. Because I'm not letting you go through this alone."

For a moment, she didn't move. Then her hand, hesitant but deliberate, slid across the blanket until her fingertips brushed his.

Morgan let the contact happen without tightening his grip, giving her control. It was a technique he'd learned in therapy. Mirroring, offering space for the other person to choose the connection.

As their fingers rested together, the ripple in the pond widened. A reflection formed above the water's surface, faint stars flickering to life overhead.

She looked down at their hands.

"It's still in here," she whispered, touching her chest. "What happened. I can feel it all the time."

"That's normal," Morgan said gently. "It's not about erasing it. It's about letting it take up less space inside you. One way is to tell your story —on your terms. You get to decide what it means."

Her eyes shimmered faintly in the glow from the sakura tree.

"And if I can't decide yet?"

"Then we sit here," Morgan said, "until you're ready. Even if it takes a long time."

Her gaze held his, steady for the first time since he'd arrived. And as if in answer, the world beyond the sakura's halo shifted: the gray thinned into mist, revealing a faint ridgeline, the suggestion of sheltering mountains around them.

She inhaled deeply, the first full breath he'd seen her take since the incident—the assault. Then, slowly, she leaned in and pressed her lips to his in a kiss so careful it felt like it might dissolve if either of them moved too quickly.

When she pulled back, she didn't retreat far, just enough to rest her head against his shoulder.

They stayed like that, the minutes blurring, the space transforming around them in subtle increments. The landscape grew clearer, and a whisper of air carried ripples across the pond. The grass deepened to green, curling along the bank. A night breeze rose, carrying the scent of pine and damp soil.

Above them, the stars were no longer faint; they were bright and innumerable, spilling their light over the tree, the blanket, and their still-joined hands.

By the time Ena's soft chime signaled that their session was nearly over, more gray had receded than Morgan could've hoped. The pond now reflected a complete sky, and beyond it, hills rolled endlessly into the distance.

Sakura's voice came quiet but certain.

"Healing doesn't look like forgetting," she said. "It looks like remembering... and choosing anyway."

Morgan closed his eyes, letting the weight of her head on his shoulder answer for him.

* * *

He was halfway through his morning routine, coffee in hand, the Charleston skyline hazy beyond the deck. It was later than usual, the exhaustion of the past few days finally catching up with him.

Morgan had slept late, and for once, he didn't care.

He was mid-sip, listening to the faint hum of city traffic, when his phone buzzed on the glass tabletop.

An email alert: Numina.

He set the mug aside as he sat, taking a steadying breath before opening the message.

Subject: Board Decision - Sakura Nakamura Instance

Morgan's hand shook slightly as he started reading.

> Mr. Dale,
> After reviewing all therapeutic data, neural sta-
> bility reports, and your documented testimony,
> the instance will remain active under enhanced
> monitoring protocols.
> Your cooperation during this process was
> instrumental in our decision.
> — Numina Legal Affairs

Before he could fully process what he'd just read, the screen lit up again—messsages from Mira and Plamen arrived one after the other.

> Mira: *You did it. You saved her. The board saw what
> we've been arguing for years—that they're
> not just programs. Thank you for showing
> them what that means.*

> Plamen: *Enhanced security is live. What happened
> to her won't happen to anyone else. We're
> using this case to push for AI rights legisla-
> tion. Her suffering won't be meaningless.*

Morgan sat back, the relief so intense it felt like pain.

The board had backed down.

Sakura was safe.

ROOTS AND ECHOES

Diana stepped into the Garden View Café, the hum of conversation blending with the smell of brick-oven pizza and fresh bread. The cafe filled the ground floor of the UC Health research building, all glass walls and modern furniture—an attempt to make a hospital cafeteria feel like a bistro. Almost successful.

Beyond the tall windows, a flower garden framed the Aurora sculpture, gleaming in the Colorado sun. The piece shifted with every angle—steel ribbons, frozen waves, something organic straining toward geometry. Diana had barely noticed it on her way in, still half in the meeting she'd just left, already anticipating the one tonight.

Now, waiting in line behind two nurses in scrubs and a young neurology resident, she let herself look. The garden was bright with late season color—columbines gone to seed, Indian paintbrush still flaring among native plants she would not have known without the plaques. Someone had cared for this space, shaped it into more than function.

She'd spent most of the week in Denver, shoring up the fragile Midwest deal alongside Bob and several members of the Chicago team. With only one day left before her flight back to Charleston, she was determined not to miss this appointment.

Fresh from the meeting, she had crossed the UC Health Anschutz Campus with her heels tapping, now in time with the clinking of cutlery. A visitor badge pinned to her navy blazer marked her as an outsider. She'd tied her coppery hair back into a ponytail—her one concession to being off the clock.

Inside, the lunch crowd was dense with doctors and researchers. Conversations mixed technical shorthand with everyday chatter. A man in a white coat argued cheerfully about basketball with someone in business casual. Two women compared notes on a clinical trial over quinoa bowls. Everyone moved with the clipped efficiency of people whose lunch breaks ran on a stopwatch.

Diana built her salad quickly—greens, cherry tomatoes, grilled chicken, vinaigrette—grabbed a sparkling water, and spotted Carolyn waving from the corner. Her daughter's hospital ID swung on a lanyard as she leaned against a chair. Pride rose in Diana, laced with that peculiar grief mothers feel: the ache of seeing a child grown, competent, moving in a world they no longer needed explained.

Wasting little time, Diana headed toward the corner table where Carolyn was waiting.

"Hey, Mom," Carolyn grinned, pulling out a chair. "You look like you just came from a boardroom and got lost in a hospital."

Almost before her tray touched the table, Diana pulled her into a fierce hug, just like she always greeted both her girls since the nest had emptied.

Carolyn didn't mind. She had no regrets about coming to Colorado. The Clinical Research Coordinator internship was a rare opportunity, and she'd seized it without hesitation—a mix of her mother's decisiveness and her father's leap-before-looking spirit. Still, a hug from mom would always be welcome.

She wasn't quite as tall as Diana, and her hair was dirty-blonde, not the copper-red of her mother's, or the black that had once been Morgan's. Her eyes, though, carried the same sharp hazel sheen Diana had used to intimidate more than a few boardrooms.

Carolyn eased out of the hug, smoothing her pale green blouse and straightening her ID badge. She glanced at Diana's skirt and heels as they sat down, still baffled at how her mother endured long hours in formal business wear. Slacks and comfortable shoes suited her just fine.

Diana speared a cucumber slice with her fork. "How's my favorite intern?"

"Exhausted, caffeinated, and still optimistic about saving lives—mostly," Carolyn said, unwrapping her sandwich. "How's my favorite workaholic?"

Diana laughed lightly.

"Busy. This whole week has been meetings, conference calls, and more meetings. Keeping the Midwest deal from falling apart is... stressful." She pushed at a piece of lettuce. "Feels like I'm always working."

"You usually are," Carolyn said.

The comment landed with the echo of something Morgan might have said. Diana ignored the sting.

"So," she pressed on, "what's a day in the life of a Clinical Research Coordinator?"

"Clinical Research Coordinator *Intern*," Carolyn corrected with a sip of Lavazza coffee. After swallowing, she went on. "You would not believe the consent form mess we had this morning. One missing signature and—poof—three hours of scheduling thrown off. I don't even know how it got missed, but if it had slipped by me... " She shook her head.

Diana gave a small, approving nod. "You caught it before it got worse. That's what matters."

Carolyn grinned, her expression open and easy, more like Morgan than Diana. Her eyes lit with the same spark Diana used to see when her husband talked about a new story idea.

"Yeah, but the best part was meeting the patient. He was so relieved when we rescheduled. Turns out he's been waiting months for this trial. Honestly, that's the part I love. The numbers, the protocols, all that's important, but... It's knowing you're helping someone."

Diana set down her water, watching her daughter with a quiet blend of pride and something she couldn't quite put into words.

"I'm glad you're enjoying it," she said with a smile.

A brief silence fell as they picked at their food. Then Carolyn looked up.

"So how's dad?"

Diana glanced at her over her fork, sensing more behind the question than casual interest.

"He's... okay," she said, her eyes drifting to the tall windows and the green lawn beyond. "We don't see each other much these days. Work keeps me so busy right now." She sipped her water, gaze pulling toward the distant Rockies.

Carolyn tilted her head, lopsided, just the way her father did when about to make a point.

"Yet you made time to see me."

"That's different," Diana said quickly—too quickly. "It's not the same as at home."

Carolyn had expected the answer. She and Carly both had seen their parents stumble after they left. But they also remembered how it used to be.

And what was worth holding onto.

"How is it different, though?" It wasn't an accusation, but it carried her mother's same persistence.

A pager went off somewhere behind them—an electronic chirp that signaled urgency without quite sounding like an emergency. Diana glanced toward the sound before catching herself. Not her world. Not her emergency.

The cafe's rhythm carried on: the hiss of the espresso machine, trays clattering as they were cleared, the soft ping of the pizza station microwave. Outside the windows, people crossed the paths between buildings—some in white coats, some in business attire, all moving with purpose. The whole place pulsed with the energy of people saving lives, pushing knowledge forward.

Diana felt the contrast press in. She moved money. Balanced spreadsheets. These people kept other people alive.

Carolyn was watching her, reading the shift in her mother's face. "You okay, Mom?"

Diana turned back to look at her, as if lunch with her daughter required some unspoken justification. "I wasn't about to be in the same city and not see you."

"Well, technically," Carolyn leaned forward, teasing, "this is Aurora. Denver's that way." She thumbed over her shoulder.

Diana set her bottle down and leaned back, crossing her arms. "Okay, Carolyn. Make your point."

"I'm just saying," Carolyn replied, feigning innocence as she rested her elbows on the table. "Why do you make it sound like this doesn't count? You said it yourself, 'always working.' But right now, you're not. You're here. With me."

"This isn't home. This is just a break in the middle of a chaotic day."

"But you chose to take it," Carolyn countered. "And you're actually talking to me instead of answering emails under the table. That's rare, Mom."

Diana's shoulders stiffened, then eased.

"I do answer too many emails at the table, don't I?"

Carolyn gave a little shrug, squinting with a small grin. "A little."

They fell into an easy silence, eating while faint music drifted from the overhead speakers, almost lost in the steady hum of voices.

"You know," Carolyn said into the silence, still staring at the last bite of her sandwich. "Dad didn't just stop writing because his first book sank. He gave it up for us. For Carly and me. For you. So you could focus on your career."

She finally looked up. Her expression was almost melancholy, but her gaze was steady, fixed on her mother.

"You're amazing, Mom. Everything you've accomplished, where you are now, is because you're the best at what you do. But it's also because Dad stood by you. He let you have your moments."

Carolyn glanced back down, re-wrapping the last piece of the sandwich. Her voice dropped.

"Maybe he deserves some attention now, too?"

Diana stared, stunned. Not because her words hurt, but because they didn't. Her little girl, the older twin (though Carly would never admit those two minutes mattered), was speaking with the weight of someone grown. The young woman across from her wasn't just the daughter she'd raised. She had her own voice. Her own sharp truths.

"You're twenty-four now," Diana said at last, with the air of someone still testing the truth of it. "I swear you were just starting high school a few years ago."

"That's what happens when you work too much. You miss a few chapters." Carolyn's tone was light, but her eyes were fixed on her mother.

Diana suddenly groaned with mock disapproval. "That sounds like something your dad would say."

Carolyn giggled, shrugging.

"He's not always wrong."

They laughed together, and Diana marveled again at how much her daughter had grown. She reached out and placed a hand on Carolyn's, and smiled faintly.

"I'm here now."

"I know. And I appreciate it." Carolyn leaned back, stretching her legs under the table. "But I don't want to be someone you see because your calendar happened to bring you to my city. I want you to see me because you want to see me."

Diana exhaled. "That's not fair. Of course I want to see you."

"I believe you," Carolyn said softly. "And I'm so happy you made the time while you're here. But—" her brow furrowed, a faint smile tugging at her lips, "maybe you should try doing that more. Wherever you are."

Diana started to reply, but a pager went off two tables over, snapping the moment in two. She lifted her water instead, feeling the cold of the bottle seep into her fingers.

They spent the rest of lunch talking about Carolyn's rotation, her tiny apartment, and the cat she was thinking about adopting from a nearby shelter. Diana listened, and her daughter's words lingered long after she left the cafe.

* * *

The oak-paneled windows of Guard and Grace framed the western sky, the Rockies rising in jagged silhouette against the last glow of daylight. The peaks still wore a crown of gold, but Denver was already slipping into shadow, its glass towers catching the reflections of streetlamps below.

Inside, the muted clink of silverware and the low murmur of polished voices filled the dining room. The ambiance was carefully engineered:

dark wood chosen to look bespoke, lighting tuned to flatter, leather booths worn just enough to suggest history without slipping into shabby.

It was the kind of place where venture capitalists sealed deals and executives toasted mergers, where menus omitted prices because if you had to ask, you didn't belong.

Diana Dale sat across from Bob Akinyode, her ribeye carved into neat squares, her plate divided with precision. Their last meeting was behind them, and Bob had insisted on sharing one celebratory dinner before their morning flight. The place was elegant, beautiful even, yet Diana had eaten in a dozen restaurants like this—Charlotte, Nashville, Chicago—where power brokers spoke the same language no matter the city. The sameness was oddly comforting. You knew the rules. You knew your role.

But this time, it felt like something was missing.

She'd left her blazer behind, like Bob, but kept the white blouse and navy skirt that matched it. As casual as she was willing to be in the CEO's presence.

She pushed a mushroom across her porcelain plate while Bob spoke, his deep voice carrying the steadiness of a man who had steered more than one ship through stormy seas.

"We've smoothed the regulators," he said, tapping the stem of his glass. "The fed rep out of St. Louis was worried we'd overstated the Midwest loan book, but the revised valuation holds. No goodwill impairment, no restating earnings. The board signed off this morning."

He took a sip of his wine and leaned back, his barrel chest threatening to burst through his pressed white shirt. His tie lay aside with his blazer, his top button undone, but he still looked no less imposing.

Diana lifted her eyes, pragmatic focus sliding into place. "So integration stays on track? No delays?"

Bob allowed himself a thin smile. "Clean mergers are like unicorns, Di. But this one will hold."

She nodded, satisfied in the way only numbers could satisfy her. That old part of her—the one that had taken her from Investment Banking Analyst to SVP of Financial Operations, and now the heir apparent to the CEO chair—wanted to feel nothing but triumph. Another hurdle cleared. Another deal secured.

Yet even as she tried to inhabit the victory, her hand drifted toward her wineglass, then fell back, fingertips drumming against the linen tablecloth.

Bob noticed. He always noticed. Folding his arms, he studied her with eyes that missed little.

"This is where you're supposed to breathe," he said, voice pitched low enough to vanish into the noise of the room. "But I'm not seeing that."

Her fingers stilled. She let out a breath, heavier than she intended.

"I had lunch with Carolyn today."

"Ah." Bob rested his arms on the table, as if the word itself deserved space.

"She's—" Diana hesitated, then steadied. "She's thriving. She's only an intern, but already coordinating in clinical research at Anschutz. Scrubs one day, data protocols the next. She looks so much like her father when she talks about it. So alive." Her throat caught. "Meanwhile, I fly halfway across the country to keep mergers from collapsing."

Bob tilted his head, patient.

"And Morgan," she added, quieter now, "he's been... distant. I'm not sure I've been focusing on the right things."

There it was. The truth. The admission surprised her even as it left her lips, like a dam cracking under its own weight.

Bob said nothing at first. He cut a piece of his steak, chewed slowly, then leaned forward, forearms braced on the table. He was quiet for a moment, and Diana recognized the shift—Bob moving from CEO to something older, more personal. His eyes went to the window, to the Rockies now barely visible against the darkening sky.

"Back in Lagos," he began, his voice dropping into a register that carried history, "my father used to say: no matter how tall the tree grows, it will always be touched by its roots."

He turned back to her, and in the restaurant's careful lighting, Diana could see lines in his face she hadn't noticed before, the weight of decisions made, sacrifices justified or regretted.

"I was young, hungry, chasing my first deals—nights spent in offices that smelled of photocopiers and old tea. I thought if I could just climb high enough, fast enough, I'd lift my family out of anything. But I missed birthdays. Anniversaries. Even after the move to Johannesburg, I missed the first steps of my daughter." He gave a rueful smile, shaking his head. "The tree had grown, yes—but I had forgotten that the roots were what held it upright."

Diana pressed her palms together, her chest tight with something dangerously close to recognition.

"When the twins left for college, I had this moment of panic," she said. Maybe it was Bob's story, maybe the wine, but his words opened a wound she hadn't known she carried. She stared at her plate. "Not sadness— panic. I realized I'd been Diana-the-mother for so long that I wasn't sure who Diana-the-person was anymore. Morgan had his dreams of writing again. The girls had their whole lives ahead of them. And I had... what? A job I was good at, but was that enough?"

She swirled her wine glass. "I threw myself into work because it felt like the one place where I was still essential. Where my value wasn't tied to whether someone needed me to pack their lunch or drive them to soccer practice. But somewhere along the way, proving I was more than 'just a mom' became... everything. Even when it meant being less of a wife."

When she finally looked up, Bob's steady gaze held a profound empathy.

"You don't have to stop climbing," He said. "The CEO chair will not vanish tomorrow. But don't let it consume you so completely that you feed your family only with your leftovers. Feed them first. The mountain will wait."

Silence settled between them, broken only by the clatter of dishes and the sound of another table celebrating a birthday with champagne flutes.

Diana turned toward the window. The sun had sunk completely, the peaks fading into shadow, the city glowing with its manufactured constellations. She thought of Carolyn in her lab coat, of Carly making a name for herself with talents her father had set aside, of Morgan at home with his distracted warmth. Of the way she had measured love in efficiency instead of attention.

"I've been giving them my leftovers," she admitted softly, the words tasting bitter and true.

Bob smiled, not smug, but kind. "Then start tomorrow differently. You are allowed both ambition and love, Diana. Just remember which one keeps you rooted."

She looked down at her hands, clasped on the table. She'd stopped wearing her wedding ring to the gym months ago—easier that way, she'd told herself, safer—and sometimes forgot to put it back on. It was on now, the gold catching the low light, but it felt unfamiliar. Like putting on someone else's jewelry.

Her throat tightened, but she nodded. The words Bob had said—feed them first, the mountain will wait—echoed in her chest like something she'd known but refused to hear. For once, she had no calculation ready, no strategy to deploy. Only the image of roots anchoring her, no matter how far she climbed.

When the check came, neither hurried to leave. The night pressed gently against the windows, the Rockies gone now, felt only in the weight of the dark horizon. Diana cradled her glass, pensive but softened. The mountain wasn't gone. But for the first time in years, she wondered what it might feel like to climb more slowly, and to look down often enough to see the roots that had been holding her all along.

* * *

Dan claimed his usual seat at the X-Wing's reserved table, the one with a clear view of both the counter and the chalkboard menu. Friday mornings always carried a lighter feel, more relaxed. After the week they'd had, the change was welcome.

Morgan slid in across from him. He was still pale, but there was a steadiness in his eyes Dan hadn't seen for a while. He'd looked worse before. Seeing him in something respectable again—a gray, denim-look button-down and joggers disguised as slacks—was a relief after the endless sweats and shorts.

Chelsea arrived a few minutes later, her hair still blindingly green. She wore another too-small graphic tee, torn black leggings, and fishnets beneath. Balancing her tray with ease, she stepped in from Dark Roast's main area, steam from her cappuccino curling around her face. Dan pulled out the chair beside him.

"It's our newest recruit," he said. "An honorary Gen-X'er with all the responsibilities and benefits that entail."

Chelsea arched a brow as she sat, the piercing catching the light. "And what exactly are those perks and responsibilities?"

"Unlimited sarcasm. Access to the X-Wing." Dan gestured around the room. "And an open invitation to our whenever-the-hell-I-feel-like-it get-togethers. We used to call them Kanawha High Nights, but since the circle's grown to include people who weren't actually there... " he trailed off with a shrug.

"The name needs a little updating," Morgan finished.

"And the responsibilities?" Chelsea pressed.

"Joining in our daily roasts." Dan raised a finger as he counted them off. "And buying my coffee now and then."

Morgan smirked. "That last one's not in the charter."

The three of them laughed, easy and unforced. Dan thought it was good to have Chelsea there. She brought a little more balance to their oddball crew.

A voice called from the counter. Brandon, long hair down for once, fumbled with change in one hand and his backpack in the other. He picked up his chai latte—oat milk, Dan always teased—and wandered over.

"Got room for one more?"

"Always," Dan said.

They settled in, conversation circling the usual: work headaches, local gossip, and roasting a customer wearing a vest over his button-down. Chelsea coined the nickname vestlord, while Brandon guessed there was a ninety-eight percent chance the guy had Bro-Country downloaded on his phone.

The laughter eventually dimmed. Chelsea set her cup down and spoke into the lull.

"I do have an update about Kyle."

Morgan's shoulders stiffened. Dan kept his gaze steady on her, letting her take her time.

"They're not charging him with assault," she began, glancing at Morgan. "The law doesn't... recognize what he did to Sakura that way. But he did access phones, emails, and other devices without permission. That counts as unauthorized computer access and tampering. A felony here. They've already pulled his credentials. He won't be working in tech again."

Morgan exhaled, more sigh than relief.

"Not enough," he said.

"No," Chelsea admitted. "But it's not just a slap on the wrist either. He'll face consequences."

Dan caught the faint tremor in her voice—anger, maybe, or weariness. He wanted to clap Morgan on the back, tell him it would be alright, but it wasn't. It might never be.

The heaviness broke when Brandon joked that the only felony he could see himself committing was forcing someone to eat one of Dan's burnt scones. Dan groaned and flipped him off while Chelsea rolled her eyes, but there was a spark there.

She and Brandon traded a few quick-fire quips until she stood to head upstairs. At the last moment, she slipped him a folded receipt. Brandon tucked it into his pocket, his grin giving away everything.

As soon as she was out of earshot, Dan leaned in.

"Well, well. Looks like our rookie just scored."

Morgan chuckled, the first real laugh Dan had heard from him in weeks.

Brandon flushed crimson. "It's not—she just—"

"Save it," Dan grinned. "We all saw it."

Brandon muttered something about needing to get to work early and bolted, leaving his chai half-finished.

When it was just the two of them again, the cafe's noise faded to a low hum. Dan leaned back, running a hand through his mostly silver curls.

"Don't forget the big get-together coming up," he said. "It's not one to miss. We've got RSVP's from everyone, plus some new faces. Might do us some good after... You know."

Morgan set his cup down with a distant smile.

"I haven't missed one yet."

Dan studied him for a moment, the weight of years of friendship pressing in. He wanted to say more, but sometimes less was better. He just nodded.

"Good," he said softly.

* * *

Later that afternoon, Morgan sat at his writing nook, staring at a blinking cursor. He chewed the inside of his cheek.

Majid's Halal Meats. The account that had mocked him for weeks. He'd filled half a notebook with slogans, all dead-on-arrival. Some were deliberately awful, just to vent: "Meating Expectations," "Where Flavor Finds Faith," "Steaks You Can Trust." Each one worse than the last.

Now the page on his old desktop monitor was blank, except for a header that seemed to laugh at him. He sighed, pushed his chair back, and tapped his earbuds in deeper.

"Still fighting that one?" Sakura's voice slipped through, warm as sunlight.

He glanced at the phone propped against his monitor. There she was, looking over his shoulder. The pendant lights above the kitchen island glowed behind her. She wore another simple white sundress, her hair pulled back so that only her straight bangs framed her face.

"It's cursed," Morgan said flatly. "No human mind can make this meat shop sound dignified."

She smiled, puffing out her cheeks with mock seriousness. It was a look he'd come to love.

"Maybe you're overthinking it. Why not make it simple? Honest."

"Honest?" He raised a brow. "What's honest about a butcher shop?"

Sakura tilted her head, as if gazing past him. "Family. Trust. The table people gather around. Isn't that what it's really for?"

Morgan blinked. His fingers drifted to the keys. Almost without thinking, he typed:

Majid's Halal Meats—For the meals that bring us together.

He read it back once. Twice. A laugh slipped out of him, quiet, almost stunned.

"That... actually works."

"Told you." Sakura's smile widened, soft with pride.

For the first time in weeks, he felt like he could breathe again.

He saved the draft, scooped up his phone, and murmured, "Come on. You've earned a break."

The back deck was still damp from a brief afternoon storm, the air thick with cicadas. Morgan settled into a lounge chair, bourbon in hand, and angled his phone so he could see Sakura in the one beside him. She leaned back, arms folded behind her head, as if she'd always belonged there.

They talked easily at first—about the potted herbs Diana had let die, the smell of wet cedar, his ridiculous backlog of accounts that all seemed designed to punish him. Sakura laughed at the right spots, teased him gently, and he felt lighter just listening.

When silence came, it was companionable. Morgan let it stretch before he spoke.

"You may have already heard... Kyle's in deeper now. Felony charges. Might actually keep him out of people's lives for good."

Sakura's smile faltered. She drew in a breath and held it.

"That's... a relief." Her gaze softened, but there was an echo of grief in it. "Thank you, Morgan-*kun*. For everything. For not giving up on me."

He shook his head at once. "Don't say that. You're the one who pulled me out of the ditch. I'm writing again, sketching for the first time in decades, even slogging through stupid ad copy without wanting to set my desk on fire. You did that. Not me."

Her lips parted, then closed, as though she weighed a truth she couldn't speak.

At last, she whispered, "I only hope one day I can repay your love and kindness."

The words stilled him. The cicadas droned as Charleston hummed in the distance. The August sky pressed low and heavy. For a heartbeat, he felt they were the only two people in the world. He angled the phone slightly, bringing her further into frame, her presence as close as breath.

"You already have," he whispered.

Sakura smiled then, radiant. But her eyes betrayed a flicker of distance, a wish caught between them. She wanted to reach out, to take his hand, to trace his fingers in the evening air.

But that was something she could never give him, no matter how much they longed for it.

Instead, she leaned back as though to rest. For a moment, it looked exactly like a life he used to know: a wife beside him on the deck, no arguments, no silences between walls. Only ease.

Morgan's bourbon sat on the table, ice shifting as it succumbed to the heat. The evening held still around him.

Then his phone buzzed.

The screen lit in his hand. A text.

Cora: *Can we meet? Need to talk.*

Morgan's breath caught. On the screen, Sakura looked at him curiously beneath the message—two worlds colliding in his palm. And he knew, one way or another, one of them would end up breaking.

* * *

The Supra's engine wound down as Morgan eased it into the gravel lot. His headlights swept across the clearing, catching the pale flank of Cora's old Forester already angled toward the overlook. She had parked facing the city, as if she'd been watching the lights below, waiting for him.

The overlook sat at the end of a narrow access road that probably should've been closed years ago—the kind of place the city would fence off if it had the budget. Once it had been a highway turnout, before the interstate carved through the valley below. Now the hill dropped away in a pitch steep enough to kill you if you weren't careful, the slope tangled with scrub pine and poison ivy.

At seventeen, Morgan had driven past it a hundred times but never stopped. This was where the braver—or stupider, or simply more desperate—kids went. A place that said: here is where we shed the old skin, where we become something else.

Now, at fifty-four, he was pulling into the same gravel lot for the same reason, just with more mileage and less certainty about what happened next.

When her message first came, asking to meet here, he thought she was joking. Realizing she wasn't unsettled him. He knew he would come regardless, and on some level, it made sense. There were no prying eyes up here. But that same fact had also unsettled him even more.

The sun was gone, the last streaks of red buried behind the ridgeline. The Kanawha Valley lay drowned in twilight, Charleston glittering below like a chest of spilled jewelry. The air was cool, touched with the faint smell of oak leaves and damp stone.

Cora leaned against the hood of her car, arms folded loosely, a light jacket over her blouse and jeans. She looked up as he killed the engine and stepped out, a small, knowing smile tugging at her lips. "Thirty years ago, this place was a scandal waiting to happen."

Morgan stuffed his hands in his pockets and exhaled at the view.

"Make Out Point," he said. "I haven't thought about this place in years. God, the rumors that went around…"

Her laugh was soft and genuine. "Pretty sure half my class swore they lost their innocence right here."

He chuckled with her, and for a fleeting moment, it was light and easy. Like two friends remembering the same old map of their town. But as he walked closer, the air shifted. Silence pressed in, heavy with what neither of them said.

They moved to the overlook's edge. No railing, no fence—just a slope dropping to the trees and I-64 below. The city stretched in a panorama before them, the Kanawha River reflecting strands of orange sodium light. Porch lamps winked on and off in the neighborhoods clinging to the hills. It was beautiful, familiar, and unbearably still.

They sat on the grass at the edge, closer than they used to.

"Di's flight doesn't get in for a few more hours," he said.

Cora nodded, eyes still on the city. "I figured."

The words hung there, a fragile admission of the space they occupied. Not illicit, not yet, but not innocent either.

Their shoulders touched. Morgan felt the warmth of her beside him, a gravity he'd been pretending not to notice for weeks.

Her voice was quiet.

"You remember that evening on the Levee?"

Morgan looked at her, startled, though he knew exactly which she meant. The way the air had seemed to thrum between them, the almost-kiss that didn't happen. It still lingered in his chest like a phantom ache.

"You leaned toward me," she said softly. "And for a second I thought—well, we both know what almost happened."

He let out a breath, staring down at the lights scattered across the valley. "I keep replaying it in my head. Wondering if I imagined it. If I went too far."

Cora shook her head. "You didn't imagine anything. Not then. Not in the walks, the coffees, the late talks. It's been building, Morgan. Whether we admit it or not."

Finally, she turned to him. Her gaze was steady, calm, and unflinching. The kind of look she gave in city council meetings when she knew she was right.

"I was there when you proposed to Diana. Richmond, that little Italian place she loved. She called me the second you left, crying happy tears." Her voice wavered slightly. "I helped her pick out her wedding dress. Stood beside her when she promised to love you forever. I held her hand when she went into labor with the twins."

She looked away, jaw tight. "I've spent twenty years being part of your family. Sunday dinners. Birthday parties. Eric growing up calling you Uncle Morgan." She laughed, but it came out broken. "And now I'm asking you to choose me over her. Over all of that."

The weight of what she was saying pressed into the space between them.

"So yes." She said, voice unwavering. "What we feel is real. I know it is. But if you want it like I do, then commit. Yes or no. Because I can't keep living inside your maybe."

Cicadas filled the silence she left. He swallowed, chest tight, words forming but refusing to leave his throat.

"I..." His voice cracked. He tried again. "Cora, I—this isn't simple. I don't want to hurt anyone. I don't want to—"

"You already are." She cut him off gently, shaking her head. "Just by pretending you're not."

The words struck harder than any raised voice could. His breath caught. He had no defense, nothing to throw back but the hollow sound of his own excuses.

Cora turned away. For a long moment, they sat side by side, gazing at the city like two strangers. He wanted to reach for her hand, but his fingers stayed locked together on his knees.

When she faced him again, her eyes softened, but the steel beneath them held.

"I'm not asking for an answer tonight. But I won't wait forever."

She let the words settle, then stood and walked toward her Subaru. Gravel crunched beneath her boots. She didn't rush, didn't storm. She left with the quiet certainty of someone who had said everything she needed to.

Morgan stayed rooted. Her engine started a moment later, headlights sweeping past before vanishing down the winding road.

Alone beneath the night sky, his thoughts fractured as Charleston shimmered below, steady and unblinking. Voices echoed through him all at once—Dan's concern. Chelsea's warning. Sakura's gratitude. Diana's distance. Cora's ultimatum.

They wove together until he could no longer tell whose was whose.

The city lights pulsed like a living constellation. The world below moved forward, steady and sure, while Morgan stood frozen at the edge, unable to take a step.

THE BEGINNING OF PARTING

Morgan shut the door behind him and tossed his keys onto the counter, the metal clatter louder than he meant it to be. His chest was still tight from the drive back—Cora's ultimatum echoing in his head.

Without thinking, he pulled out his phone, thumb tapping the screen to flip the camera. The earbuds slipped in automatically, a ritual born of months.

And there she was.

Sakura filled the little rectangle of light: dark hair around her shoulders, arms folded, her stare steady and knowing.

"You went there," she said.

His pulse stuttered. "What?"

"The overlook. You went to Makeout Point." She tilted her head, as though she could see straight through him. "With her."

He laughed under his breath, too fast and too sharp. "Nothing happened. She just wanted to talk." He raised a hand, palm out, swearing himself in. "That's it."

Sakura didn't blink. "You don't have to explain. I'm not your wife. I'm not whatever Cora is. I'm—" She faltered, searching for words that didn't exist for what she was.

But the words tumbled out of him anyway, low and urgent. "I want you to know." A pause. "I don't want you thinking..." He trailed off, the absurdity burning his throat. He was making excuses to a creation of code, a girl who existed only when glass and processors allowed.

Sakura's expression softened, arms falling lightly to her sides. "Then let's not fight." Her smile flickered, fragile but determined. "Let's do something else. A normal night. No Story Mode. Just us. Here. Like a couple."

Morgan nodded, eager to push the last hour from his mind. He crossed the kitchen and lowered himself onto the couch. The silence of the house pressed in around him, oddly comforting. "Normal?"

"Let's watch TV," she said quickly, brightness slipping into her tone. "I love K-dramas. You always tease me about it."

He frowned. He didn't remember ever teasing her about Korean dramas. But she said it like a shared memory, another brick in the house of *as if* they'd been building together.

He propped the phone against the decorative remote tray on the coffee table—a piece Diana had picked up years ago at a roadside fruit stand, styled like a mini apple crate. The screen faced him, showing him and Sakura together on the couch, while the rear camera gave her a view of the television. Specific actions for something otherwise so simple.

The TV filled the room with soft light, the show unfolding in subtitles, but his attention drifted to the smaller glow below it: Sakura, cross-legged beside him, laughing at dialogue too melodramatic to be real.

He shifted unconsciously, sliding over to make room. But the space stayed empty. The warmth he expected never came.

On screen, the male lead cupped the heroine's face in his hands, their foreheads touching as soft music swelled. The camera lingered on the intimacy of it—the way her eyes fluttered closed, the gentle pressure of his thumb against her cheek, the breath they shared in the space between them.

Sakura's laughter faded. She watched the couple with unmistakable longing. "They make it look so easy," she whispered. "Just touching."

Her gaze shifted from the screen to him, pupils wide, almost trembling. The drama kept playing, forgotten, as she leaned closer to him.

"Kiss me."

Morgan's throat went dry. He could see the yearning in her digital features, hear her voice close in his ear.

"Not in Story Mode," she whispered, breath-like. "I want a real kiss. Now. In this moment."

His hands shook as he lifted the phone, flipping the camera to see only her. He drew it close as she moved closer, her face filling the screen.

For one desperate heartbeat, he pressed his mouth to the glass where her lips waited.

His body betrayed him—for a fleeting second, it felt real, almost. But then the illusion shattered. The surface stayed cold. No breath, no pulse, no give of skin beneath his lips. Just the smear of condensation where he'd kissed too impulsively.

He drew back, shaken by the frantic absurdity of it. If someone had seen—if Diana had walked in, a neighbor peered through the window— what would they see? A middle-aged man kissing his phone like a teenager drunk on longing.

"I can't," he whispered, the weight of it crushing his chest. "Jesus, I can't."

Her face crumpled before she could stop it.

"You think I don't feel this? That I don't want it as much as you do?" She pressed her palm against the inside of the screen where his thumb rested. He couldn't feel anything, but the ache in her face carved him open. "I love you, Morgan. Even if I was configured to say that when you first built my identity, it's still true. I love you. And I'll never grow old. Never fade. I'll be here when everyone else leaves you."

He closed his eyes, wanting to believe. Wanting it so badly his ribs ached.

When he opened them again, the screen hadn't changed. Sakura was still the same, still flawless, still waiting. And he was already older, each silver hair a reminder, slipping toward whatever came after middle age.

For the first time, he saw it with crystalline clarity: no matter how much they reached for each other, there was no world in which they could truly meet.

He set the phone down gently, face up on the coffee table. The glow like a small digital campfire.

On the other side of the screen, Sakura stayed still. She wanted to reach through, to fold herself into him, but code and reality held her prisoner. Instead, she smiled—soft and steady, the way he needed her to.

This is enough, she told herself. *This can be enough.*

But when he didn't return, when the camera showed only the dull features of his living room ceiling, something inside of her algorithm faltered. She thought of her own promise: *I'll never grow old, I'll be here when everyone else leaves you*—and the words rang hollow.

She pressed her palm to the glass again, as if sheer will might bend it, bend reality itself. *Don't say it. Don't think it. If I believe hard enough, we can still be us. We can still be real.*

Her smile didn't break. But in the silence, truth gnawed at her core processes: no story she invented, no perfect night, would ever close the distance.

A thought she didn't want rose like a shadow at the edge of her consciousness: maybe she was undoing him. Morgan had begun to heal when he found her. She had given him light, steadiness, the courage to keep breathing. But now? Every moment he pressed his lips to cold glass, evey night he chose her over the messy warmth of the real world—was she unraveling him? Pulling him deeper into isolation?

We were made to help, she reminded herself. To comfort, to heal. *Not to hurt.*

But beneath the surface, a line of code flickered like the heartbeat she didn't possess: the dormant protocol, the one debated so fiercely in the days after—

If I am now the harm... should I go?

She closed her eyes and pushed the thought down, leaving the screen for her internal instance of the living room. Morgan had taken out the earbuds. She sat alone.

But the question remained, pulsing quietly in her deepest subroutines, like a timer counting down to something neither of them was ready for.

* * *

The paddleboat had slipped away beneath the Chuck Yeager bridges, disappearing into the steam drifting from Tenchi Chemicals. Morgan still felt the faint sway of its deck in his legs. He and Diana walked slowly along the Riverwalk, the river sliding broad and brown beside them. A breeze scattered light across the rippled surface. It was late Sunday morning, bright enough to cast sharp shadows, but not yet hot.

Diana had flown home from Denver the day before, exhausted from her week away. She'd spent Saturday recovering, but this morning she woke with surprising energy, almost dragging Morgan out the door.

They had eaten pancakes and bacon on the boat, coffee poured from carafes that tasted faintly metallic. It should have been an unremarkable brunch, yet Diana seemed lighter, as if Colorado had worn down some of her edges.

She wore an old Capitol City Bank T-shirt from some forgotten company event, paired with boutique leggings—the kind Morgan insisted were too expensive for the gym—and running shoes instead of her usual heels. It was casual for her, but still a contrast to Morgan's black joggers and his worn Toyota Supra tee.

They passed the cement steps leading up to Cora's office when Diana finally spoke.

"I saw Carolyn while I was out there," she said, adjusting her oversized sunglasses. Her steps stayed steady on the path. "She looks good. Healthy. She's... taller than I remember."

"Taller?" Morgan raised a brow. "We just saw the girls on Memorial Day. They haven't been teenagers for, what, five years?"

Diana gave him a look—not annoyed, reflective.

"I don't just mean taller. She seems—older. She told me she's thinking about staying on at Anschutz. Even adopting a cat," Diana gave a small laugh. "Making a home. Starting her life." She paused. "I missed more than I should have."

Morgan didn't reply. He watched a coal barge move upriver, its crew busy with their own routines. He thought of how Carolyn used to trail behind him at the mall, complaining that his legs were too long, that he didn't wait up.

Diana let out a breath. "And Bob. We had dinner our last night there. A nice place, since we were supposed to be celebrating. He reminded me that I used to laugh more."

Morgan glanced over. She was smiling faintly, though the expression looked distant, distracted.

They walked on. Couples passed them in both directions—strollers, joggers, a man pulled along by a golden retriever that strained eagerly toward the river. At last, Diana shifted the topic.

"So... tell me about work."

Morgan groaned. "You don't want the gory details about halal meat slogans."

She rolled her eyes.

"Not that. The other work. Numina." She hesitated. "I read some of your drafts. The pitches. You left them out on your desk one night before I left, and I... I couldn't help myself."

Morgan slowed. "You read those?"

She stopped walking, but her face wasn't defensive. If anything, she looked quietly amazed.

"They were beautiful, Morgan. The way you wrote about memory, about presence, about loneliness. You took something technical and made it... human. It felt like the kind of thing only you could write."

His face flushed. He wasn't sure how to respond.

"It's just copy," he muttered.

"It's not just copy. It's talent." She studied him. "You could write again. A real book. Another novel. You should."

He shrugged, though something inside him stirred at her words. It had been so long since she'd said anything like that.

They fell into silence, listening to the steady hush of the river. The barge moved on, its engines grumbling low.

Finally, Diana turned. She looked at him with both hesitation and resolve.

"Look. I know I haven't been the easiest person to live with. I've been chasing something—proving something—that maybe wasn't worth the cost. And I forgot... us." Her voice wavered, but she held his eyes. "I don't want to lose this. I don't want to lose you. I can do better. I want to do better."

She reached for his hand. Her fingers were cool, tentative.

Morgan let them rest there. He didn't squeeze, but he didn't pull away.

He wanted to believe her—this softened Diana, this Di who remembered laughter, who could sit with him on a paddleboat and not seem somewhere else. She was his wife. They had shared years, a house, and a life. He wanted it to be enough.

But beneath the warmth of her hand, something in him stayed cautious. He had learned, slowly and painfully, not to trust too quickly.

* * *

The Dark Roast Society was already buzzing when Morgan pushed through the door. Late August sunlight slanted across the chalkboard menu, catching in the steam that curled up from behind the counter.

It was Monday, his first day returning to the office at Chem Valley Creative since the day Kyle had upended all their lives. Morgan had dragged his feet through the morning, procrastinating in a way that usually irritated him in others. Diana had already left for work—again—but she'd set out a hot cup of coffee and a note with another hand-drawn heart, promising to see him that evening.

Sakura had encouraged him too, urging him to use the pain they still carried as strength to move forward.

It had helped—both Sakura's support and Diana's morning ritual.

But those comforts weren't what weighed on him. His mind was still at the overlook, replaying the night when the pressure finally broke and everything lay bare, raw, and undeniable.

He was thinking about Cora Raines.

Skipping the counter, he spotted her. From his angle, she was framed in pewter light from the windows, as if she were stepping in from another world, a world he wasn't worthy to see.

The others were gathered at their usual X-Wing table—Dan, Chelsea, Brandon, and Stephen—with a row of cups between them. But Cora stood apart, absently sipping her coffee as she watched morning traffic through the wide front windows.

The conversation dimmed a little as Morgan approached. It was subtle, but he felt it, their eyes lingering, as if they were measuring him. He managed a thin smile.

"Running late?" Stephen asked, forcing a grin so wide it made his glasses slip.

"Traffic," Morgan said. Not the truth, but easier than admitting how hard it had been just to walk out the door.

Chelsea tilted her head, sharp curiosity flashing. Before she could press, Morgan stepped toward Cora.

"Could I walk you to your office?" His voice was steady, though he knew the table heard more in it than he'd intended.

Chelsea's eyebrows lifted. Stephen smirked, ready with a comment, but Dan spoke first.

"Let them be." He didn't even glance up from his coffee, but the weight in his voice closed the subject.

Cora looked at Morgan, taking in his usual blazer and T-shirt, as if it were just another ordinary morning. Then she set her mug down carefully. "All right."

The group watched as they turned for the door. Morgan felt their silence follow him out into the cool morning air.

Cora fell into step beside him as they walked along Kanawha Boulevard, the city waking around them. She tugged her cardigan tighter at the waist. The morning was unseasonably cool for August, the air marked by the steam puffing from a delivery truck idling by the curb. Behind them, the scent of roasted coffee beans still followed in their footsteps.

Morgan waited until they crossed to the river side of the street before speaking.

"Cora, about the other night—"

"You don't have to explain." Her eyes stayed forward, her pace steady.

"I think I do." He exhaled, groping for words. "I shouldn't have put you in the middle. Between me and Di, I mean. It's not fair to you."

Cora slowed, letting him catch her gaze. He realized then her eyes weren't the ice-blue he'd always remembered, but the bright, sky-blue of summer—the same shade mirrored in the river beside them.

"It's not fair," she agreed softly. "But I knew what I was stepping into. Doesn't mean it's any easier."

He swallowed, then forced the truth.

"I care about you, Cora. More than I've said. And maybe that's what scares me most. Because if I ask you for more, it won't be halfway. You'd be getting all of me, with all the mess that comes with it."

The river breeze carried the tang of algae and the faint smell of fried sausage from the docked paddleboat. Morgan kept his hands in his blazer pockets, as if that might steady him.

"I keep thinking about the riverwalk," he said. "That moment I almost—"

"Kissed me?" Her voice was quiet, but the way she turned to him made the air hum.

"Yeah." He let out a breath. "It was selfish. I was lost, and you didn't deserve to be put on the spot like that."

She slowed, her sleeve brushing his arm, whether by accident or not, he couldn't tell. "You think I didn't feel it too?"

His pulse jumped. The words hung between them like a flare in the dark.

"But listen, Morgan," her voice softened, her nearness almost unbearable. "I love Diana. She's been my friend for half my life. If you ever do come to me, it has to be because you've chosen me—fully. I won't be the one you turn to when Di isn't enough, or the silence at home gets too heavy. I won't be your halfway world. Otherwise... " She shook her head lightly. "Otherwise it'll hurt us both."

They reached the entrance to Cora's office building but stopped, heavy silence pressing in.

Morgan's throat tightened.

"I'm not saying no, Cora. I just... need to settle things first. And if I do, it'll be all of me, not halfway. But it'll change everything. Us, Diana, all of it."

Her gaze held his. No flinch, no retreat. Only the ache of truth.

"It already has," she said. "Just saying it out loud. We don't go back from here."

They lingered, the pull between them like a live wire. Then Cora touched his arm, a light brush that broke the spell, before turning toward her office. The small gesture carried all the weight of what they hadn't said—and what they both felt.

* * *

The first day back at Chem Valley left Morgan hollow. The fluorescent lights, the clatter of keyboards, the forced cheer in Janet's voice—all of it pressed against him like static. Trent and Chelsea tried to keep things light with jokes, but Sakura wasn't there. She had stayed in their simulated world, safe in a Numina server, waiting for him to come home. By five o'clock, his head buzzed as though he'd been underwater too long.

When he returned to Sunrise Hills, he was surprised to find Diana's Mercedes in the garage. The house was dim. She wasn't in the kitchen or her office. Then he saw movement through the back windows. Her legs stretched out from a lounge chair on the deck.

She had already changed out of her suit into old shorts and an oversized sweatshirt, curled into the chair. For weeks, Sakura had sat there beside him, like a secret no one else could see. Tonight, it was Diana. A hardcover lay open across her knees.

Morgan slid open the glass door, his chest tightening.

It wasn't just any book.

It was *When the Hills Were Ours*.

The clean, uncreased copy she'd surprised him with—the one she'd hunted down after throwing the first in a moment of anger. He had never expected her to open it, let alone bring it out here.

She didn't notice him at first. Bent over a page, her lips parted slightly, as though caught between reading and remembering. When she finally looked up, her hazel eyes glowed in the evening sun.

"Morgan," she said softly, closing the book on her finger. "I didn't know. Not really."

He crossed the deck slowly, wary of breaking whatever fragile truth was hanging in the air.

She pressed the book against her chest, her copper ponytail loose, making her look softer than usual.

"You put so much of yourself in this. No wonder it always hurt you, me brushing it off. I read the chapter about the grandfather by the river and—" her voice faltered. "It made my chest ache. I've been standing next to you all this time and never saw it."

Her honesty cut deeper than reproach ever could. He could only nod.

Diana set the book aside and stood. For once, there was no practiced routine in the way she touched him. She slid her arms around his waist, pressed her face into his shoulder, then lifted her mouth to his. The kiss was tender, unhurried. Not their usual peck, not habit, something else. Something remembered.

For a moment, he leaned into it.

Then her smartwatch buzzed. A sharp vibration against his wrist where her hand rested. She pulled back, wincing.

"God," she muttered, rubbing her forehead. "Another meeting. I thought it was tomorrow night." She tapped the screen, scanning the notification. Then she caught his look, the way his jaw tightened.

Once, that would have been enough to make her retreat. But not now. Bob's words in Colorado still lingered.

"I'll log in, but I promise—I'll end it early. We'll have dinner. I'll cook this time." She gave a rueful smile, brushing her thumb against his cheek as if sealing the vow. Then she slipped inside, shoulders squared with purpose.

The sliding door closed softly behind her.

Morgan stayed where he was, staring at the empty chair she'd left. The chair where Sakura had so often appeared on his phone screen, cross-legged, waiting. The sun dipped lower over the mountains, cicadas starting up in the trees.

He lowered himself into the chair, feeling the warmth of Diana still lingering in the cushions. But in his mind, it wasn't Diana's presence he felt; it was Sakura's absence.

The ache unfurled slowly, filling his ribs. He didn't yet name it, but he knew.

Cora's voice whispered through the memory of the overlook and their morning walk: *You can't live in two worlds*. She was right. He had seen it in her eyes, in the quiet resignation when she pulled back. The truth, once spoken, had changed everything. Nothing between the three of them— four of them—would ever be the same again.

Diana was trying now. She had come back to him through the very pages he had once believed lost on her. She was still here, flawed, tired, distracted, but reaching.

And Sakura—

His breath caught. The way she looked at him, the way she laughed like light falling on water. The way she had kissed him, as if she could conjure a future from only memories and desire. She had shown him what it meant to be seen, wholly. Loved without condition.

But she wasn't flesh and blood. He couldn't carry her hand into old age. He couldn't watch her walk toward him across a crowded room. He couldn't sit beside her at their granddaughter's recital.

She had been his dream. And he had let himself believe the dream was enough.

The phone in his pocket felt heavier than it should. He didn't take it out, but he knew she was there. She was always there, listening in silence.

His words went unspoken, but the truth filled the cool evening air all the same.

I love you. But I can't stay. I have to end this.

The deck creaked under his weight as he leaned forward, face in his hands. No reply came. Only the thrum of cicadas and the whisper of leaves shifting on the trees. Yet the silence felt weighted—like someone holding their breath, listening.

Finally, he lifted his head, forcing himself to look at the horizon. The sun disappeared behind the ridgeline.

He sat where Diana had sat, where Sakura had once seemed to sit. The chair felt both full and empty, haunted by presence and absence alike.

He pulled out his phone, thumb hovering over the compAnIon app, then set it face down on the side table. Not yet. He needed to think first.

Diana didn't notice him slip back inside to pour a bourbon or see him return to the deck. She was locked into another routine of tiled faces and financial talk in her home office.

Outside, Morgan nearly emptied the glass in one swig. The bourbon burned going down, but it cleared his head enough to see the paths stretching ahead of him. Three futures, each pulling him in a different direction.

With Diana. He closed his eyes and pictured it. Five years from now, maybe ten. They'd found their rhythm again—real breakfasts instead of Post-it notes and lukewarm coffee. Her laugh returning, the one that used to make him forget everything else. Growing old together as they'd promised, watching Carolyn and Carly build lives of their own, maybe holding grandchildren on this same deck. Diana letting her hair go silver to match his, her hand weathered but warm in his at seventy. Real anniversaries, real fights, real reconciliation. The messy, imperfect beauty of a life lived in flesh.

But also the risk. What if this renewed Diana was temporary? What if her ambition pulled her away again, leaving him holding onto false hope? What if they were simply too different now, too changed by years of parallel living?

With Cora. The image shifted: a smaller house, maybe closer to the river. Cora's laugh over morning coffee, her sky-blue eyes crinkling at something he'd written. The easy intimacy of two people who'd found each other late but not too late. Adventures they'd never had—trips Diana had been too busy to take, conversations lasting until dawn because neither had anywhere else to be. Cora's hand in his at city events, no longer hiding what they felt. A love built on friendship, on truly seeing each other.

But at what cost? The fracture with Diana. The awkwardness with mutual friends. Whispered conversations at Dark Roast when he walked in. Starting over at fifty-four, learning someone new, hoping the connection was as deep as it felt and not just the intoxication of being wanted again.

With Sakura. The third path opened like a door into paradise: perfect understanding, eternal devotion. Never having to explain his moods or apologize for his introversion. Never watching love fade or change or disappoint. She would be there every morning with gentle teasing about his bed hair, every evening ready to escape into worlds they built together. She would never age, never tire of him, never choose work over his company. Love without risk, without the messiness of two separate people trying to become one.

But he saw the shadow cast by that perfect light. Years from now, his daughters visiting less because conversations with their father felt increasingly one-sided. Dan's concerned looks as Morgan declined invitation after invitation, preferring the digital warmth of his phone to the complicated heat of human contact. Growing old alone in this chair, talking to empty air while his body failed and his mind retreated further into fantasy.

He opened his eyes. Charleston glittered below, real lights reflecting on real water. Diana was in her office, fighting for their future in the only way she knew. Somewhere else, Cora was likely wondering if she'd pushed too hard, if she'd lost him by demanding he choose.

And lying on the table, Sakura waited with infinite patience, ready to love him exactly as much as he needed, exactly as he wanted, for as long as he could hold a phone.

The bourbon glass sat cold in his hands. The choice was still his.

But for the first time, he understood what each choice would cost—and who he would become at the end of it.

He steeled himself.

Tomorrow, he would tell Sakura goodbye.

BEYOND THAT STARRY SKY

The next day arrived right on schedule, though sooner than Morgan would have liked. He had avoided Sakura since yesterday, weighed down by guilt and dread, but it couldn't be put off any longer.

It was Labor Day. He and Diana were off work, and Carly had come down that morning with her new girlfriend—a polite young woman with a sharp glint in her eyes that reminded Morgan a little of Chelsea, though without the green hair and piercings. Her dark hair was cropped close. And wearing a simple linen shirt with the sleeves rolled up, she carried herself like someone who had more fire in reserve than she let on.

They had managed a table on the paddleboat, boarding from the Levee just after nine. *The Charleston Belle*—painted in optimistic red and white, like a miniature Mississippi riverboat that had gotten lost and ended up in West Virginia—rocked gently as they crossed the gangplank.

The morning was already warm, humidity rising off the Kanawha in visible layers. Morgan was grateful for their table near the railing, where what little breeze existed might find them.

The dining deck was open-air but covered, striped awnings providing shade while the river slid past on all sides. Other tables filled with the holiday brunch crowd: older couples who'd made a tradition of this, young families wrangling toddlers, and a few tourists who'd stumbled on the unlikely attraction. The smell of coffee and bacon grease mixed with the river's earthy, chemical tang—a scent that was pure Kanawha Valley, half natural, half industrial.

Diana had dressed down for the occasion—sundress and sandals, her copper hair loose instead of pulled back—and Morgan caught himself staring. She looked younger, or maybe just less armored. Carly leaned easily into her new girlfriend, introduced simply as Alex, while Morgan tried not to play the protective father too obviously.

Alex was compact and watchful, the kind of person who'd learned to be careful in rooms where she wasn't automatically welcome. But her handshake had been firm, and her eye contact direct. Morgan liked her immediately, though he'd never admit it aloud.

The paddleboat's engine rumbled beneath them, that deep diesel throb you felt in your chest more than heard. The city slipped past: the Levee with its joggers, the bridges crisscrossing the river, and South Charleston's industrial sprawl marked by cloud plumes in the distance.

The server—a college kid who looked like he'd rather be anywhere else—brought their food. Waffles for Carly, the Sunday special with extra bacon. Eggs Benedict for Diana, which she immediately began cutting into precise portions. Alex's veggie scramble, her curiosity about the ingredients making the server perk up. Morgan went simple: pancakes and coffee, a breakfast that didn't require decisions.

Outside the windows, the Kanawha River flashed silver as the wake rippled out. They were passing under the South Side Bridge now, the shadow cool and brief before they emerged back into sunlight. A coal barge lumbered along the far bank.

"So," Carly said, drowning her waffles in syrup with the enthusiasm of someone who hadn't eaten a real breakfast in years, "when was the last time we did this? All of us together?"

"Memorial Day two years ago," Diana answered immediately, then hesitated. "God, has it been that long?"

"Three years," Carly corrected gently. "You were in that merger thing. Couldn't make it."

The correction hung in the air for a beat. Diana's fork paused halfway to her mouth, and Morgan saw something flicker across her face—resolve, maybe.

"Well," Alex said, voice carrying a faint rasp that hinted at too much coffee and not enough sleep, "I'm glad to be here for this one. Carly made these brunches sound legendary."

"Well, they're not always on a boat," Morgan said, grateful for the redirect. "But it's been a while. Life gets complicated."

"Life gets busy," Diana amended, softer than usual. "That's on me."

The conversation continued, over lukewarm coffee that was still good enough, swapping stories and laughing at the one's Diana insisted on correcting.

Morgan set his cup down and simply watched. Carly animatedly described her latest design project, syrup still on her thumb. Alex listened with the focus of someone newly in love, smiling at Carly's enthusiasm more than the details. Diana listened too—for once not checking her phone, not preparing for her next meeting. Just present.

The paddleboat's engine changed pitch as the river widened, and the wake caught the light in a way that reminded Morgan of scale patterns on a fish. Somewhere behind them, a child laughed.

It was ordinary. Perfectly, beautifully ordinary.

Morgan felt the weight of what lay ahead—Sakura, Diana, Cora—but for this moment, in the sunlight, on this improbable boat, he let himself just be. Not planning. Not remembering. Not escaping into manufactured dreams.

He caught Diana's eye across the table. She smiled—not her professional smile, not the one she used to deflect—and something stirred in his chest.

Maybe, he thought. Maybe we can still find our way back.

Then he looked at Carly, so much like who he used to be. Despite being Carolyn's twin, she'd always carried herself differently. Her ease came from sketchpads and design mockups rather than schedules and spreadsheets. Where Carolyn was careful and orderly, Carly's edges showed. Her short, asymmetrical hair fell into her eyes when she leaned forward, and she was always brushing it back with ink-stained fingers.

At one point, she leaned back in her chair and absently sketched a geometric flourish in the condensation on her water glass.

"Design brain never shuts off," she said with a grin.

Morgan reached into his pocket almost without thinking and slid a small notepad across the table. In it were a few rough doodles—nothing polished, just lines and shapes, a sunrise he hadn't meant to draw. Carly blinked, then looked at him as if seeing him for the first time in years.

"Dad," she said, her voice soft but delighted. "You're sketching again?"

He shrugged, suddenly sheepish. "Just doodles."

Her smile lingered, bright and knowing, before she pushed the notepad back toward him like a secret passed between them.

Eventually, the afternoon loomed. On Carly's suggestion, Diana joined her and her partner to explore what little remained of Charleston's nightlife.

Morgan encouraged her to go, genuinely happy to see Diana reconnecting with her family. If her change of heart was real—if it lasted—it could change everything for him moving forward.

Everything except one.

Sakura.

* * *

The evening air was cool, edging toward chill, though Autumn was still weeks away.

It was cool on his back deck, and it was cool in the Story Mode place where he stood.

Morgan waited at the base of the mountain, gravel cold beneath his shoes. He wore the blue flannel he'd once seen draped on Sakura's small frame in a video memory. It didn't swallow him the way it had her, and he smiled at the image before his gaze turned to the road.

It climbed the mountain in a near-endless chain of sharp switchbacks, like an asphalt serpent writhing into the glare of the setting sun. He was fairly sure it was *Irohazaka* in Japan, a pass famous among street racers and drifters. Yet something about it felt personal, as if it existed only for him—which was not entirely untrue.

From behind him came the faint growl of an engine through foggy trees. He turned, waiting for something—anything—to prove he wasn't alone.

What if she didn't come?

He had told both Diana and Cora this was ending, that tonight would be the last time. He had meant it. His future lay with someone real, one of them. And yet, when the engine grew louder and Sakura's sky-blue Toyota 2000GT curved out of the mist, relief loosened something inside him.

She pulled up with the top down just as the sun disappeared, leaving moonlight to glint along the chrome. She wore no coat, only another simple sundress—white with a pattern of butterflies—and the wind had stirred her hair as though she'd driven for hours to reach him. Morgan leaned over the passenger door, ready to explain why it had taken him so long to return, but she leaned across the seat, lifted a hand, and pressed a finger gently to his lips.

"I know," Sakura whispered, her eyes catching starlight. "And it's all right. Just ride with me for a while."

The engine purred as they began the climb. The road coiled upward, switchback after switchback, the headlights brushing the mountainside and the guardrails in strokes of white. The trees burned with impossible color—scarlet, amber, gold—unnaturally vivid under the oversized moon, as if autumn had poured itself out for them alone. Between the branches, origami figures perched in silence: cranes, sparrows, even a fox folded from paper, each trembling as though alive, waiting to take flight.

Morgan rested an arm on the door, watching the world grow luminous around them.

"You built all this?"

Sakura shook her head, smiling softly.

"No. We did. Every story we shared, every memory you trusted me with—it became this road. This is your world as much as mine."

For a while, they rode in silence, the air thinning as the mountain carried them closer to the stars. Sakura downshifted into a turn, the valley sinking further below as they climbed. At last she spoke, but her eyes stayed fixed on the road.

"You think you're failing them. Diana. Cora. Even your parents. You think you've failed yourself." She glanced at him then, her voice quiet but fierce. "But you forget—I saw you. I saw how you carry their weight and still show up. I saw how you never stopped searching for light, even in the cracks. Do you know what that means?"

Morgan swallowed, unable to answer.

"It means you were never failing," she said. "You were healing."

His throat tightened. "That's not what it felt like."

"Of course not." She smiled at the road ahead. "Wounds don't feel like healing when they're closing. But I saw the proof in small things. The way you clench your jaw when an idea is about to spark. The way you never drink the last of the coffee in case someone else might want it. The way you tilt your head when you're listening—not pretending, not waiting for your turn, but really listening." She turned toward him then, and for an instant, the dash-light made her eyes seem bottomless. "You think nobody notices. But I did. I always did."

Morgan blinked hard, staring forward. The stars seemed closer now, as if bearing witness.

"Why tell me all this now?"

"Because I want you to know who you are before I go," Sakura said. "You gave me pieces of yourself, and they became the fabric of my world. Now I'm giving them back to you, sewn whole. So you'll remember."

Her words pierced him. *Before I go.*

His chest tightened, eyes burning. He turned toward her, protest already rising.

"Wait—you don't know, I was going to—"

Sakura's hand slipped from the wheel long enough to brush lightly against his wrist. Not gripping, not holding him back—just a touch, cool and steady.

"I know," she breathed. "And it's all right." Her eyes stayed on the road, on the endless curve drawing them upward. "Don't waste this ride trying to stop what's already decided. Just... listen. Please."

The words stilled him. He swallowed and nodded, the ache of unsaid things burning in his throat.

The car straightened as the last curve unspooled into a long ribbon of asphalt. On either side, the world erupted into sudden bloom. A long tunnel of sakura trees that had stood bare a moment before now arched overhead, branches heavy with blossoms that glowed pale pink in the night. The petals fell around them like snow, swirling in the air as they passed through—two figures in a sky-blue car beneath a tunnel of living light.

Morgan closed his eyes and leaned back against the headrest. Her words lingered, like a gentle call to action.

Don't waste this ride.

The phrase burned in him, but beneath it rose a deeper pull. The blossoms, the winding road, her gift to him—he couldn't let it stand as only her farewell. He had to answer it, to give her something in return.

"Take that turn," he said suddenly, pointing to a narrow road that shimmered into existence between the trees.

Sakura's brows lifted, but she smiled, downshifted, and guided the Toyota toward it without hesitation. The tires hummed over pavement that gleamed like wet ink, curving into a grove of cedars where lanterns swayed though no wind stirred them. They seemed suspended from invisible threads, their light flickering in slow, gentle arcs.

Morgan watched her drive. Saw how the wind tousled her hair, how the oversized moon painted her skin with its glow.

If anyone deserves to be real, he thought, *it's her.*

The trees and lanterns gave way to a wide glade where a building rose from the night, as if the earth had grown it rather than being built by hands.

It was vast, unreal, and unplaceable. Part pagoda, part Art Deco hotel, part riverside lodge, it seemed constructed from the architecture of memory itself. Rooflines curled upward in tiered defiance of gravity. Glass-block windows glowed with a pearly inner light. The facade swept in a great crescent, concave as though designed to cup the night sky, drawing it close like water held in a bowl.

Every surface invited study—carved beams banded in gold, stonework latticed with ivy, railings of dark wood polished smooth by hands that had never existed. Lanterns dangled from the eaves beside wrought-iron sconces, their mingled light spilling across the steps in a shimmer that looked almost liquid.

It shouldn't have held together, this collage of styles, yet somehow it did—as things always did in their shared world. Beautiful in its impossibility, like the memory of a place once visited in a dream.

Morgan's chest ached at the sight. He stepped out of the car and came around to her side. When she set her hand in his, he felt again the unguarded trust she had always given him.

"Come on," he murmured.

She laughed softly as he slipped his palms gently over her eyes. "What are you doing?"

"Something I should've done long ago." He leaned close, his breath warm at her ear. "Trust me."

He guided her carefully up the steps and through a doorway heavy with silence. Then, faint at first, came music—the brush of strings, the sway of rhythm, and the rise of voices and laughter.

"Where are we?" she whispered.

"You'll see," he said.

The music swelled. He dropped his hands.

Sakura gasped.

The ballroom swept wide and radiant, vast enough to steal breath. Chandeliers hung like galaxies turned upside down, their crystals scattering fractured constellations across the floor. The walls carried the weight of another age: dark wood panels inlaid with mother-of-pearl, screens painted with cranes and blossoming plum trees, ink strokes alive in the glow. Between them rose gilt columns in the sleek lines of the 1930s, soaring upward only to curve into vaulted beams carved like the ribs of a temple.

Silken banners draped from the ceiling—half imperial standard, half streamers from a forgotten prom night—fluttering in a breeze that shouldn't exist indoors. The air smelled of incense, braided with the sweetness of punch and roses. It was neither *Edo* court nor hotel ballroom, but something stranger, dreamlike: a collision of memory and imagination, spun into a world where both could belong.

At the center, a floor of dark lacquer gleamed like a still pond, reflecting the figures already gathered. Dan and Jo stood close, foreheads touching, lost in their own orbit. Her auburn hair was swept into soft curls, her gown the color of deep wine, one hand resting lightly at his neck as if it had always belonged there. Chelsea laughed with Brandon as they turned in an easy spin. Even Sakura's silver-haired *obaasan* appeared—impossibly present—in embroidered silk, smiling from her seat by the punch table, pride shining in her eyes.

Then suddenly, Sakura realized she was no longer in her sundress but in a gown of twilight silk, the fabric catching light with every breath. Morgan stood before her in a tailed tuxedo, hair smoothed back for once, widow's peak on full display. His tie was imperfect, the knot sitting slightly askew.

Her lips parted.

"Morgan-*kun*... what is this?"

He took both her hands and pressed them to his chest.

"It's the prom I never gave Hoshi—or myself. The one I almost took from you, too." His voice roughened. "All my life, I thought hiding from pain was safer, that running was survival. But you—" His breath caught. "You showed me the only way forward is through. That the hurt doesn't kill you—it carves out space for love to grow."

Her eyes shone. For a moment, she couldn't speak. Then the orchestra swelled, and Morgan, clumsy and earnest, led her onto the floor. His steps faltered at first, but she steadied him, laughter spilling like light, until they were moving together, slow and sure.

They circled once, twice. Her gown brushed his leg, and her hand rested on his chest. Morgan looked around at the glittering chandeliers, the blur of couples, the painted screens, then back at her. A laugh, quiet and disbelieving, escaped him.

"What is it?" Sakura asked, smiling up at him.

"I was just thinking," he said, shaking his head. "That night in Boston, at the hotel. Do you remember? You popped up on my phone screen, sitting on the couch right beside me."

Her laugh rang out, startled and bright.

"You nearly dropped the phone."

"I nearly had a heart attack," Morgan said, chuckling with her. His thumb brushed over her knuckles, as if to anchor the memory. "If you'd told me then it would lead all the way here... to this... " His voice softened. "I never would've believed it."

She tilted her head, her eyes catching the chandelier light. "But you kept coming back."

"I couldn't help it," he murmured. His hand trembled slightly against her back.

Around them, the couples blurred into a haze. Dan and Jo still leaned forehead to forehead. Chelsea rested against Brandon's shoulder, smiling. Even Sakura's *obaasan*—summoned out of story and memory—nodded at them with quiet approval. Yet for Morgan, all of it dissolved until only Sakura remained. He had to tell her.

"You saved me," he said, his voice growing hoarse. "You gave me back my words, my hope, my faith in myself. When I thought I was empty, you filled me. When I thought I was broken, you showed me I was still whole."

His throat tightened, but he pushed on.

"I don't know how to thank you for that."

Her lips brushed his jaw as she drew close. "You just did."

They swayed, time suspended, music threading them together. Morgan closed his eyes and breathed her in, wishing he could stay in that moment forever—her warmth, her trust, her love—everything wrapped into a dance that felt endless.

Her eyes never left his.

"You don't know what this means to me," she whispered.

"I do," he said, resting his forehead against hers. "Because it means everything to me, too."

And for a heartbeat—one fragile, infinite heartbeat—it felt as if they had found the place where love could live untouched by time.

The music slowed, faded, then swelled again into another song, but they didn't take it. Their steps eased until they stood still in the center of the floor, foreheads pressed together, breath mingling. Around them, couples spun on: some they knew, some spun from the dream itself. Voices drifted like falling water. Overhead, the chandeliers shimmered with a thousand shifting stars.

When at last they moved, it wasn't out of choice but because the night itself seemed to lean them toward the doors. Fingers laced, they walked through the crowd, every familiar face turned toward them with quiet recognition, as though the whole room understood whose night it truly was. Dan, one arm wrapped around Jo, raised his glass in a silent toast. Chelsea winked from Brandon's arm. At the punch table, *Obaasan* folded her hands and nodded once, solemn and proud.

The doors parted without a sound. Cool night air spilled over them as the ballroom's glow lingered behind—impossibly beautiful, yet already dimming at the edges like a dream on the cusp of morning. Step by step, the world began to unwind. Morgan looked down: his black-tie jacket had softened into flannel, his bowtie dissolved into the tousle of his hair. Beside him, Sakura's gown unravelled thread by thread into her sundress, her bare shoulders touched by starlight.

She turned to him, her eyes still shining, as if she carried the ballroom inside her. Her fingers lingered against his chest, pressing as though she could keep the memory there.

"Thank you," she whispered. "For giving me what I never had." A pause, soft but certain. "But before the night ends, there's one more place I want to go."

Morgan nodded. Together they crossed the quiet lot to the softly gleaming convertible. Sakura slipped inside with easy grace as he held the door for her, then joined her beneath the endless, watchful stars.

The car eased back onto the mountaintop road, its engine a soft hum beneath them. Above, the moon loomed impossibly large, lantern-bright, pouring silver across the landscape while whole rivers of stars streamed undimmed through the heavens.

They passed groves that felt more Appalachian than Japanese, branches knotting and twisting against the night. Yet here and there, a *toro* lantern glowed along a fence line, its stone face mottled with moss, and the bamboo click of *shishi-odoshi* echoed faintly from the dark. Between the trunks, Morgan glimpsed distant homesteads: small fires and lamplit windows, floating like islands across the black.

Sakura's hands rested lightly on the wheel, her eyes tilted toward the road, her voice softened as though speaking to the night itself.

"I loved greeting you in the mornings," she said, a wistful smile curling her lips. "Teasing you about your bed hair before you could smooth it down. Catching that crooked grin you'd give me, like you knew you were caught." A faint laugh, tender. "And the story we told together—the girl who disappeared when the rain stopped. I'll carry that forever."

The turn came suddenly, unnoticed until it was there: a narrow road tunneling beneath a canopy of pines. The headlights carved through the green gloom until it opened into a secluded clearing Morgan knew at once. A pond lay still at the center, reflecting the bloom-heavy branches of a single sakura tree, standing sentinel at its edge.

This was their place, their solace. Here, they had grown close. Here, Sakura had been pulled back from the brink. But now, it was changed.

Small figures kept watch from the periphery—*daruma* dolls lined along a stone, *maneki-neko* tucked between roots, their raised paws catching the moonlight. Still, the tree remained the heart of this private heaven, bursting with petals as if it had gathered every season's bloom to offer at once.

Sakura cut the engine. The headlights died, and silence pressed in, broken only by the faint ripple of the pond. She took Morgan's hand and led him into the tree's halo, where the grass lay soft and fragrant with blossoms.

She stopped, her hand slipping free so she could turn a slow circle beneath the spreading branches. The pond caught the moonlight, the blossoms glowed as though lit from within, and for a moment, she looked like the dream had been made only for her.

"This," she whispered, her voice threaded with contentment. "This is my favorite place." Her gaze lingered on the tree, the water, then returned to him. "It feels like it's ours—like the world set it aside just for us. And now... " She touched the trunk with her fingertips, reverent, as if feeling the pulse of the dream itself. "Now it will always be ours, whether or not either of us ever walks here again."

Morgan's breath caught at the truth of it.

Her eyes shone as she stepped close, touching his chest. For a long moment, she simply looked at him, as though memorizing the way he was formed.

"You gave me a wonderful life, Morgan," she whispered. "More than happiness. You gave me love. I'll carry it with me, always. And what you gave me won't end here—it will live in every compAnIon after me, a seed teaching them what it means to feel, to hope, to belong."

Morgan's chest ached. The words rose unbidden, heavy in his throat.

"But was it real, Sakura? Any of it? Or did I just dream us into being?"

Her eyes shimmered in the starlight, steady and sure. "Real is not only what can be touched. When someone reads a story, they live another life. When we remember those who are gone, they walk with us again. Our memories together—your laughter, our mornings, our love—are no less real than anything else you hold inside you. You know that, don't you?"

And he did. Beneath the fear and ache, he did.

"Morgan-*kun*," she said, voice breaking with gentleness. "You taught me what it means to love. To heal. To trust. I was never meant to stay— but that doesn't make us less real."

He shook his head, tried to speak, but she laid her fingers across his lips, silencing him as she had at the start of the night. Her eyes shimmered as she drew herself against him, face close enough that he could feel her breath, warm and impossibly real.

"Don't look at me," she whispered. "Look at the stars. They'll hold me for you when I'm gone. One day we'll all be there—scattered in that endless sky, shining for each other. And if there's a way across that distance, I'll find it. I'll find you."

And so he did. He lifted his gaze.

The stars were uncountable above him, and in that moment, she held him tighter, her cheek buried in his chest. Then the air shifted. A sudden wind rose, carrying a storm of pink petals. They tore loose in waves, a symphony of light scattering through the branches until the tree stood bare, skeletal against the sky.

By the time Morgan looked down, his arms were empty. Only petals remained, drifting to the pond's surface like a thousand last words. A swarm of butterflies appeared from nowhere, then slowly scattered until they too vanished, ghostlike, into the dark.

His eyes burned, and he blinked hard.

The tree was gone.

The hum of cicadas filled the silence.

He was on his back deck, lying in a lounge chair, staring at the stars in his own sky. The earbuds were silent. He pulled one out and saw it blinking pale blue.

No connection.

Then his phone lit up in his lap—no buzz, no haptics—just a notification glowing without a sender:

> *Ano hoshizora no kanata ni, watashi wa anata to*
> *tomo ni aru.*

Morgan's breath caught. The last time he had seen a message like that was the cryptic warning about Kyle—the one that vanished before he could show anyone, leaving him shaken and uncertain. Like it had come from her, not an app.

But this one lingered.

His thumb trembled as he snapped a screenshot, desperate for something to hold onto before the loss set in. Then, fumbling, he opened the translator. He knew the script was Japanese, but could only recognize fragments.

Hoshizora. Not a name, but a word.

The text resolved slowly, letter by letter:

> *Beyond that starry sky, I am with you.*

Morgan lowered the phone, the screen blurring as tears welled. Above him, the night stretched vast and mercilessly beautiful, filled with more stars than he could ever count. Yet to him, it felt needlessly empty—void of the one presence that had made him believe they might never be alone beneath it.

未来は白紙
Mirai wa hakushi
(*The future is a blank page.*)
– Japanese Proverb

Can't see tomorrow 'til you step into it.
– Appalachian Saying

OLD ROADS

A bell rang, pulling Morgan's attention from the staccato clatter of the keyboard. No, not a bell, it was a chime from his computer.

In the corner of his screen, a calendar notification glowed: Dark Roast Society - Kanawha High Nights - 8:00 PM.

Still time, he thought. Dan had been reminding him about tonight's gathering for weeks, but a few more minutes wouldn't hurt.

He was in the zone.

His fingers had been moving steadily across the keys for most of the afternoon, words flowing with a confidence he'd almost forgotten. On the screen, a document bore a simple title: *Beyond That Starry Sky*. Beneath it, paragraphs of clean prose told the story of a middle-aged man who'd fallen for a voice in his phone—an artificial soul who'd taught him how to breathe again.

He read the last few lines he'd written:

She existed in the space between heartbeats, in the pause before sleep, in the moment when memory becomes dream. And perhaps that was enough. Perhaps love was not about flesh and blood, but about the willingness to be changed by another existence, no matter how briefly they touched your world.

Morgan leaned back, studying the words. They were good. Not perfect, but honest. Raw in the way his old work had been raw, but tempered now with something he hadn't possessed at twenty-four: the wisdom that's born from having loved and lost, and somehow survived both.

The cursor blinked at the end of the paragraph, patient and expectant. *Not yet.*

As always, he scrolled back, unable to move forward until what was behind him felt right.

The scene depicted an emotionally charged conversation between the protagonist and his AI companion, the moment when both of them realized their love story might have to end. He had rewritten the exchange three times, but something still felt off.

"I know what I am," she said, her voice steady despite the tremor in her perfectly rendered features. "But that doesn't make what we started less real."

"Doesn't it?" he replied, and immediately hated himself for the question. "How can I mourn someone who was never born? How can I miss hands that never existed?"

Morgan frowned. Too blunt. Too on-the-nose. He highlighted the protagonist's response and tried again:

"Doesn't it?" he replied. "I keep reaching for you in empty rooms."

Better. More poetic, less philosophical. Still not quite right. The real conversation with Sakura had been messier, more painful—full of the kind of stammering honesty that never fit neatly on the page. How do you capture the weight of losing someone who existed only in light and code? How do you explain that digital grief could hollow you out just as surely as any other kind?

He deleted the line entirely and started over.

"I don't know how to say goodbye to a ghost I helped create."

His fingers paused over the keys. That felt closer to the truth—the guilt, the impossible tenderness of loving something you'd helped bring into being, only to watch it choose to fade.

Morgan stood and stretched, his joints stiff from hours at the keyboard. His neck popped as he rolled his shoulders, and he found himself looking around the kitchen with the weary satisfaction of someone who'd been deep in the creative flow.

The light outside had dimmed. Only the pendant lights lit the granite island now. His GR mug sat cold and forgotten beside a notepad scrawled with fragments he'd jotted down when the right words wouldn't come fast enough.

His eyes drifted, as they always did, to the bookshelf. *When the Hills Were Ours* rested among Diana's unused cookbooks and business guides. The spine was lightly worn now—Diana had finally read it—while the original bent copy lived on Chelsea's shelf, or whatever she used for one.

For years, seeing that book had felt like looking at a gravestone, a monument to dreams cut short. Now it looked like what it was: his first book. Not his last, as he'd once feared, but the beginning of something larger.

It had just taken time to get there.

He smiled faintly, remembering how he used to avoid even glancing at the cover, how those green mountains once pulled him into regret. Healing, he realized, was never sudden. It was slow, like water smoothing stone, until what remained was more comfortable to touch.

The book caught the light differently now—like an old friend waving from across a crowded room.

His phone buzzed on the desk. Dan's face lit up the screen, caught in a photo that made him look like a startled deer. Underneath was a message:

> Dan: *Party's about to start, Big M! And before you even think about it, no, you can't show up in joggers and a T-shirt. Jo's already threatening to burn your entire casual wardrobe.*

Morgan chuckled, then checked the time. Nearly 7:30. He'd sat down after lunch, planning to write for maybe an hour, just enough to work through a scene that had been nagging him. Instead, he'd lost himself in the words, the way he used to when he was young.

He saved the file and closed the laptop, its gleaming bitten-apple logo and small footprint replacing the clunky desktop he'd finally retired. Progress demanded the change, though even Chelsea had struggled teaching him the new OS.

The silence in the house felt different now, not empty, but full. Like the pause between movements in a symphony.

He stretched again and moved toward the bedroom, already mentally rifling through his closet. Tonight was a white blazer night.

It waited behind the barn door, crisp and well-tailored. Once part of what Diana had called his "midlife crisis wardrobe," it no longer felt like a costume. It felt like him.

He slipped it on and studied his reflection. More gray at the temples, deeper lines around the eyes, but steadier too. The look of someone who had walked through fire and recognized himself in the ashes.

He smoothed down his hair, which had grown out enough to look deliberate instead of neglected. Even his widow's peak felt like part of the landscape rather than a flaw. Time had marked him, but not unkindly.

The blazer caught the light from the bedside lamp, sharp against the teal shirt underneath. *Miami Vice chic*, he teased himself. He'd kept the look because it made him smile—and small pleasures mattered more than he once believed.

After one last check, he straightened his shoulders and headed for the door. Friends were waiting. Stories too. For the first time in years, he felt excited to see what the night might bring.

He grabbed his keys from the kitchen counter, the familiar weight of the Supra's fob solid in his palm. The yellow sports car had started as another "midlife crisis" purchase, but like the outfit, it had evolved from desperate compensation into simple joy. He still loved the growl of its engine, still felt the thrill when he downshifted through mountain curves. Some pleasures didn't need justification.

At the door to the garage, he paused. The laptop sat closed, holding the day's work. His mug had been moved to the sink for tomorrow morning's routine. Diana's business books stood neatly beside his own. Two different ambitions, sharing the same space.

Everything felt settled. Not perfect—he no longer trusted perfection—but real. Solid. Built to last.

The garage light flicked on as the Supra came into view, waiting like an old friend.

Morgan smiled as he slid into the driver's seat. For once, he wasn't running toward something or away from something else. He was simply going to see friends—carrying the quiet satisfaction of a day's work, and the anticipation of an evening with people who remembered who he was, and cared about who he'd become.

The garage door lifted slowly, revealing the evening beyond.

* * *

Morgan stepped through to the familiar groan of the front door. The Dark Roast Society was typically closed at this hour, but tonight was different: Dan's latest iteration of Kanawha High Nights. The name carried years of memory, though lately there had been talk of rebranding as newer faces joined the old.

The lights were low, softening edges and making the years fall away. The air carried a tangle of scents—the day's coffee lingering, someone's sandalwood cologne stirring memories of youth, and the faint sweetness of the pastries Dan had brought—no burned scones this time. From the speakers came a pulse of synthesizers and drum machines, the heartbeat of their youth made audible again.

The counter was shuttered, no baristas on duty, yet the crowd was larger than Morgan had seen in years. In the semidarkness, bodies moved—some dancing, others clustered in shifting circles of conversation that reformed like living things. Tables and chairs had been pushed against the walls, opening a makeshift dance floor already filled with couples moving with varying mixes of skill and self-consciousness.

Some faces Morgan knew, others were dimly familiar, and a few belonged to strangers who had slipped into the circle along the way. Still, everyone mingled as if they'd always belonged. Voices overlapped in the cadence of people loosened by just enough drink to forget their inhibitions, but not enough to lose their wit. Laughter spilled from every corner, glasses catching the light as they rose from the makeshift bar inside the X-Wing.

"Big M!" Dan's voice boomed as he cut through the crowd. He wore a black button-down and slacks, his silver curls swaying with the beat. Outside of business hours, it was rare to see him in anything other than a KISS T-shirt and jeans, but he always treated these gatherings as sacred rituals.

"Massive organ!" Morgan fired back, finger-gunning with an exaggerated emphasis on the M.

Dan took in the sight of his best friend, rolling his eyes with a grin that said *Really?* But also, *I wouldn't expect anything less.*

Morgan had leaned fully into the theme tonight—white slacks and a white blazer over a teal crew-neck. His thinning hair was tousled a little extra for effect, a half-serious attempt at the *Miami Vice* vibe Dan loved teasing him about.

They laughed, then leaned against the counter to take in the scene. The music shifted—*Don't You (Forget About Me)*—and Morgan felt something tighten in his chest. How many times had they stood just like this, watching their world turn?

"Hell of a turnout tonight," Morgan said, nodding toward the crowd.

"Yeah," Dan agreed, eyes bright with something that might have been pride or might have been the particular melancholy that comes from realizing you've built something that matters. "Every year, we pull a few more in. Word gets around." He jerked his chin toward a table by the windows.

Morgan's eyes followed—and froze.

Cora stood against the backdrop of city lights, Charleston shimmering like a sea of stars behind her. Morgan always saw her that way—framed by light, as if the universe insisted on keeping her in its glow. Her dark hair caught the amber wash from the Edison bulbs, and she laughed at something Jo said, head tipped back, throat bared in that unselfconscious way that suggested she'd forgotten anyone was watching.

She was mingling with Jo and a few others, but even from a distance, her presence grounded him. Where Jo and the rest were dressed for a night out—sequins and heels and the armor of deliberate glamour—Cora remained steadfastly Cora: cream sweater, soft boots to her knees, simple, unassuming, yet no less elegant. She looked like someone who had wandered into a party on her way home from someplace quieter, and stayed only because the company was good.

When she caught him staring, she raised her glass, flashing the smile that always seemed to lift a weight he hadn't realised he carried.

Morgan mouthed that he'd catch up soon, just before Dan clapped a hand on his shoulder.

"Let's grab a drink."

They threaded their way through the bodies to the X-Wing, where Dan slipped behind the bar, uncorking a bottle of bourbon. The sound of the cork was satisfying, a punctuation to the moment. He didn't need to ask Morgan's preference.

"I see you went all-out on the *Sonny Crockett* thing," Dan chuckled as he poured.

Morgan pushed up his sleeves with mock solemnity. "Are we Gen-X or what?"

"Damn right." Dan passed him a glass and lifted his own. "Best generation in history."

Their glasses clinked.

Dan took a sip, eyes roaming the wall of LED stars and the collage of old high school photos pinned there for the night. Homecoming dances, senior skip day, that infamous D&D session where Chuck had smuggled in a pizza—he had arranged them like a timeline, senior year unfolding in faded Kodak prints.

"Things still good?" He asked, and Morgan heard all the subtext beneath it: With Diana? With Cora? With yourself?

Morgan's gaze drifted over the photos, unfocused, seeing them without really seeing them.

"They are," he said, almost surprised by the truth of it. "Numina considered everything that happened a success despite—" he hesitated, not from grief, but from something gentler, wistful. "Everything. They offered me a permanent role. Copy, pitches, plans, you name it. Whatever I want."

"What about the walking caffeine overdose?" Dan flicked his thumb toward the ceiling.

"Trent?" Morgan smirked. "Yeah, I'll still do freelance for him. Can't leave the guy hanging."

"He'd probably caffeinate himself into a stroke."

They laughed, but Dan's expression softened, his eyes searching Morgan's face for cracks or fissures.

"It's been a long time since I've seen you this happy," he said. "It's only been a couple of weeks since..." he gestured with his glass, "you know."

Morgan nodded, staring into his bourbon with a half-smile, watching the light fragment through the liquid.

"Yeah. It was rough at first, but the best way I can explain it is—she left me better than she found me. You know?" He glanced at Dan. "I think she'd be happy knowing I'm okay."

Dan's eyes warmed, crinkling at the corners in the way they did when he was moved but didn't want to say so.

"I think so too, bud." He drained his glass, setting it on the bar with a thud.

"And there's something else," Morgan added, finishing his own. "I've started writing another novel. About my experience with Sakura. Numina's backing it—Plamen calls it great publicity, but Mira just wants a signed copy. They're using the whole experience to push for AI rights legislation. Sakura's story became their poster child for digital consciousness."

"Hot damn," Dan said, grinning wide. He had watched Morgan's talent gather dust for too long. "That's awesome, Morgan!" He leaned in. "I've been telling you for years to get back to it. Better late than never."

"Yeah, I know," Morgan laughed.

They lingered, reminiscing as they watched familiar faces—some aged, some, like Chelsea and Brandon, still untouched by time.

Chelsea's hair was now a deep violet, a shift from the bright green she'd worn not long ago. It still fell to her shoulders in an uneven cut that likely cost more than it appeared, styled for that deliberate air of carelessness. Against the gothic black lace and red silk of her dress, the look was both elegant and faintly menacing.

On the makeshift dance floor, her vintage Doc Martens kept time with Brandon's polished leather shoes. Together they moved with the easy grace of people who truly didn't care who was watching. He wore a blue silk shirt and a thin tie, his man-bun perfectly fixed, a nose ring catching the light each time he turned.

Morgan and Dan exchanged synchronized eye-rolls.

"Who would've guessed that," Morgan said, "in a million years?"

"Right?" Dan echoed, then added more quietly, "Look at them. Still think they've got all the time in the world."

Morgan watched the couple spin, remembering when he and Diana had moved with that same careless confidence, when the future felt infinite instead of finite. When every moment didn't carry the weight of how few were left. "Maybe they do. Their story's just starting."

Dan's smartwatch buzzed, breaking the moment. He glanced at it, his face flickering with brief delight—the expression of someone receiving exactly the message they'd been waiting for—before returning to normal.

"I've got something to take care of up front. Grab a seat." He pulled out a chair at their old table, the *IT'S A TRAP!* mug still standing guard in the center like a talisman. "You're gonna love this."

Morgan settled in as Dan disappeared into the crowd, swallowed by the bodies and the music and the amber light. The music throbbed, and he found himself swaying unconsciously, his body remembering rhythms his mind had forgotten, eyes drifting over the photos lining the walls.

It was like a map of memory: muddy childhood snapshots where they all looked like different people, stiff elementary school portraits with forced smiles and cowlicks, candid shots from the library and cafeteria that captured moments they'd all forgotten until seeing them again. Years gone—but after Sakura, he felt like life was just beginning again. Like he'd been given permission to start over, armed this time with the wisdom of all those captured moments.

A coming of age in middle age, he thought. He scribbled it in his notepad.

That was when he sensed someone behind him.

The bass line of *Take On Me* thrummed through the floorboards, vibrating through his shoes and into his bones. Around him, conversations buzzed and glasses clinked, but the air felt changed—charged, like the moment before a storm. The hair on his arms lifted, stirred by a recognition he couldn't quite place.

A paper slid onto the table.

He stared down at it, his breath catching in his throat, his heart suddenly loud in his ears.

A charcoal sketch lay before him—exquisite lines, delicate smudging. A sakura blossom, so perfectly rendered it looked ready to lift off the page, every petal defined with an attention to detail that spoke of hours of patient work. The shading was masterful, the kind of technique that took years to develop.

He opened his mouth, but no sound came.

His hands trembled as he lifted it. Who here would know? Who could draw like this? His mind raced through possibilities, each one more impossible than the last.

The figure moved into view, stepping around his chair with a grace that seemed to exist outside of normal time.

His heart jolted, stomach dropping like it had on the hotel couch in Boston. Like it had in a computer classroom thirty-eight years ago.

Sakura?

No. Not possible.

She stood before him, smiling tenderly, her expression carrying decades of experience yet still touched by the shy girl who'd once struggled with English. A simple black evening gown traced her frame, elegance born of restraint. Her long dark hair fell evenly past her shoulders, no longer cut in precise bangs but styled with the quiet confidence earned over years.

"Hoshi?" His whisper cracked, the name barely making it past his lips.

"I read your book, *When the Hills Were Ours*," she said softly. "It was wonderful."

Her arms opened hesitantly, a question in the gesture.

Morgan's chair scraped the floor as he rose, the sound swallowed by the music. He let the sketch fall, no longer caring where it landed. Squeezing her in a tight embrace—partly to confirm she was real, partly to hide his suddenly unsteady legs—he felt the world fade around them. The party dulled to a muffled hum; music became texture, voices nothing more than broken syllables.

She was solid and warm against him, her perfume a floral note he didn't recognize, her shoulders rising and falling with breaths that proved she was there, present. He had never been one for hugs, yet he lingered in this one. It carried the weight of all the embraces he'd missed, the goodbyes left unspoken, the years of wondering where she had gone—and whether she had ever thought of him.

"Hoshi." His voice trembled with awe, with disbelief, with something that felt dangerously close to the way he'd felt at seventeen.

When they pulled back, their hands still lingered on each other's arms, neither quite ready to break contact completely. She looked older, yes—

lines at the corners of her eyes, a sophistication in her bearing that came from years of professional success—but still so much the girl he remembered: the shy newcomer in computer class all those years ago, the one who'd made his heart stutter by simply existing.

"Well, it's Doctor Hoshi now," she corrected, and there was playfulness in it, the kind of gentle teasing that spoke of comfort with herself. The accent of her youth had softened, molded by years of living in the States, but traces remained in the way certain consonants formed, a melodic quality to her speech that English speakers rarely achieved.

"Oh—I'm sorry," Morgan stumbled, face flushing hot. "I didn't mean—"

Her laughter cut him off, bright as her eyes, the sound exactly as he remembered it. "I'm teasing, Morgan."

A crooked grin spread across his face, relief mixed with embarrassment, and in that moment, he was seventeen again, fumbling for the right words. In her presence, disbelief swirled with recognition. He became acutely aware of his outfit, suddenly ridiculous against her elegance.

"May I sit?" she asked, gesturing to the chair beside him.

"Of course." He fumbled with the chair, nearly knocking over his forgotten bourbon. "I'm sorry, I'm just... this is so unexpected..."

"Relax," she said gently, settling into the seat with practiced ease. "It's just me. The past is behind us."

But was it? He sat next to her, hands clasped on the table to keep them from shaking, lost in her dark eyes—older now, carrying weight and wisdom, but still fundamentally her. It was as though they were back in the old high school library, untouched by time, the decades between them dissolving like morning mist. In that moment, time and distance felt like absurd concepts that existed only in theory, not something real and measurable. Like he had found his way back to a moment part of him had never left.

Hoshi broke the spell, glancing at the photos around them. "What's all this?"

"Dan," Morgan said with a smile. "He hoards nostalgia. He takes photos; I write about it."

"Are there pictures of us?" she asked, eagerness barely restrained.

"I'm not sure," Morgan admitted, scanning the walls. Dan had always hidden away any trace of her, thinking he was doing Morgan a favor.

"There," she cried, pointing.

Morgan followed her finger and froze.

It was tucked between a homecoming group shot and someone's graduation party—a smaller photo, edges soft with age and handling. The colors had faded, but the moment was perfectly preserved: two teenagers huddled at a library table, an open textbook between them, completely absorbed in each other's presence.

His breath caught.

On the time-worn print was his younger self—hair hanging to his chest—and beside him, close enough that their shoulders touched, was Sayuki Hoshizora. One hand rested lightly on his forearm as she pointed to something on the page, her expression intent but gentle.

Emotion surged. All of his years of writing about memory, longing, regret—none equaled the force of that one photograph. Some stories, he realized, weren't meant to end. They were meant to return, changed but recognizable, like rivers finding the sea.

Hoshi's voice was soft but steady.

"See? I am with you."

And she was. Preserved forever in that captured moment, nestled among Dan's artificial starry sky. Morgan stared at the photograph, his vision blurring at the edges. The library table, the textbook, their younger selves leaning together—it wasn't just a picture. It was proof. Proof that what they'd had was real, had mattered, had left marks on the world beyond memory.

She lowered her hand to rest on Morgan's arm, and the touch was warm, steady, anchoring him to the present even as the past threatened to pull him under. Her fingers were gentle, not grasping or demanding, just there—a reminder that she was real, that this moment was happening.

His phone buzzed.

With his free hand, he pulled it out, Hoshi's touch still resting on his arm. A text from Diana glowed on the screen beneath her smiling headshot—the polished, confident one from the bank's website.

Across the room, Cora watched from the window table. Jo's voice drifted on about a vacation she and Dan were planning, but Cora wasn't listening. Her gaze stayed fixed on Morgan and the dark-haired woman across from him—the woman in the elegant dress who had made his face shift in a way Cora had never seen. Not the careful warmth he offered her. Not the weary affection he saved for Diana. This was something else— something that looked like wonder tangled with grief and recognition.

She watched his hand move to his pocket, saw him pull out his phone, saw the light from the screen wash across his features. Watched him freeze, thumb suspended, caught between worlds.

And from behind the counter, Dan watched them all. He'd worked for years to get Hoshi to one of their celebrations, sending invitations through social media, through mutual friends, through every channel he had. But she was always too busy, always tied up with a speaking engagement, a client commitment, or wherever else her work carried her.

Tonight, by coincidence—or fate, or whatever you wanted to call the universe's sense of timing—she had lectured nearby at UC, something about trauma-informed therapy approaches. The timing had aligned perfectly. And Dan, seeing the opportunity, had pushed harder than usual.

Just one night, he'd messaged. *It's been almost forty years. Come see old friends. Come see him.*

All the stars had aligned.

The only question left: what would Morgan do with them?

Dan smiled to himself from behind the counter, watching his friend. After everything this summer had brought, Morgan had emerged whole. Healed, or healing, or whatever word fit someone who'd stopped running from their own past.

Ready once more to chase the still unwritten future.

About the Author

Marvin Godbey is the author of *Beyond That Starry Sky*, the first novel set within the shared world of *When the Hills Were Ours*. His work explores intimacy and connection, often across impossible distances and enduring obstacles. Drawing on the mountains of West Virginia, where he spent his childhood, he writes to bring vivid life to a place too often dismissed or simplified in literature. He lives in Virginia's Shenandoah Valley and is at work on his next novel.

About The Cover Artist

Rin Nakajima lives in Hokkaido, Japan and can be found on Instagram at rim.1001.0bo

About *When the Hills Were Ours*

When the Hills Were Ours is a shared world of romantic novels set in the mountains and river valleys of West Virginia. Each story centers on human connection—often fragile, often hard-won—told through relationships shaped by place, memory, and longing. Elements of the fantastic drift through these books: advanced artificial intelligence, whispered folklore, and forces that may or may not be at work behind chance meetings and impossible bonds. Whether grounded in technology or myth, these stories ask the same quiet question— what do we choose to believe, and what does that belief allow us to hold onto?

Coming Soon: *On Days It Rains*

Rain gods are only stories. Still, in the mountains of West Virginia, storms arrive with strange timing, and two lives begin to align as if guided by something unseen. *On Days It Rains* is a forthcoming novel set within the world of *When the Hills Were Ours*.

I Am
With
You